SERVICE

Lauren Mooney is a writer from the East Midlands. She works in theatre and audio drama, and has co-run Kandinsky Theatre Company since 2015, making award-winning shows across the UK and Europe. She is a graduate of UEA's Creative Writing Prose MA, where she held the David Higham Scholarship. She lives in East Sussex with her husband Stewart and their tortoise, Sacher Tort. *Service* is her first novel.

SERVICE

LAUREN MOONEY

MANILLA
PRESS

First published in the UK in 2026 by
MANILLA PRESS
An imprint of Bonnier Books UK
5th Floor, HYLO, 105 Bunhill Row,
London, EC1Y 8LZ

This is a work of fiction. Names, places, events and
incidents are either the products of the author's
imagination or used fictitiously. Any resemblance to
actual persons, living or dead, or actual
events is purely coincidental.

A CIP catalogue record for this book is
available from the British Library.

Hardback ISBN: 978-1-78658-628-5
Trade paperback ISBN: 978-1-78658-629-2

Also available as an ebook and an audiobook

Epigraph from 'This is the First Thing' from *The Complete Poems* by
Philip Larkin. Reproduced by permission of Faber and Faber Ltd.

1 3 5 7 9 10 8 6 4 2

Typeset by IDSUK (Data Connection) Ltd
Printed and bound by CPI Group (UK) Ltd, Croydon CR0 4YY

The authorised representative in the EEA is Bonnier Books
UK (Ireland) Limited.
Registered office address: Floor 3, Block 3, Miesian Plaza,
Dublin 2, D02 Y754, Ireland
compliance@bonnierbooks.ie
www.bonnierbooks.co.uk

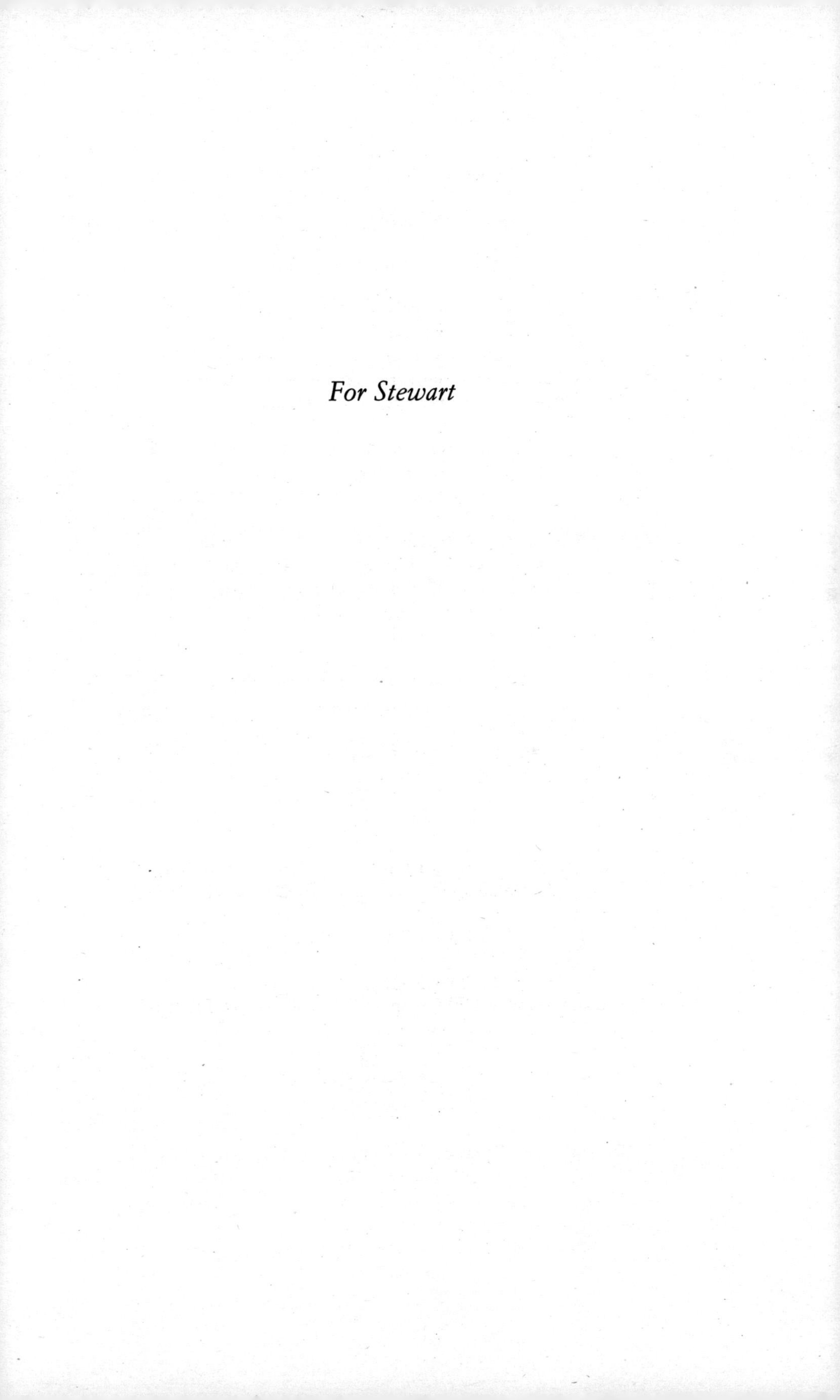

For Stewart

This is the first thing
I have understood:
Time is the echo of an axe
Within a wood.

Philip Larkin, *This Is The First Thing*

I.
Noise

JEANNIE SURFACED SHORTLY BEFORE MIDDAY. She blew into the office with her scarf trailing, wishing each of us good morning, one by one, like the Queen. I stood up from my desk and went into the kitchenette to make her coffee. I'd worked with Jeannie long enough that we no longer needed to discuss such things; I was attentive to her needs.

As I stood watching the water boil, I wondered if, actually, it was too late in the day: Jeannie could be funny about coffee after eleven. She said it affected her sleep, that green tea was better, even though as far as I knew, green tea was just as caffeinated.

Her voice drifted through from the office, where she was talking to my colleagues. '*So* sorry if you've been trying to reach me,' she said. 'I was in a meeting all morning. It took *hours*.' As the person who scheduled all Jeannie's meetings, I thought this unlikely to be true. She'd blocked out the time herself, listed in her diary as a private appointment, but as soon as she walked in, it became clear that she'd actually spent the morning having her hair blow-dried.

All things being equal, I decided it would be wisest to bring the sparkling water through first, lightly refrigerated, and ask about the coffee. I put a small bottle and glass onto the tray Jeannie bought last year, 'to make things easier', and took everything through.

Jeannie was in her own office, a little room off the musty open-plan where the rest of us sat. We rented the basement of an overpriced building in Bloomsbury, where all the other companies seemed more important than us; possibly this was why we had so few windows. Most of the ones we did have belonged to Jeannie, whose office was nicer in every way, a dusky lilac to our mud-brown, mood-lit where ours was strip-lit, with her wide, teak desk tucked into one corner. I don't know if she'd noticed the disparity. Nobody ever mentioned it.

I stood in the doorway, holding my little tray, and watched her bustle about, pouring bottled water into one of her plant pots, tossing her jacket onto a peg and throwing the windows open. She did all this with the air of someone returning not to a room they'd left twenty hours ago, but to a closed-up country pile after a long winter. Watching her was like watching a character from the books I'd loved as a teenager; Jeannie had a profile bred to be observed throwing the dust cover from a grand piano and saying, 'There, just like in Grandmama's time.' This wasn't baseless prejudice; she really had grown up in a country house. She'd told me years ago, 'A very small one', while we were drinking free wine at a work event. I sometimes wondered how small a big house could be.

Jeannie turned and saw me. 'Danielle,' she said, face breaking into a smile. 'Lovely. Pop down there. Are we meeting?' I put the water in front of her, on the desk, where she'd pointed.

'We can,' I said. 'Green tea? The kettle's boiled.'

'Oh, you angel. Please.'

One point to me, I thought, enjoying my usual rush of satisfaction at a job well done, a need correctly anticipated, before the inevitable self-disgust. How deeply I wanted to please her. What a worm. I went back to the kitchen.

I had been Jeannie's PA for four years. She was the founder-director of our charity, Hodgepodge, and the leader of our fearless team: the two of us, plus Nick, who did finances; Mollie, nebulously on *programme*; and Femi, who ran our social media. I'd taken the job when I was young and desperate, figuring that, although it wasn't clear to me what Hodgepodge did, it would be obvious once I actually started working there. Unfortunately, I still wasn't sure.

Our tagline said that we were *'for ideas'*. But which ones? Some, according to Jeannie, were *'in our remit'*, while others were *'definitely not a Hodgepodge sort of thing'*. Broad, but sure. Ideas! Which in and of themselves were definitely . . . good?

It troubled me, at first, that I wasn't sure how to answer when people at parties said, 'So what do you do?' Saying I fetched things for Jeannie would have been accurate, but depressing; saying I worked in an office only invited more questions. 'Doing what?' they'd have asked, and I would have had to start talking about Ideas. Luckily, there had been a pandemic, and the parties hadn't really come back, or not in the same way. Now that people only rarely asked me what I did, it didn't seem so important to have an answer. Day-to-day, Hodgepodge ran a mix of poorly attended talks, events and exhibitions, but I didn't need to worry about any of that, really – my job was to run Jeannie.

I filled the pot with loose-leaf tea and poured hot water on top. I never used teabags because Jeannie said she could taste the paper in the drink, even though I had hinted several times, conversationally, that teabags weren't made with paper anymore. Had they ever been? Whatever. I loaded up my tray and took it back through the open-plan. I passed my colleagues, in headphones. Nobody looked up from their screens. The door to Jeannie's office was still open.

'Come in, come in,' she said with faux-conspiratorial cheer, as I put the tray on her desk. This was a tone she often adopted, like we were sisters going into a treehouse to share secrets, when actually I was coming into Jeannie's office to perform basic tasks for her. I shut the door behind me, and we were alone.

'So,' she said. 'How are we today?'

'Fine,' I lied. 'How are you?'

Jeannie looked out of the window. 'Well, Edward's back in his old room,' she sighed. 'Money's run out again. So much like his father, *completely* unrealistic.' Edward, her youngest son, was a little older than me, thirty-one or thirty-two, and still trying to make it with an East London electronic band called Feather Gamblers. I'd actually seen them live, footing the line-up at a one-day festival in Victoria Park that Jeannie had made us all go to last year. They were fucking shit.

'Sorry to hear that,' I said.

Jeannie shrugged decorously, skinny shoulders rising and falling, and ran a hand through her great crest of newly blow-dried hair. She was very glamorous for a woman in her late sixties, with a thin frame, delicate gestures and angular, well-made clothes. I sometimes wished that I would look as good at her age, despite knowing that I wouldn't. People who've never been frightened about money don't get older like the rest of us. She pointed to the little stool by her desk and said, 'Come on then. What have I missed?'

The stool was too short, or I was too tall for it, but I scrunched myself into my usual spot and began to run through my list: meetings Jeannie had scheduled for the afternoon, calls I'd taken that morning, things people had emailed me to ask her, presumably because they'd already tried emailing her themselves and had no reply. Technology was not her strongest suit, skill-wise, though she approached it with more faith and enthusiasm than I did.

Quite a lot of the messages I was relaying came from Jeannie's friends, but then quite a lot of her friends had become donors to Hodgepodge, or involved in some way with the panels, talks and exhibitions; they were speakers, writers, thinkers, broadcasters, commentators, MPs. Jeannie was what was known in our industry as *well-networked*, meaning she had one round of powerful allies from her own boarding school and another from her sons', the well-heeled parents of their well-heeled friends.

I sometimes worried that the whole company, with all its indefinable works, was just a plaything of Jeannie's, an extension of her lifestyle, relationships and willpower. At other times I thought, come on, four other people work here! But the fact remained that I spent a lot of time relaying voicemails from vaguely famous people about boozy lunches that would or wouldn't happen as planned, holidays in the south of France, and people's weddings.

'And,' I said, coming to the end of my list. 'Brett's out, so we need to rethink.'

Jeannie was applying lip balm with her middle finger; she stopped, and looked up at me, brow creased. 'Brett. Remind me.'

'That journalist who was going to chair the DPDI event? He can't do it anymore.'

This was one of our panel discussions, designed to get *ordinary people* to grips with *real issues*; in this case, online privacy laws. Ours was a guilt-based economy, focused on things people knew they should be worrying about, but had little time for. This made sense to me – it was perhaps the only thing about Hodgepodge that did – but we never seemed able to capture the *ordinary people* market.

'Oh dear,' said Jeannie. 'That's soon, isn't it?'

The panel was two days away. 'Quite soon, yeah.'

'And Mollie's so busy with the season launch!'

I agreed that it was bad timing.

'Could you put some names together? Or are you too stretched?'

'No, I can help,' I said. 'I'll make a list. I think that's everything.'

I was standing to leave, but Jeannie said, 'Hold on. Are you sure you're all right, Danielle? You look tired.'

I stopped, turned. Jeannie was watching me with narrowed eyes and an inscrutable expression. I was surprised: it was nice of her to notice, or if not nice, at least unusual; Jeannie was ludicrously, almost comically self-absorbed. Then I realised *tired* was probably code for the fact that I'd spent the last fortnight drinking too much, sleeping too little, not washing my hair enough, and generally looking like a big piece of shit.

'I'm fine. Just some personal stuff going on,' I said. I made my voice slightly husky in an attempt to convey huge depths of bravery, and also that I didn't want to talk about it.

'Do you want to talk about it?' Jeannie asked.

I shook my head. 'No, I'm fine.'

'All right. Well, let me know how you get on with the DPDI chair. And Danielle?'

I stopped with my hand on the doorknob, waiting for something, though I wasn't sure what. Some wisdom, maybe, or a pep talk. 'Yes?'

'I need a few things for tonight, but I ran out of time this morning. Could you be an angel . . . ?' Jeannie slid a piece of paper across the desk, a hurriedly scrawled list, folded around her bank card.

I tried to remember what tonight was. An event? Some work thing I'd forgotten? I picked the list up, scanned it, and realised she was asking me to do her food shopping again.

My job before Hodgepodge was horrendous, so I tried not to mind, but there had definitely been, over the last few years, an encroachment – a blurring of boundaries between Jeannie's work and life. By which I mean that she was more and more regularly asking me to do things that were unrelated to my job, and I didn't know how to handle it. There had always been ambiguities, of course: the panellists who were also Jeannie's friends, the work messages that were also party invites. Maybe that was what had made it so tricky to pinpoint when, exactly, we'd crossed a line. But I was increasingly sure that, at some point, we had.

'Of course,' I said, pocketing the list. 'No problem.'

*

'It's like £300 *a day*, no joke,' said Femi.

We were in the Waitrose round the corner from the office, Femi holding a supermarket sandwich and two bags of Popchips ('they never put enough in them'), me gripping a basket of stuff for Jeannie. Femi had come to keep me company, but so far, she'd spent most of the time doing maths.

'I've been trying to work out what I earn in a day,' she went on. 'Because that's like – let's say for the sake of argument, fifty-two weeks in a year, though I get annual leave – but it's paid leave, so we're being paid for all the days in the year, right? Even the ones we don't work.'

'Yeah,' I said, though I hadn't been following, and wasn't sure if this was true. I was holding a packet of lemongrass and trying to decipher Jeannie's terrible handwriting. Surely it said lemongrass? There was definitely a *g* in the middle.

'So, fifty-two weeks, that's 260 working days.'

'Did you just do that in your head?'

'Fifty-two times five, it's not that hard. You just times fifty-two by ten, and then – no, I can see your eyes glazing over,' she laughed. 'Anyway, I earn twenty-four grand a year, and divided by 260 days that's like ... ninety-two pounds a day. *Before tax.* And I bet she doesn't even pay tax because who's going to check?'

Last night, Femi's housemate Dee had revealed that she was moving out, because she was making enough money from OnlyFans to rent a place alone, and no longer needed to live in a houseshare. Femi, it seemed, had been doing maths near constantly ever since.

Femi was my only real friend at work. We were the most junior staff at Hodgepodge, or as we sometimes called ourselves, 'the most shat-upon'. I was a few years older, but we were still both in our irresponsible twenties, even if only narrowly in my case. Femi was trying to become a journalist and did a lot of badly paid freelancing, sometimes during office hours; she worked very hard, just not for us. She was able to use phrases like 'poorly optimised' and 'excellent metrics' to blind Jeannie, an enthusiastic but slapdash user of the internet, with science. Jeannie still sometimes asked me to find the 'best tweets' on certain issues, and print them out so she could read them, like a sort of almanac. Femi ran rings around her.

'So she's earning, what, £200 a day more than you?' I said, putting the lemongrass into my basket. (Fuck it.)

'Yes,' said Femi. I whistled like a man in a film who'd seen a really big shark. 'Exactly. It's like, no wonder you don't want to share a bathroom with three people anymore, I wouldn't either.'

The supermarket was heaving with the office crowd, but it was quieter in the dried goods aisle, away from the meal deals. I picked up a bottle of soy sauce. 'Does she like it?'

'Soy sauce?'

I laughed. 'No, the OnlyFans thing. Does she like the work?'

Femi shrugged, put down the rice wine she'd been holding. 'Sure. Dee said she doesn't mind getting her tits out, but she's not so into the Twitter.'

I must have looked blank.

'Apparently she mainly gets new OnlyFans followers when her tweets go viral,' Femi went on. 'So that's like, a big part of it.'

'Wow,' I said. The only viral tweets I could think of were by @dril, the anonymous guy who said things like, 'IF THE ZOO BANS ME FOR HOLLERING AT THE ANIMALS I WILL FACE GOD AND WALK BACKWARDS INTO HELL'. I couldn't picture how that could be converted into charging people to see your tits. 'What . . . does she say?'

'Dunno. She won't tell me her Twitter name, she said it's too personal.'

'But she showed you her OnlyFans? That's not too personal?'

'Are you kidding? Her arse is amazing. If that was me, I'd be forcing people to look. Though it was weird seeing the room across the hall in, like, a porn context. Makes you think about the porn houses.'

'What are you talking about?' I put brown rice into the basket and checked Jeannie's list: sea salt next.

'Just the houses they film porn in. I mean they look like Airbnbs most of the time, don't they? Blank walls, generic art.'

'They probably are.'

'Hey, would that be a good listicle? Could I sell that? Interior design in porn?' Femi stopped to make a note on her phone.

'Oh God.' I'd forgotten avocados.

'What?'

'I have to go back. I have to go back to the vegetables.'

Femi laughed. 'Okay, no, you're on your own, sorry. I'll wait out front.'

I waded back through the tide of men in suits, women on hands-free calls, everyone harried and ignoring each other, to the avocados, which were out of stock. 'Great,' I said out loud, to nobody.

I swung back through dried goods for cashews and ginger tea, and then the list was done. While I was paying at the till with Jeannie's card, I realised I'd forgotten to pick myself up any lunch. I wasn't going back in there. I'd have to stop somewhere else.

Femi was leaning on the front wall, vaping, when I got out. She was the only person I knew who made vaping look cool. I watched her a moment before she turned towards me, imperious and confident in her nineties corduroy jacket, designer glasses and braided bob. Hackney-trendy, but in an ex-goth way, and far too cool to be stuck at Hodgepodge forever. My heart contracted with fear. I wanted good things for Femi, but if she got out of this job before me, I would die.

'Come on,' she said, and we started back to the office.

'What were you telling me about your housemate?'

'Oh, yeah,' Femi said, offering me a Popchip from bag one. I declined. 'So apparently she tweets this mathematically exact mix of like, emotional vulnerability, one-liners, and side-boob. Irresistible combination. But she said that's what makes it feel like work, having to get the tweets right.'

'Wow.'

'Yeah, she's tried making stuff up, but those never land, only ones about how she's *actually* feeling – stuff that involves a piece of her. Like, her real soul.'

I agreed that it sounded like a lot of emotional labour. We reached our building, took our cards out for the scanners by reception. 'At least our souls are nothing to do with it,' I said.

'Yeah,' Femi said. 'Still. Nice to be rich enough to live by yourself.'

I was too needy to live alone, but I knew what she meant. Until a fortnight ago, I'd shared a flat with my boyfriend, Chris, a pandemic situationship that we'd both allowed to drag on longer than it should. I wasn't overly sad about the break-up, which seemed inevitable, but I was dreading having to live in a houseshare again.

'Yeah. That would be nice.'

We went back to work.

*

Ever since the break-up, I'd been staying on my best friend Anita's couch. She lived in a big ex-council flat in Whitechapel, with high ceilings and those really good windows you can open in two directions. It was a sparse, strangely furnished flat, because it had a rotating cast of housemates who never seemed to be able to move out with all their belongings, but Anita had been there years and had the second-biggest room, and said she would die before she moved again.

Either through seniority, skillset, or because none of her current housemates were that into cooking, the kitchen seemed to belong to Anita more than anyone else. We would often eat long, leisurely meals in there, recipes she'd learned to make on one of her courses. Anita was a rampant self-improver, though not in a modern, Always Be Optimising way – she was simply one of life's joiners-in, like those retirees who go indefatigably from WI meeting to language class, but in the body of a twenty-nine-year-old who worked in marketing.

Tonight, we were enjoying a risotto she'd perfected on a three-day Italian cooking intensive. It was spectacular. We'd nearly finished when her housemate Nice Pete burst in, shouted, 'I cannot fucking believe it,' and threw his backpack on the floor. I'd never seen him raise his voice before. We stared.

Nice Pete – whose name implied the existence of a second, less-nice Pete who I had never met – was the only one who'd lived in the flat longer than Anita. The other rooms were occupied by an American PhD student whose name I could never remember, and Nads, a twenty-three-year-old personal trainer, who lived in the box room and hated me.

That's not fair. We didn't really know each other, but I'd been staying on their couch for two weeks, and she kept making loaded comments about how she needed the communal space for her pre-work workouts, and I always slept in too late. I didn't understand how anyone could need to exercise before going to work in a gym all day (???), but I still felt guilty. I'd had the box room in houseshares before and it was shit. I just didn't have anywhere else to go.

'What happened?' Anita asked.

Nice Pete looked embarrassed. He picked up his rucksack and muttered, 'Sorry.' I wondered if he was talking to us or the bag. 'But my fucking bike got stolen *again*. That's the second time this year.'

We made sympathetic noises. Pete opened the fridge and began rummaging around in there, while explaining that he'd come out of a pub to find it gone, even though he'd had a really good, quite expensive D-lock. 'Bastards must have brought an electric saw,' he said, and emerged from the fridge holding a yogurt.

'Sorry, Pete, that's shit,' said Anita. It was hard to know what else to say: everyone we knew who rode a bike had had it stolen at least once.

'That's London for you,' I added lamely.

'Yeah,' said Nice Pete. He opened the yogurt and stood for a while in silence, licking the lid and staring out of the window. Then he moved on to the main event. There was something thrilling about watching an angry man eat a banana yogurt. Maybe I was ready to live in a houseshare again, after all.

Anita glanced at me. I could tell she was wondering how long we'd have to mourn Pete's bike before we could go back to our conversation. Eventually he sighed, rinsed the yogurt pot out, and put it into the recycling. 'I'm gonna go tell Nads about my bike,' he said, and left.

'Phew,' I said. 'Yikes.'

'Poor guy.'

'So what were you saying about that man you hate?'

Anita had been telling me about her new enemy, a colleague who kept trapping everyone in pointless meetings with long, boring stories. 'Yeah, so now he's started reheating fish in the office microwave every day, some kind of fad diet. Fish in an open-plan office, I mean, Jesus Christ.' I made a sympathetic face. 'And not just at lunch – several times a day. I think it's a protein thing, for like . . . powerlifting?'

'I thought that was chicken?' I said, remembering a man I'd seen eat a Tupperware of chicken and broccoli at a party at 1 a.m.

'Well for this guy, it's fish,' she said. 'The whole office stinks.'

Anita and I met at university, in the first week, when she got too drunk at a roller-disco and all the cool girls from her floor abandoned her. We were in the same halls, so when I saw her being sick into a bin, I'd recognised her, scooped her up and got her home. We'd been inseparable ever since. We still were, even though she'd become organised and sensible in the last few years, started ironing her bedsheets, paying into a pension and drinking less, using the money she saved by not buying twenty Marlboro Gold every time she was battered to pay for her courses. Did I feel immature in comparison? Yes, sometimes, but I was too busy benefitting from the fruits of her labour to mind.

'Anyway,' she said. 'How was your day? You got back late. Was it busy?'

'Um,' I said. There was an unwritten rule in our friendship that you were allowed to complain as long as you made it funny. 'Oh. Well, in the afternoon, I just kind of . . . couldn't work? I was too, like – *ugh! This job!* You know? It's draining the life out of me! I think I was hungry? I got distracted doing Jeannie's shopping and forgot to buy lunch. So I went for a walk, but then I just sort of disassociated in the park for ages, and when I got back, I had loads of stuff to do, so, yeah. That's why I was late!'

Anita was looking at me, and I realised I hadn't succeeded in making any of this funny, I'd just said several depressing things in a loud voice. 'Are you okay, Dan?'

I waved a hand. 'Fine. I need a new job, we know that. But now I have to move house in like, three months – four – I've been wondering if I should just stick it out till everything's sorted and stop applying for stuff? I don't know.'

Soon after the break-up, I'd called our landlord to ask if Chris and I could move out early, seeing as we could no longer live together, and neither of us would be able to afford the flat alone. Our landlord had explained that, because of the contract, he could only let us out if we paid, upfront, the four months' rent remaining on our lease, while I tried to say 'Mmm,' like we had the money to seriously consider this. So Chris and I had agreed we should each find somewhere free to live for two months – first me, then him – until the contract was up in February, when we could get our deposits back and move on. Staying in the same one-bedroom flat was too depressing to contemplate, we'd have ended up sleeping together out of politeness. But now I was in a strange position, with months of inertia between me and my life starting again.

'Dan,' Anita said slowly. 'I actually . . .' Then she stood up, shut the kitchen door, stuck the radio on. Houseshare privacy. My heart sank. 'I have to talk to you about all that.'

Somehow, I knew what was coming. Like I'd been waiting for it. 'Oh, shit. I'm out, right? You need me off the couch.'

'Ugh, I'm so sorry,' said Anita, her large, brown eyes wet with guilt. '*Please* don't be upset.'

'I'm not,' I said. Was I? I didn't know. I was stressed, obviously, but mainly I didn't want Anita to feel bad; it wasn't her fault.

'But I do feel bad,' she said, when I pointed this out.

We went back and forth a while, an inane feedback loop of guilt, until I said, 'This conversation is stupid. Let's go outside and smoke the really old cigarette I found in my desk this morning.' Neither of us technically smoked anymore, but we deserved a treat.

'Okay,' said Anita.

There was a scrubby little park at the back of Anita's block. We sat on a bench there, in our jackets, breath fogging as I clicked her lighter, shook it, tried again. I was surprised by how cold it was, though I shouldn't have been. October already. The weeks since Chris and I broke up had been strange, suspended; the cold was a reminder that, outside my life, the world was still turning. Dark nights ready to roll in.

The lighter caught, and an acrid, stale taste hit the back of my throat. I coughed. It really was a very old cigarette.

'Wow,' Anita said, watching me. 'Great trailer.'

'No, it's nice,' I lied, trying to stop coughing. She laughed, and I did too, but her eyes were still glassy when she lifted the cigarette from my fingers.

'It's been really nice, living with you again,' she said.

I looked at Anita, with her neat, dark hair, her fringe that was elegant without being try-hard, her work clothes that somehow looked freshly ironed after a day in the office. She was right. It had been nice. We'd lived together at university, and then for several years when we first moved to London, until Anita started earning real money and moved, apologetically, to zone two. We'd stayed close, of course, but deep in the soul of our friendship, we were housemates, at our happiest when we were both wearing pyjamas.

'Yeah,' I said.

She took a drag and immediately started coughing. 'Wow. This is fucking rancid.'

'Anita, don't feel bad about the couch thing, okay? It's so great that I was able to stay this long.'

She shook her head. 'But where will you go?'

I didn't have an answer to that, so ignored it. 'Anyway, I've known this was coming since Saturday, so it's not really a shock.'

She frowned. 'What was Saturday?'

'Um,' I said, trying to think of a non-embarrassing way to say that I had been woken at 3 a.m. by the sound of her and Nads having a drunken row in the kitchen, in which Anita kept repeating, voice shrill and defensive, 'Dan's had a hard time! She's having a hard time!'

'Nads just sort of dropped some hints that she was done, you know? Which is fair enough.'

Anita frowned. 'Yeah. I mean, full disclosure, it was Pete's decision. But he fancies Nads, so she probably just asked him.'

'Why was it Pete's decision?'

'Well, it's his flat.'

'What?' I said. 'Do you mean because he's like . . . been there the longest?'

Anita snorted. 'Dan, it's *his flat*. His dad owns it. I'm sure I told you that?'

'But,' I said. 'But – he was talking about paying rent like two days ago. He said something to me *specifically* about having to pay rent.'

'Oh, yeah, he does that. He said he doesn't want it to be weird, so he always says "rent" instead of "mortgage", to make it like – well, yeah. Less weird.'

I wasn't sure this did make things less weird. I took a big drag of our disgusting cigarette, which at least lit up all the parts of my brain it was supposed to light up, and began mentally reviewing all the interactions I'd had with Nice Pete over the last fortnight.

'I'm sorry,' Anita said, into the silence.

I shook my head. 'No. Stop. We agreed.'

'You know if it was up to me, you could stay the whole two months.'

I smiled. She was so busy and together and nice. My life might be a shambles but at least I had Anita. 'Honestly, it's fine. When am I out?'

'I've got him to agree to one more week. I hope that's okay.'

It was better than I'd feared, and I felt a rush of gratitude. 'That's amazing, thank you. I'll get on it tomorrow. I'll find somewhere. Don't give it another thought.'

*

That night, I stayed up on the couch for a long time after Anita went to bed, drinking wine and scrolling on my phone. Her living room was familiar, comfortable, with its sunny yellow walls, small TV and assorted collection of Monet prints, tacked up with that no-nails stuff for renters, that guaranteed not to rip your paint off, but always did. The prints belonged to Maja, a former art history student, working in finance, who'd left them behind when she moved out. This couch had been my second home for years, a place to crash after nights out and late dinners, whenever I couldn't be bothered to brave the night bus back to South London. Now it was my only home. And soon I would be – where?

The room was too quiet, so I turned the TV on and flicked backwards, through the news and radio stations to the late-night sales channels. Even though I lived in the world of streamers, I had never been able to break this habit from my youth. I didn't buy anything, but found the sound comforting, like white noise. Tonight, a man called Brian was trying to sell me a chunky necklace. He grinned with large, false teeth, shouting, 'Mega deals! Mega deals!'

Presumably at some point I fell asleep. I must have, because the next thing I knew, I woke to find the room in darkness and the TV off. One of Anita's housemates had presumably heard it blaring and come in. Embarrassing. That would be a mark against me, although I remembered blearily that I was already out, so what did it matter now? Then I realised I was not alone.

A jolt went through me. From where I lay on the sofa, very still, I could see someone standing in the corner of the room, behind the television.

I couldn't make out who it was, but the shape was unmistakeable, definitely a person, definitely somebody (Pete?) standing there in the dark like a freak, while I slept. *Now that he's throwing me out*, I thought, *he's going to try and sleep with me before I go, thinking I'm sad and drunk and ready for a rebound.* I was gearing up to tell him to fuck off when I realised it wasn't Pete at all.

The certainty was sudden, indescribable, something shifting in the room, like when the light changes or fails in some subtle way before a thunderstorm. Not different for any obvious reason, but different, different forever, because suddenly I knew it wasn't Pete – it wasn't any of the people who lived in this flat.

My heart thumped in my chest. Stupidly, I tried to say, 'Hello?' like that would help in a home invasion, but nothing came out of my mouth. It was round about then that I realised I couldn't move.

I wasn't tied up or anything – I just couldn't move, like all the telephone lines to all my limbs had been cut. I was sending the signals, but no one was getting them. Panic rolled through my body as I tried to sit up, go for the light, and all the time the stranger stood there, calm, backlit by the dull glow of streetlights through the windows, watching me. Nothing worked.

I tried to calm myself. I must be having a nightmare. But I could see all the familiar trappings of the living room so clearly: Maja's prints, Anita's cushions, Pete's laundry on the rack. How could a dream have so much detail? The figure looked wrong in the middle of these everyday things, hunched, quietly breathing, seeming to expand and contract with each breath.

Still unable to move, I had no choice but to lie and watch it, waves of horror breaking across me the whole time. And yet, the more I watched, the more certain I was that this wasn't a person at all. It was more like a shadow, an absence. It began to move. Not as a person would – more like the way fog rolls over a field. It moved like a wall closing in, and then it was there, above me, a darkness, hands on my face. I screamed.

That was when I woke up on the couch. I don't think I'd really been making a noise, but there was a sound caught in my throat, panicked and involuntary, as I scrabbled to put the lamp on.

In its light, the room looked ordinary. Empty. The TV was indeed off, blinds still open, everything just as it had been, except that I was alone. I searched for my phone, which had fallen down between my body and the couch; it was 4 a.m. My heart was in my throat and I didn't want to lie in the dark again, couldn't, somehow, bear the thought of it.

I got up to close the blinds, then put the TV back on, muted, with some kind of soap opera playing. I lay there for a long time, light on, watching the characters' mouths move with no idea what any of them were saying. I don't know how long it took me to fall asleep again. A long time, I think.

*

And then I was back at my desk.

It was bad inside my emails: the DPDI panel was the next day, Thursday, and we still didn't have anyone to chair. Also, Jeannie had sent me several long, rambling emails late at night, about some paint samples she wanted me to order. I'd forgotten that she was repainting her home office and needed testers before she could make a decision. She'd sent a few links and some names, asking for 'those and similar x20 or so options', which seemed insane to me, like way too many, but who was I to say? I'd never painted a room before.

It was hard to focus on the pointless shit Jeannie wanted me to do. I had one week to find somewhere else to live in London, for free, for nearly two months. But I must know someone who could help. I switched windows, work email to personal, and opened a new draft, to make a list:

1. *Mum?*

She would definitely put me up, but there were several problems here. Firstly, I hadn't wanted to worry her, so I hadn't actually told her yet that Chris and I had split up. I was still thinking of a way to phrase it that sounded *fine*.

Secondly, she'd had her hours cut at work last year, and moved into a one-bed flat, so there wasn't much room for me, and I didn't really want to spend two months sleeping on her couch. Thirdly, she still lived in my home town, near Birmingham, which was too far to commute to London, and too expensive.

Could I work remotely? We'd all done it in the pandemic, planning meetings in the Hodgepodge group chat, but Jeannie had made it clear that when the lockdowns ended, my job needed to be done in person. Mollie and Nick worked from home about half the time, and Femi was allowed one day a week, but Jeannie wanted me in, boots on the ground, to answer calls and make coffees. I guess it made sense. My job was mainly errands.

If the housing situation got really desperate, I could always quit and stay on Mum's couch. I wanted to leave Hodgepodge anyway, didn't I? But the thought of going back to that town with no job, and no flat in London – nothing to hold onto, nothing to bring me back here – was not good.

It was the thing I'd been scared of ever since I got out of that town in the first place. Having to crawl home with my tail between my legs. Bumping into an old teacher in the pasta aisle of Morrisons. 'Come back, have you?' they'd say. 'Aw, well, it's tough down there,' with an air of kindly finality that implied I was home, now, for good. No. Better to have a job I didn't love and keep clinging onto the city I'd chosen, where, unlike my home town, no adult man had ever shouted 'GOTH BITCH' at me in the street for wearing eyeliner.

2. Dad?

Not an obvious one because we rarely spoke, beyond Christmas cards and the odd text. Dad went back to Scotland and remarried after my parents split up, when I was five, and we hadn't been close since, which to be honest I thought was his fault, because he was the adult, though I'd been an adult well over a decade now and hadn't made much effort either. Anyway, whatever. Same problem as Mum, I couldn't commute to work from Scotland, but I wanted to stay with him even less.

3. Anita

Always the next person on the list. But no, obviously not.

4. Ben

Ben was my other best friend. He would definitely put me up for a bit, but he rented a studio so small that it didn't even have a couch. It was nowhere near big enough for two people. It wasn't really big enough for one person. Ben had so little storage space that he'd had to sell or give away most of his possessions before he moved in, a situation I'd described as insane, and he'd described as 'medically necessary', after a houseshare with some friends went south. The housemates in question had started sleeping together, and he'd had to pretend not to notice, which was fine, until they broke up without ever having got together. It was harder to pretend once they were having screaming rows in the middle of the night, and by the time they were both trying to sleep with Ben, to get revenge on each other, he'd told me that if he couldn't live alone from now on, he would drown himself. (Another reason not to impose.)

I looked at the list, wondered who else I could add. Obviously I had more than two friends, but I wasn't really in touch with any of them enough to ask for such a huge favour. I'd got lax since the pandemic, let a lot of things slide. Anyway, like Anita, like Femi, they were all in house-shares, so it meant making a nuisance of myself on another communal couch.

I put Femi's name down anyway, with a question mark, just in case.

5. *Femi?*
6. *Chris???*

Could I really admit defeat and go back to my own flat? Even seeing his name on the list was depressing. Two weeks ago, we'd sat down like grown-ups and agreed on a plan; I could picture his face, eyes rolling behind his wire-rim glasses, if I called this quickly and asked to come back. He would be so *irritated*. Also, it had been a mutual break-up, but really, if we were honest, more his idea than mine, and calling your ex, begging them to let you stay on your own couch, was too embarrassing. I may not have much, but at least I had my pride.

Jeannie arrived then, doing her queenly wave, so I got up to boil the kettle. While I was standing in the kitchenette making coffee, I heard Jeannie talking to Mollie about the DPDI panel, which I still needed to sort out, and hadn't.

'Morning, Danielle,' Jeannie said, as I put the coffee down on her desk. Dusky lilac, so much nicer in here. 'Was that all clear about the paints?'

'Yes,' I said, though I'd barely looked at the emails. 'Absolutely.'

I went back to my own desk, under the strip-lights, and opened the links Jeannie had sent in the night. There were greens called *lichen* and *sap*, blues called *sardine* and *coppice* and *sloe*, reds and purples, *harissa*, *menagerie*, *church roof*. Every room on the website was beautiful. I thought about sleeping in show homes; about the Christmas film I'd loved as a kid, where a family lose their flat and stay, secretly, in a department store. I imagined hiding in the big John Lewis, sleeping in their comfortable beds; it would be an easy commute to work from Oxford Street. I could walk.

While I added the yellows Jeannie wanted to my basket (*sand, biscuit, old stone*), I wondered why this was my job. Not Hodgepodge generally, though I often wondered that, but the paints specifically. Yes, Jeannie had said she was repainting her home office, but wasn't this too many colours for one room? I wondered if she was actually painting her whole house, and getting me to buy the samples on the work card. Then I wondered if I cared. Clearly this was stretching the boundaries of my job, but was it really worse than the time she'd got me to go to Fortnum's and do all her Christmas shopping? ('Not *all* of it, Danielle. Just the bits.') No, probably not. I got the work card from Nick, and bought the samples.

Anita texted, checking in. I'd left early, and she was worried I was upset, trying to avoid her. I said I wasn't, I'd just slept badly. She sent a bunch of hearts, then a short video of her colleague's fish revolving in the microwave, with the caption, *I will kill this motherfucker*.

I went back to the internet, and looked up some flats around Streatham, where I'd been living. I did the maths on exactly how badly I couldn't afford them. It was very bad. Then I looked up houseshares and did the maths on what it would cost me to take one now, before my lease was up. The answer being: £3,000 of debt.

I went to the bathroom to sit by myself in one of the cubicles and breathe deeply. I wondered whether crying would make me feel better, so I closed my eyes, put my hands over my face. *Go on then*, I thought. Nothing happened. I was too scattered, or too tired – I had slept so badly.

An image surfaced in my mind. The figure I'd seen in the night. How it moved. Strange, the way something so inhuman, so disembodied, could feel so actively malign. I knew it was only a nightmare, but I felt a shudder run through me all the same. I took out my phone and googled 'Figure by my bed'.

Several articles about ghosts came up on the kind of cheery, recycled web pages the broken internet age was full of, called things like Answer Me! and Wonder That and Let's Discuss, all barely useable through the mist of a million pop-ups. One website advised that spirits would often 'stop by' in the night while you were sleeping, and that if you 'didn't enjoy' their visits, you should simply 'tell them to go!' The next article was more like an agony aunt column, where the questioner had written, 'Help! For the last few nights I've been woken by a dark figure standing over my bed. Should I get my house exorcised? I don't want to tell my new boyfriend in case he thinks I'm crazy.' Commenters were advising her to burn sage, salt her window ledges, *get out of the house, girl!*

A reminder pinged. Jeannie had an eleven o'clock meeting, and I needed to sort refreshments. I threw some water on my face at the sinks, and went back to work.

I made coffee, arranged biscuits on a plate, poured sparkling water. I took everything upstairs and got a meeting room ready, fixing the blinds how Jeannie liked them, setting the thermostat to twenty-three. While I did all this, I thought about £3,000, how little it was to some people and how much to others. It wasn't crazy debt. Maybe it would be worth it for all of this to be over – just to take a room in a houseshare and get on with my life. But I had no savings, and I'd spent eight years in London steadily ticking down the credit card debt I'd accrued at university. I'd been free of the repayments for just six months. I couldn't bear to go back there so quickly.

Back at my desk, I opened Twitter and scrolled. I opened the BBC news website and scrolled. Then I closed it again because it was all too depressing. I went back to Twitter and searched *DPDI*, looking for high-ish profile people who'd been talking about internet privacy. I scanned a couple of impenetrable articles, tried to work out how to contact the people who'd written them. I found one journalist, Luke, whose tweets were actually quite funny, and who had a contact form on his website. I wrote to him, then a couple of the others.

The phone rang: Jeannie's ex-husband Hugo, the father of her children, calling to check on Edward. He'd been to the flat and found no sign. I said he was staying with Jeannie again. 'Money run out, did it?' said Hugo, laughing. 'All well and good, then. You might let her know I called? Cheerio.'

I went back to the house website in case anything incredibly cheap had come up in the last twenty minutes, even though the numbers I was looking for would be impossible. I searched in Streatham, in Whitechapel, in Norbury, in Tooting. I found a website for people who were paying minimal rent and topping it up with jobs for their landlord: pastry cheffing, au pairing, gardening. The problem was, I already had a job, and also, I didn't have any skills. I went back to the house website and, to torture myself, flicked to buying instead of renting, and set £400,000 as the minimum price. I scrolled for a while through photographs of places I would never be able to afford, because I'd always spent 50–60% of everything I earned on rent, and had no savings, and even if I didn't go back into debt, now, for this, there would be something else eventually, wouldn't there.

Red-brick, wisteria-covered cottages in the Cotswolds. Multi-floor mansions in Highgate. High-ceilinged apartments in Whitstable. The colours of all those lovely walls were slightly familiar. *Lichen. Sap. Harissa. Church roof.* Flicking through well-lit photographs of beautiful kitchens gave me the same feeling I used to get playing with doll's houses as a kid: all the little rooms, the little people, all pretend.

My work emails pinged. The journalist with the funny-ish tweets, Luke, was free tomorrow night and happy to chat about chairing the panel. My ennui dissipated instantly. I was a genius! I had solved the DPDI thing all by myself, probably. I couldn't wait to tell everyone. Then I saw that one of my uni group chats was going crazy, with thirty-two unread messages. The first, from Ben, said: *WHOSE SEEING MY SHOW THEN CUNTS?*

Ben had been out of London for weeks, on tour. In all the chaos, I'd forgotten the show was finishing with a run at a pub theatre, starting tonight. The other messages were pointless back-and-forth from people I liked but never saw anymore, so I messaged Ben directly: *free ticket tonight?*

He answered immediately: *On the door. Drinks after?*

Obvs, I replied.

Ben was back in town. Maybe everything was going to be okay.

*

Though I met Anita on my first day of university, it was another six months before I met Ben, at a drama club I'd gone to, to try and get 'out of myself' after a break-up. I say a break-up, like it was casual. Actually I'd had my heart smashed to bits by my college boyfriend, Matt.

Matt was the first great love of my life. Why, I don't know. Slim pickings in that town. He was the only boy in our A level English class who actually read the books, and apparently that was enough. I was private to the point of secrecy as a teenager – and, to be honest, I still am – so I did what anyone in my place would do. I made instant, close friends with Matt, jocular and sisterly, to ensure my crush was hidden not just from him, but from everyone I'd ever met. I worked as hard as possible to hide it even from myself. I would take it to the grave. Obviously that meant I had to pretend to be cool and normal about the girlfriend he got six weeks into college, Beautiful Emma Who Could Drive, from his Spanish class.

Matt and Emma were together nearly eighteen months, practically married by teenage standards. When she chucked him the spring before A levels, we were close enough friends that he literally cried on my shoulder about it. I felt confused, but noble; I read about nunneries, listened to Sufjan Stevens, sobbed into my pillow at night. It was fine. Normal. Until a month later, battered on cider and blacks on the dance floor of some awful Scream pub, when Matt leaned over and kissed me, like something out of an episode of *Skins*. That was it: there was no will-they-won't-they, it was just like, kiss, bam, together, and suddenly we were the Danny and Sandy of our FE college on the edge of a shit Midlands town.

I lost my virginity to him two weeks later, then pushed him to tell me about losing his with Emma, picked a fight about nothing, and cried all the way home on the bus. The whole thing was like that: volatile, frightening, like I was going to be sick all the time. I supposed I was happy, though; I must be.

We were the only people in our group of friends going to university rather than taking a year out or getting a job. We both hated the town we were from, it was one of the first things I'd liked about him, the feeling that somebody else was going to make it out. I was off to Leeds, Matt to Southampton, so we'd be pretty far apart, but we planned train journeys, weekends, trips we would take. Danny and Sandy. The future was bright. I remember people saying, 'Whatever you do, don't go to uni with a boyfriend', but I just laughed at them. This wasn't a boyfriend, this was *the love of my life*.

When I finally got to Leeds, I bored on about Matt at parties. Anita's friends used to tease me – not meanly, but still, I felt the sting of how parochial I was. The common, small-town girl, with the credit cards and the boyfriend. But every couple of weeks I'd go down on the coach to visit him and stop caring what anyone thought. They were the only times I ever really knew peace, when we were literally within metres of one another, and even then it wasn't guaranteed. I remember lying in Matt's single halls bed one night, listening to the girl in the next room come home smashed from a night out, crying a long, terrible cry like a siren. I was worried about her, but he said, 'Oh God, don't. Melissa's nuts,' and I felt a little glow of satisfaction at being The Girlfriend: not nuts; reliable; a rock.

Those moments were worth savouring because I barely enjoyed being eighteen and in love at all. It was all so huge and terrible, and I worried constantly about when we would split up, and if he loved me as much as I loved him, which frankly he obviously did not. Still – I thought about our future a lot. We'd move to London. I could see it all: the rented flat, shared things, dog, garden. Both of us would have the kind of high-paying jobs that allowed us to enjoy expensive hobbies, like the private school girls at my university, who spent their weekends climbing and hiking and generally keeping fit, instead of lying in horrible hungover pits of self-loathing like I did. I'd seen them comparing their walking shoes that cost hundreds of pounds, even though before I got to university, I would have said that surely, of all the exercises, walking was the cheapest?

So it was a blow when, in the spring of first year, the letter arrived from Melissa, the girl on the other side of Matt's wall. It said she was sleeping with him and had been for months, which had been very painful for her, because she was a feminist, and knew he had a girlfriend. Now, out of her deep respect for me, she was moved to confess the whole thing in a multi-page, agonised letter, handwritten in pink gel pen. I read the whole thing several times, wondering if it was a joke, but deep down I knew that it wasn't.

When I called Matt, he wouldn't even argue with me. He just admitted it, apologised, then hung up and blocked my number. That was that: we hadn't even been together a year, and it was over.

It sounds ridiculous to say this now, but I was so upset that I actually considered dropping out of university. I felt so much shame. Not just because he'd humiliated me: because I'd been waiting all my life to move to a city, and I'd already wasted most of the first year pining after someone who didn't give a shit about me. With all the debt I was going into, maybe I was better off drawing a line under the whole thing and giving up, going home.

I lay for several days in my halls bedroom, staring at the white-washed walls, their mysterious stains from former occupants. I hadn't got round to buying grown-up bed covers, so I rotted in my *101 Dalmatians* sheets, the desk strewn with unopened, forgotten books and unwashed mugs.

Anita snapped me out of it in the end, thank God. After the millionth day of bringing soup to my bed like I was a sick little baby, she told me it had been long enough: I needed to shower and dress and leave my room. When I said that actually, I was thinking of dropping out, she called me a cunt. Anita swore so rarely, and never the big ones; I was shocked out of my misery.

'Okay,' I said. 'Yeah.' I got out of bed.

'You need to join a club or something,' she said, opening a window.

That night, I went to Anita's room. We sat on her purple beanbag and looked at the list on the student union website. There were clubs for politics and religion and music and LARPing and salsa dancing, clubs for almost everything you could think of. I put off choosing anything until a few days later, when I was buying a panini in the student union. I stood waiting for them to heat it up, looking at the posters for club nights and foam parties, and advising you not to get crabs, when I saw one advertising auditions for the drama club's summer production of *Henry IV*. I went before I could change my mind.

I'd barely even done school plays, so I honestly don't know what possessed me, but before I knew what was happening, I'd been offered the role of a bawdy tavern wench (typecast for the tits and the accent, presumably), and found myself sitting in a draughty room with a bunch of people I didn't know.

PRINCE
Thou art so fat-witted, with drinking
of old sack, and unbuttoning thee after supper,
and sleeping upon benches after noon, that thou
hast forgotten to demand that truly which thou
wouldst truly know.

He stuck out as soon as he opened his mouth. The guy playing the lead, the charming and wayward Prince Hal, was miles better than the rest of us. Not that I didn't give the tavern wench a good college try. And some of the others were all right. But, Hal: whatever it is that some actors have, that quality that makes you want to watch them, he just – had it.

> *What a devil hast thou to*
> *do with the time of the day? unless hours were*
> *cups of sack, and minutes capons, and clocks*
> *the tongues of bawds, and dials the signs of*
> *leaping-houses, and the blessed sun himself a*
> *fair hot wench in flame-colour'd taffeta, I see no*
> *reason why thou shouldst be so superfluous to*
> *demand the time of the day.*

Something about those soft, posh vowels was a balm after weeks of teenage misery. Maybe I liked Shakespeare now? Or maybe I just fancied this guy. I didn't think so, though. I was impressed, that was all. It was nice, watching someone do the thing they were meant to be doing in this life.

After rehearsals, everyone went to the pub, and I ended up standing next to him at the bar. 'You were great, by the way,' I said, bracing myself for disappointment, a run-in with some flintily charismatic posh boy.

'Aw, thanks,' he said. 'You're new, right? Is it Danielle? I'm Ben.'

I stared, surprised by the sheer difference of him: the northern accent he'd smoothed the edges off; his gentle, polite friendliness. 'Acting's a fucking lie, isn't it?' I said, and he laughed.

That night was one of the first times I really had fun at university. I loved Anita, but her friends liked to dress up nicely and go clubbing, and I've never been able to wear hairspray without feeling like Miss Piggy. Finally, I could drink a pint in a jumper and relax. Although, like a lot of Heartbreak Havers, I flew too close to the sun in the end.

I remember the pub shutting, and going to the student union, and then the union shutting, and going somewhere else. Colours. Shapes. Ben and I were both in halls, we must have ended up alone in one of the takeaways out of town, because the next thing I really remember is crying in a chippie, saying – I don't remember what, exactly, but I know the kind of thing, because it beat at the edges of my ribcage all that spring, threatening to come out whenever I had a drink. *I loved him so much and I was just his rebound from Emma.* Ben frowning at me, impossibly patient and gentle when he said, 'Okay. Who? And who's Emma?'

Maybe it's not surprising that I transferred some of my post-break-up intensity into our friendship. We were almost exactly the same height and had almost exactly the same birthday, three days apart, so went through a phase of calling ourselves The Twins and going to parties in the same outfits, which had been sort of confusing. I was on the verge of going a bit weird before he got a boyfriend and I snapped out of it. Anyway, we'd been best friends ever since, a lovely friendship that I now paid for by watching him in all the worst fringe theatre shows in the world, Ben having gone to drama school after we graduated, and become a real actor.

I was so glad he was back in London. If anyone could cheer me up after the last few horrible weeks, it was him.

*

'So that was fucking shit,' said Ben.

I was in the middle of sending a string of horrified messages to Anita when he emerged from the dressing rooms. The show, *Liquid Animals*, had turned out to be about a man (played by Ben) with a drug addiction, coming to terms with his childhood sexual abuse via several played-out conversations with different aspects of his psyche, personified by actors who were pretending to be, variously, a lion, a dog and a fish. It was one of the worst things I'd ever seen in my life.

'No-o,' I said, so unconvincingly that Ben started laughing, and then I laughed too. He reached the bottom of the stairs where I was waiting, shrugging his jacket on with one arm, unlit cigarette clamped in his mouth, and pulled me into a hug. 'Come on. Let's grab a drink and get outside before we have to speak to anyone.'

The play had been on in a little room above a rough North London pub. Ben got the drinks in ('my round. You had to sit through that shit'), then steered us out to the beer garden. It was small and ratty, in this case meaning both 'unkempt' and, according to Ben, 'full of rats'.

'Huge bastards,' he added, lighting up. 'Keep your feet off the floor.'

'How? We're standing on it.'

'Well let's sit down then.'

We sat on top of a picnic table, with our feet on the bench, which Ben said was the only way to stay safe and, far from minding, the pub landlord had specifically told him to do it. We were the only people out there. I patted Ben on the back while he let out a long, low, agonised noise, a sort of *hurgggggghhhhhhhhhhh*. Then he clinked our glasses together, said, 'Okay. Nearly better. Cheers,' and drank about a third of his pint in one swallow.

I used to wonder why Ben wanted me to see him in things he knew were dreadful, and a few years ago had even asked. He said that if he had to do bad shows night after night, for people who were hating it and hating him for inflicting it upon them, it was nice to have at least one person in the audience who was onside, or at least didn't blame him personally.

'I know you'll think this is bollocks, but you were great,' I said. He really had been, somehow. Ben was good in everything. 'And isn't that a mark of real talent? To be good in something like this?'

Ben shook his head, not in disagreement so much as in disbelief. 'Yeah. I don't know. Who knows.' He put a hand on my shoulder and held me at arm's-length, looking at me intently. 'Anyway. How are you holding up?'

I looked back. Ben's floppy, too-long hair was in his face, and he was unshaven and drawn from weeks of touring, drinking too much, not sleeping in his own bed. I was so relieved to see him. 'Oh, fine,' I said. 'Yeah. You know.'

'Yeah?' He let go of my shoulder. 'Anita told me about the house stuff.'

I felt a flare of irritation. They were friendly with one another, but not close. I didn't like the thought of them discussing me, like a problem that needed to be solved. 'Why?'

'Well, she's worried about you,' he said reasonably. 'She thinks you're super freaked out but won't talk about it. She asked if I knew anywhere you could crash for a few weeks.'

'Do you?' I asked, too quickly.

'You're welcome at mine anytime, you know that. What?' He must have seen the look on my face.

'Come on. You live in a shoebox.'

'Two shoes fit in every box. Anyway, go on, how's the heartbreak? Are you crying? Kickboxing?'

I snorted, sipped my beer. 'I really don't think I'm heartbroken.'

'Oh,' said Ben. His brow creased, like he was trying to work something out. I wasn't sure I wanted him working anything out against my will. He opened his mouth to speak.

'Hey,' I interrupted. 'Guess what?'

Ben frowned. 'What?'

'I got Scrooged last night.'

'Like . . . the Bill Murray film?'

'Like I was haunted by – well, not three spirits, just one.'

'What the fuck are you talking about, Mac?' Ben was the last of my friends who still called me that, short for my surname, MacKinnon.

I laughed, and told him I'd woken in the middle of the night to see a dark, shadowy figure in the corner of the room. 'Obviously it was a dream,' I said. 'But – I don't know. It was weird. I could see everything in there, exactly how it looks when I'm awake, except I was asleep, obviously, and . . .' I trailed off. It was only while describing it to Ben that I saw how unsettled the dream had made me. I'd been thinking about it all day, that dark shadow. Once or twice, I'd even felt like I was being watched.

'And you couldn't move?'

'No.'

'That's sleep paralysis, isn't it?' asked Ben, lifting his pint to take another drink. He looked at me over his raised elbow.

'Right,' I said. 'And what is that?'

Ben laughed. 'It's like – when your brain gets caught between sleeping and waking. I worked with a lighting designer a few years back who got it loads.'

I sat up. 'Exactly the same? With the shadow?'

'Not exactly, but he used to wake up to this . . . He called it The Creature. I think it was a sort of goblin? And he'd find it sitting on his chest, pressing down on him, so he couldn't move.'

'Jesus.'

'Yeah, which is a whole thing. Look.' Ben took his phone out, googled *sleep paralysis* and showed me the top hit, an eighteenth-century painting of a woman thrown back across a bed with a monster crouching on her ribcage. 'Apparently the hallucinations are caused by panic? Obviously you're kind of awake, but you can't move, because your brain turns your body off when you're sleeping, so you don't, like, punch the person you're next to in the face, or jump out of a window or whatever.'

I was warm with relief. Not that I'd thought it was actually a ghost. But it was nice to know I'd experienced something from the normal spectrum of human experience, and wasn't losing my mind. 'Wait. Your friend – did you say he got it *loads*?'

'Oh yeah,' said Ben. I made a face. 'But that doesn't mean you will! It's just – it's really common. I even had it once, back when I was drinking too much.'

I tried to remember a time when Ben's drinking had been worse than it was now, and failed. 'Is that bad for it? Alcohol?'

'Think so. But Imran got it whenever he was stressed or slept on his back.'

Drinking, stress, sleeping on your back: I had definitely been doing too much of all these things since I moved onto Anita's couch. I tried to recapture the relief I'd felt before. Normal! I was so deeply normal. But the thought it might come back again, the shadow, had unsettled me. I could live with being haunted once, but it wasn't something I wanted to make a habit of.

'Do you think it's stress about Chris?' Ben asked carefully.

'Or work,' I said.

'Yeah, maybe.' Ben looked at me, nodded. 'Jeannie still taking the piss?'

'Oh, she's not so bad,' I said vaguely. It was kind of Ben to let me change the subject, but maybe it wasn't surprising. He'd probably done it for the same reason I hadn't asked about Claude, the skinny French actor from the show, who'd been the main character in all Ben's touring voice notes. Not that there were loads of them – Ben's terrible at keeping in touch when he's away – but Claude was so present in every funny story that I'd wondered if they were seeing each other. I hadn't asked, though, and wasn't going to. Maybe it was weird, but Ben and I didn't really talk about that stuff.

Other people said he was braggy about his one-night stands, like that was an accepted fact – but he wasn't, not with me. One of a few funny little bubbles in our friendship, respect for each other's privacy or something. Maybe it came from all the months we'd spent calling ourselves The Twins, like it would be the same as knowing too much about a sibling.

Also, though Ben dated both men and women, he rarely dated seriously, and the fact he only vaguely alluded to these things in front of me had made it easy to make certain elisions which I now felt guilty about. Namely that for the whole two years we were together, I'd let Chris believe Ben was gay. I'd never actually lied: I just hadn't corrected him when he assumed. It had seemed easier than trying to explain our platonic closeness, but had also been like forcing my best friend into a bisexual closet. One of the nice things about splitting up with Chris was that I no longer had to worry about either of them finding out.

'Look,' I said. 'It's freezing out here, my hands are blue, can we go inside?'

Ben laughed. 'Sure. Everyone else should have gone by now.'

The pub was quiet. Ben got a table while I bought a round, and then we sat in the corner and talked. It was like a million other nights in a million identical pubs: the high ceiling, stained and yellowed from pre-smoking-ban smoke, or possibly from the smoking lock-ins I knew still went on; the dark red carpet, over-patterned, hiding a million sins; the shaggy old dog dozing in the corner.

We talked about the tour, Femi's housemate with the OnlyFans, an actor Ben worked with last year who'd been cancelled. We discussed a popular rumour about a politician who got all his assistants to peg him. Ben swore he had first-hand confirmation, but it turned out to come from a friend of a friend of a friend. 'That is not first-hand,' I said. 'Do you need me to explain to you what that phrase means?'

At some point, after several rounds, the bell rang for last orders, and Ben said, 'I'll get us a whisky. Double?'

'Jesus Christ,' I said. 'No.' I meant no to the whole confection, but he came back with a double for him and a single for me. The pub, which had been quiet before, was now completely empty.

'So, I read this article today about rich people,' said Ben, settling into his chair.

'Oh, the leaked texts?'

'What?'

'The actor with the leaked texts.'

'No, different rich people. What are you talking about?'

It was possible that I was drunk. 'Never mind. Go on.'

'Well,' said Ben, leaning back with his elbow across the seating bank. 'Apparently there's a company in America that are trying to sell rich people "the body of an eighteen-year-old". Their own, not one they've found in the street. Because they can, like, de-age all their . . . cells?'

Neither of us having a good understanding of science, our conversations on these subjects tended to break down around this point. 'Right,' I said. 'Cell-zapping machine.'

'You're joking, but it's real. It would be like *The Fly*, but when you get out of the box, instead of being a fly, you're you, and your brain's the same, but your body's young.'

'Brr,' I said.

'You wouldn't want that?'

'Who would?'

'I would.'

'Bullshit.'

Ben laughed. 'Of course. I used to be so full of – you know. Potential.'

I rolled my eyes. 'Name one thing you could have done when we were eighteen that you couldn't do now.'

Ben thought for a moment. 'The splits?'

I laughed. I remembered his splits era well: years ago, some drunken party, Ben stupidly revealing that he'd been a teenage gymnast, and then it had become his party trick, splits requested by our friends on a hundred sticky carpets and, on at least one occasion, in the middle of a dance floor.

I was trying to bully Ben into revisiting the splits era ('this place is empty! There's nobody here!') when the old man at the bar rang the bell again. This bell was specifically for us, and it meant: please go home. 'Sorry,' we called, standing up.

'How would the machine work, anyway?' I said, putting my jacket on. 'Cells die, don't they?'

'They surely do,' said Ben, downing the end of his drink. 'Come on. I'll walk you to the Tube.'

It had started raining while we were inside, and as I fumbled in my bag for my umbrella, I tried to imagine moving again inside my younger body. Eighteen. Twenty. Twenty-three. I didn't feel so different, but I must be. How many little cells had lived and died in all that time? If that was how cells worked; I wasn't sure.

I followed Ben to the door and we stood out front, under my umbrella, while he lit a cigarette. We were both thinking whatever we were thinking. One of our comfortable silences. Ben is a talking machine and I sometimes like to believe that I'm the only friend he can be quiet with; strange vanities in our friendship, strange chasms of insecurity.

'Penny for them?' he asked.

I didn't want to say. 'Just thinking about being eighteen,' I lied.

'What about it?'

Good question. 'I was just thinking,' I said, although I hadn't been, and wasn't sure what was going to come out of my mouth. 'That – it wouldn't matter.'

'What wouldn't?'

'The machine. You know, it wouldn't matter if they could make me *look* eighteen – all the good stuff about being that age still wouldn't come back.'

I glanced at Ben, wondering if he knew what I meant. The terror and excitement, the mystery of who we would become, that hadn't been in our bodies, it had been somewhere else. 'I guess I mean the potential,' I added, trying to remember what he'd been saying before, trying to seem like I was responding to something, and not just talking. But Ben looked as if he understood. Actually, he looked sad.

'Mac,' he started, but I cut him off.

'No, stop, shut up,' I said, because I didn't want to get into it all. The website where you could pay rent with graphic design, and £3,000 of debt, and leaving Anita's couch next week when I had nowhere to go.

'Jesus, I'm your best friend, will you not talk to me?'

I felt a mix of warmth and humiliation. This was as close to declarations of love as we got, and always, always that was what Ben said: *I'm your best friend*, never the other way around.

'Look. Here's what I want to say to you, Ben, okay,' I said. I took him by the shoulders. We looked at one another very seriously. 'Do you . . . want to go and get chips?'

'Well,' he said slowly. 'Yeah. Of course.'
I cheered.

*

The booze hit me on the bus home anyway, too late to have had dinner, not enough dinner to have had, and now that I was drunk and alone there was nothing to keep me from a really good, uninterrupted bathe in anxiety. I took out my phone, opened the draft email with the list in it. Disappointingly, no great ideas had magically appeared in the last twelve hours, like that story with the elves and the shoemaker. It was the same as I'd left it that morning:

1. *Mum?*
2. *Dad?*
3. *Anita*
4. *Ben*
5. *Femi?*
6. *Chris???*

I texted Femi to say I'd stayed out too late with Ben and was going to die tomorrow. She replied immediately, and while we were texting back and forth, I thought, fuck it, spare room at Femi's, who knows, and sent a series of messages in quick succession:

Been thinking about your housemate. The moving-out one with the OnlyFans? Big question so be honest

I wasn't sure how to phrase what came next. What was I asking for? I guess I wanted to say: if she's going to move out and leave the room paid up, I want to be in it. But how likely was that? I spent a while wondering how I could ask in the right way, typing and retyping, and then I saw Femi had sent me a voice note.

'Oh God, Dan, no,' she said, voice tinny through my cheap headphones. 'I know things are rough at the moment and your tits are great, so I get it, but you're too like – blocky. Square-shaped. I don't mean it in a bad way, I have the exact same thing, it's just that all the girls who make serious money on there are very conventionally attractive . . .'

I texted back immediately.

No!

I was going to ask about your SPARE ROOM!!!!!!!

For a while, we were hysterical. Gifs. Emojis. Voice notes of us both on the verge of tears. Eventually Femi remembered I'd asked her a real question.

Soz also yeah about the room thing, Dee said tonight she's changed her mind

She's going to stick with us like six more months and then """try to buy""" can you believe it . . . if we didn't look like Minecraft men that could be us ☹

I thought about the time Femi's housemate had let her cousin crash on their couch for a fortnight, how Femi complained bitterly the whole time, the strain it had put on her household. I crossed her off my list and said goodnight. *Get home safe*, she replied.

One option left.

That was fine though, right? Femi had knocked the anxiety out of me. It was late and I was loose, spacey, relaxed, and why shouldn't I go home? It had seemed awful to me that morning, but I could no longer remember why. Something to do with pride. Well, pride might be a luxury I couldn't currently afford.

I opened my WhatsApp thread with Chris. It was depressing in there, full of cosy, unsuspecting, pre-break-up chats about needing bread, and if our neighbours were leaving their dog alone too often. In the fortnight since the split, we hadn't texted, keeping our intermittent personal admin to email and calls, like colleagues. But now I spent five or so minutes composing a message that was clear but firm.

Hey Chris! Hope you're well. Just to say I've hit a bit of a speedbump with housing because Anita's housing situation has changed and so I think we're going to need to review the decisions we made. All in all I think it might just be easiest for me to stay on the couch until you're able to go back to your mum's. Is that ok? I can stay at Anita's one more week so let's chat housing practicalities tomorrow? Hope you're well xxx

I'd pressed send before rereading, but it seemed fine. I thought it struck a good balance between asking permission and presenting the situation as a fait accompli, although if I was sober I might not have used the word housing three times, or said I hoped he was well twice. Still.

To my surprise, *Chris is typing . . .* appeared almost immediately. After less than a minute his reply popped up:

Hey Dan, I'm okay, hope you are too. That's not going to work I'm afraid. Hope you can sort something else! C xx

I blinked. I began writing without actually thinking what I was going to say, a string of question marks and capital letters spilling out under my thumb until I came to my senses, erased everything and looked out of the window. I had presented it as a done deal. How could he just say no? It was my flat too. I was paying half the rent. Perhaps he didn't understand.

Hi Chris, I replied. I don't know what it was about our break-up that was making us communicate with this chilly, professional tone, but I didn't seem able to stop. For a moment I thought of our first date, the Sam Smith's pub where we'd stayed till closing, doing tricks with the beer mats and sharing bags of peanuts – it had been nice, hadn't it, us? We'd had a nice time. I managed not to say any of this.

Sorry to ask, I know it's not what we agreed, but I've already tried a lot of different things, can't work remotely, can't stay with folks etc, nobody I know has a spare room going so I think I have to come home and we'll just work it out. I know it's not ideal but that's where we're at now. So is that ok? X

This time he typed for much longer. I watched the late-night London streets pass as I waited for his message to appear. Shut pub, shut shop, shut supermarket, open takeaway, flats, small houses, big houses. All those people.

Hey Dan – totally get it's tricky but think I'm gonna have to say no here. I don't think it would be a good idea because as we agreed we need the space to get used to living separately, seeing other people, etc. Obviously I sympathise and really hope you can sort something but I'm sure you will! Cxx

Seeing other people? I laughed. We'd only split up twenty minutes ago. Then I felt that cold-water feeling, that heady moment of drunken clarity where you just *know* something, suddenly you just completely know it. I'd muted Chris's Instagram straight after we split, but now I went looking for it. There was nothing on his page – nothing visible to me, anyway – but I knew what I was hunting for.

I scrolled down his photos, through ten months of bollocks, his five-a-side football team, our ill-fated camping holiday, until I found the one he'd put up for his work's

Christmas last year. He'd tagged the Dutch girl he was always boring on about, *Lina*, so I clicked her profile – and there he was in all her fucking stories. They'd been out for dinner tonight. The bastard. The lying-by-omission little prick.

I didn't think about what I was doing, back in our message thread, pressing the call button. It was midnight, or maybe after, but I knew he was awake because he'd been texting me, and anyway we were both night owls, that was Our Thing. He cancelled my call, so I tried again. Cancelled. I called again, and this time he answered.

'Dan,' he said.

'Since when?'

'What are you talking about?'

'When did it start, you and Lina?' I began tearing into him: how I knew, how the signs were there, asking if we'd crossed over or he'd waited a respectful three and a half hours from our break-up before getting with her, and had we crossed over, did we cross over?

'No,' Chris said forcefully. 'Dan, I didn't cheat on you. I wouldn't do that.'

Yeah, but Lina. He'd always liked her. And I *knew*. I could *feel* it. I was like a lawyer summing up in one of those American procedurals: BAM, slamming folders of evidence down on the desk. I was definitely drunk. BAM, another folder of evidence. Chris shushed me, and I heard the unmistakeable creak of the bed as he got up, went into the living room. No reason to do that unless you were leaving somebody behind.

'Oh my God, is she there? Is she there *right now*?' I was maybe shouting. A woman a few seats behind me said, 'Babe, shut up.'

Only three stops from Anita's anyway, so I stood, rang the bell, then swaggered down the stairs one-handed and graceless, Chris still talking in my ear.

'Danielle, we split up,' he was saying. 'We agreed it was for the best. We don't love each other. There's literally nothing to be upset about here.' He sounded so calm.

I felt a spike of anger. What did he mean, we didn't love each other? How did he know? How was he so sure about everything all the time? 'Chris,' I said, helplessly, voice thick with booze and sadness. I was standing in the street. The bus had gone. 'Please. I just want to come home.'

'I know. But it's over. And you don't really want that anyway.'

'Yes, I do,' I said, but I didn't mean I wanted us to get back together, and I thought he probably knew that. Even my anger wasn't even really about him, was it? It was about Matt, and anyway, I believed Chris despite myself: he hadn't cheated on me; he'd always been nice. No, we didn't love each other – but I still needed somewhere to sleep. 'Can't you both just stay at hers?'

'We agreed two months each,' he said slowly, calmly. 'That's fair. That's what we agreed. Dan, how would you feel if we made all these plans and said all this stuff and then I called you drunk at midnight demanding to come back early?'

'I'm not drunk,' I said, which was a stupid lie.

Chris laughed. 'Okay,' he said.

'I don't have anywhere to go!'

'You'll work something out. You've got loads of friends. It's just a couple of months.'

'Seven weeks,' I said petulantly.

'Exactly.' Fuck, I'd lost the thread and shot myself in the foot. 'If you need anything from the flat before then,' he went on, 'text me, and we can arrange for you to pick it up. Otherwise, we're sticking to what we agreed. I'll give you the key in seven weeks. Okay?'

'I have a key,' I said. Of course I did: it was my flat. Half mine. For now, anyway. There was an uncomfortable silence. 'Oh my God,' I said. 'Have you changed the locks? You have, haven't you?'

For the first time, he sounded embarrassed. 'Lina said . . .'

'Oh, just fuck off,' I snapped. I cancelled the call.

*

Anita's flat was quiet. Not surprising at 1 a.m. on a school night, but I felt too weird and uneasy to be alone. I wanted to see Anita, I'd even have settled for Nads, but there was nobody in any of the communal spaces, no sound bleeding out of anyone's bedrooms, not so much as credits rolling on a laptop. Silence. They were all asleep.

I made up my couch-bed, stumbling over the cushions, ungainly. The walk back from the bus stop had taken a long time. As soon as I hung up the phone, I realised I'd

59

got confused, thought a betting shop outside the window was another, different betting shop, closer to Anita's. I'd got off way too early. The walk took nearly half an hour, but there were no other buses due for ages, and it was raining, so I'd had no choice. In the end, I was so angry and cold that I'd bought a whisky miniature from a corner shop to cheer myself up. I regretted everything now, cold and wet and whisky-drunk, feeling sorry for myself as I spread the sheets out on Anita's couch.

Finding somewhere else to stay was for the best. I couldn't be making and dismantling my bed every day for the next two months, or even seven weeks. It lacked dignity.

I threw on my pyjamas, rolled myself into my sleeping bag, turned off the lamp and dropped into a light, restless sleep. It was like this sometimes when I'd drunk too much, or had a lot on my mind, an almost feverish inability to relax and turn my brain off. For hours I tossed and turned, half certain there was something I was meant to be doing, that someone needed me. But I must have slept, because I woke in the darkest part of the night to find that I was not alone. The figure was there, in the corner of the room, exactly as it had been the night before. It was back, just as I'd feared.

Feared? No. Like I'd known it would be.

I tried to move, speak, tell it to go away, but it was impossible. I couldn't so much as lift a finger. In the dark, I heard the sound of my voice rattling in my throat like something caged.

This wasn't real, of course. Soon, I would wake up. But as I lay on my back, the shadow in the corner of the living room rippling with static, it felt nothing like sleep paralysis, or even a nightmare. I was absolutely certain: something terrible was going to happen.

*

And then I was back at my desk.

I must have looked as bad as I felt, because Femi emailed me a photo of a dog holding a cocktail glass with a fake headline, *SOURCES WONDER IF MACKINNON WILL SURVIVE DAY*. There was no hiding from Femi, so I replied, asking her to go to McDonald's with me at lunch. She winked at me over the desk, which I figured meant yes.

Jeannie got in just after 11. I made coffee, took it through on the tray with sparkling water, tried to keep my hands from shaking. Mercifully, she didn't want to meet, because it was the day of the DPDI panel and she needed to focus on preparing her introductions. I gave her a thumbs up, then went to the toilets to be sick.

I threw up for a surprisingly long time. I hadn't been able to face breakfast, so it was all liquid. That didn't feel great. I stayed there a long time, kneeling on the tiled floor, holding my hair back from my face, and wondering if there was any corner of my life I hadn't completely tanked. Here I was, single again at twenty-nine, just when people I knew were starting to settle down, talk about marriage, kids, mortgages. I had a job I hated, running around after Jeannie, and no prospects, no career ladder, no idea where I was going. Nowhere to live. And now I was banned from my own couch, because my ex was sleeping with a Dutch girl who was skinny and blonde and still had freedom of movement in the EU. I was fucked.

At least the vomiting seemed to be over. I spat into the toilet bowl, wiped my mouth, scrubbed a hand over my face. I was well-practised at being hungover at work, but I'd gone too far this time. Whisky on a school night, not enough dinner, and I'd slept exactly as badly as I'd deserved to.

Standing over the sink, I met my own eyes in the mirror. Thick eyebrows. Long, boyish face, pale and slightly sweaty. *What are you going to do now, then?* I thought. Something moved out of the corner of my eye, and I turned to look over my shoulder, but I must have been mistaken: I was alone in here. Thank God, because the vomiting had been – loud. Unbecoming.

I washed my face a few times with cold water and began to feel better. *Okay*, I told myself, *here we are, baby. Rock bottom! It has* got *to start getting better and this is where it starts!* I was on my period, so I'd brought my bag to the bathroom; the cramps weren't helping my sense of bodily catastrophe, but at least I could make myself look less like a corpse. I had a hairbrush, mints, a small amount of make-up. While I was dabbing concealer onto the bags under my eyes, I remembered my Emergency Lipstick and dug it out. I rubbed some between my thumb and forefinger, pushed it onto my cheeks like blusher. I was worried I'd look like a clown, but actually it was fine, like I was just the kind of pale, sweaty woman who, for some reason, had lots of healthy colour in her cheeks.

Jeannie opened the door, and I jumped.

'Oh Danielle, that's great,' she said immediately, looking at the lipstick in my hand. 'It's so nice to see you making a bit of effort.'

I was too surprised, for a moment, to speak.

Jeannie dropped her voice conspiratorially. 'You know,' she went on. 'You don't have to just put lipstick on when we have events – you could do it for normal days, in the office. I know what your generation are like, but I promise it wouldn't make you a bad feminist. And do you know, making the effort might even give you more confidence? More *oomph*.' Then she winked, and went into one of the stalls, leaving me standing there.

It was the same stall I'd just been sick in, and I thought, *I hope it doesn't still smell like vomit in there*. Then I thought that actually I hoped it did. I went back to work.

*

That evening, I took the lift up to the big events room at the top of the building, to set up for the DPDI panel. Mollie, who was in charge of our 'programme', came to help. For twenty minutes or so, we moved furniture around – clearing tables, putting out chairs – while making polite small talk. 'I'm so looking forward to this,' said Mollie.

'Me too,' I lied.

'Have you read the bill?'

'Of course,' I said, which was also a lie; I'd read a short summary online after we agreed to do the talk, no more than that. I considered telling her that I sometimes got my news from the 'how to talk to your children about the news' section of the BBC website, because I found the ongoing soap opera of steadily worsening geopolitical crises so completely overwhelming that I needed it explaining to me like I was ten. But she already didn't respect me, and I didn't want to make things worse by being honest about who I was. 'So how's the house stuff going?' I asked instead.

'Oh, God,' said Mollie. She'd been trying to buy a house with her husband for months, but the three-bed in Denmark Hill had fallen through, and now they were struggling to find somewhere in-budget, with a garden, that wouldn't need years of work. 'Bit of a nightmare. No good leads and time is of the essence . . .' She'd told me before that she wanted to start trying for kids as soon as they were in, given she planned to have three, and not *too* close together. ('Not, like, Irish twins, you know?' she'd said, a phrase I'd never heard before and which seemed vaguely offensive.)

'That sounds stressful,' I said.

'It is! Have you seen those studies? After a bereavement, buying a house is one of the most stressful experiences you can have.'

I laughed bitterly, but managed to turn it into a cough. I usually managed to get on okay with Mollie, and I knew buying a house was horrendous, because everyone said so. Her concerns were just so *alien*. She was only a few years older than me, thirty-two to my twenty-nine, but she was always worrying about deeds of transfer and solicitors, while I worried about spending over my food budget because I was too bored to get through the working day without Jaffa Cakes. My complete financial insecurity wasn't just tiring, it was infantilising. And the worst part was, I knew this wasn't only in my head, and that actually, Mollie noticed it, too. I tried not to mind, but today it felt unbearable. I wanted to be a grown-up with a mortgage; now I no longer had a rented flat, and in a few days, I would even lose the couch I was staying on. No wonder Mollie always talked to me like she was an adult, while I was only playing at being one.

The whole office treated me and Femi that way. We were Hodgepodge's naughty children, young(ish), or at least the youngest, plus there were our long lunches and not taking The Work seriously enough, and coming from the kinds of families that would never be able to drop us £80k for a deposit on a three-bed in Denmark Hill, with or without a garden. People like Mollie got funny about that stuff. Even though, if you asked her, she would have been able to say the right things about how lucky and privileged she was, I was pretty sure my interminable renting made me a less serious person in her eyes. It was like, are you not planning to get out of that beartrap? Are you not even going to *try*?

The door opened, and Jeannie swept in. 'Looking great in here, girls!' she said. There were a lot of things to be carried up from our office (bottles of wine, the crates of glasses we kept in the cupboard for events, the live-streaming equipment), but she hadn't brought any of it with her.

'Hi Jeannie,' Mollie beamed. 'Are you ready? Do you need anything?'

It was probably my job to ask that, but I didn't mind.

'Oh yes,' said Jeannie. 'Panel will be here soon – all right if we bring them straight up?'

'Absolutely.'

Jeannie turned to me. 'Now, Danielle, I know you'll be very busy setting up refreshments, but are you okay to do some teas and coffees for the panel first?' She said this very seriously, like I was an army private being given a special mission.

'Sure,' I said. I had better start carrying things now. 'I'll go and get the refreshments first,' I added, heading towards the door, wondering if either of them would offer to help.

'Thanks!' they trilled in unison as I left.

I carried the glasses, took the cold wine out of the fridge, the red wine from the stationery cupboard, brought up jugs of water. Over the next twenty minutes, the panellists arrived one by one, and I made their drinks: black instant coffee for Luke, the chair; decaf tea with oat milk for Suzanne, from a think-tank; something herbal for Maryam, from another, different, think-tank, that thought different things.

Once the panellists had their drinks, Jeannie gathered them all at the front – on the 'stage', such as it was – for the pre-game chat. I was in the middle of setting wine glasses out at the back of the room when Suzanne appeared at my elbow. 'Excuse me, sorry, what's your name?'

We'd been introduced earlier, when Jeannie asked me to make her decaf tea. I put down the glass I was holding. 'It's Danielle,' I said, as neutrally as possible. There were waves of tension rising off her.

'Danielle, okay,' she said. Her mouth was a thin line. 'Can you try this? Because I really don't think it's oat milk.' She held the cup out to me.

'Oh.'

'Just try it.'

'Do you want me to make you another?'

'I specifically asked for oat and this is – I'm sorry, I'm really not the kind of person to make a fuss, but you've put dairy in, and that's incredibly dangerous.'

I looked around. Jeannie and the other panellists were watching in silence. I felt hot and cold at the same time. I was sure I'd made it with oat milk, remembered holding the carton. Or had that been somebody else's? I was tired, out of sorts, of course I'd do something stupid like this. 'I'm so sorry,' I stammered.

Jeannie rushed over to join us. 'Suzanne, is everything okay?'

'Well, I don't mean to make a fuss, but your assistant's given me a drink I'm completely allergic to,' said Suzanne. Her voice was high and trembling.

I held out my hand for the mug. 'I'll make it again.'

'I'd had two or three sips before I realised. I mean, I could be sick.' She wouldn't give the mug to me, or stop, and I wondered what she wanted. What else could I say?

Jeannie made a cooing noise. 'Suzanne, that's awful.'

'I'll make a new one,' I repeated. Jeannie was patting Suzanne on the back and had succeeded in wresting the mug from her.

'Tell you what,' said Jeannie. '*I'll* make it.'

'Would you?' said Suzanne, like I'd poisoned her on purpose and she couldn't trust me not to do it again.

'Of course. Let's go downstairs together and we can make sure it's right.' Jeannie took Suzanne by the elbow and led her to the lift. I heard their voices as they moved away from me.

The lift pinged, and the room was silent. I glanced at the other panellists. Maryam was on her phone, but Luke was watching me. Our eyes met for a moment, then he looked away, and I was grateful. I would have loved nothing more than to disappear.

Would I get the sack? It would serve me right, hungover at work and making stupid mistakes. I tried to focus on putting the wine glasses out, the click of each one deafening in the quiet, and there was a thin, high buzzing in my ears underneath. Click. Click. I imagined Jeannie emerging from the lift, asking for a word with me. Having to call my mum and tell her I'd lost my job as well as everything else. Click. Click. Click. Then I knocked one of the glasses from the table with my elbow, and it smashed. The noise was a shock, and everyone jumped.

'Sorry!' I shouted. It was a clean break, at least, in several pieces, and I knelt on the floor, scrabbling to pick the shards up. Someone knelt beside me.

'Let me help.' It was Luke.

'No, it's fine,' I said. 'Really. I'm fine.'

He ignored me and began picking up pieces of glass. My hands were shaking. He leaned closer to me, where we were crouching on the floor, and said, 'Don't let her get to you, okay? She's always been like that. Likes to fuck with people, assistants. Don't show weakness.'

I looked up. It occurred to me for the first time that he was quite attractive. This hadn't been visible from the three Getty images of him at talks that I'd looked at while adding him to my shortlist; it was the sort of attractiveness that was not really about looks so much as confidence. I managed not to tell him this, but only just, and what I said was nearly as embarrassing: 'I really thought I got it right.'

'Yeah, you probably did. But you feel stupid now, don't you? That's the point.'

'You're saying she lied?' I said. He shrugged. 'How would you know?'

'Because Suzanne's older than she looks, and I used to be an assistant.' There was a twist in his mouth like he was hiding a smile.

I was surprised, though I didn't know why. Femi was trying to be a journalist. Lots of successful people must have started out in jobs like ours. 'Well,' I said slowly. 'Good to hear somebody made it out alive.'

He laughed. 'Danielle, isn't it? Listen . . . Wait, you're bleeding.'

I blinked, looked down. He was right: there was a slice down the side of my right index finger; I must have cut it on the broken glass without noticing. 'Oh, shit,' I said, getting up. It was bleeding so fast and so much that it was almost funny. The lift dinged, opened, and Suzanne got out alone, with a mug of tea. She didn't look at me.

'Sorry,' I muttered. 'I should, I'll just . . .'

Luke nodded as I scurried towards the lift and pressed the lower-ground button for our office. As I descended, blood dripped onto the rubber tiles. I scrubbed at it with the toe of my shoe, holding my injured hand, like that was going to do anything. Ding. I ducked into the toilets.

Back at the scene of the crime: I'd been a wreck in here a few hours ago. Now I was back because I'd poisoned a woman and nearly sliced off a finger. What a legend. I turned the tap on and ran the cut under cold water.

Despite Luke's kindness, I was mortified. If I wasn't incompetent, then Suzanne was a monster who'd pretended I was, just to one-up me; either way, my job was to make little drinks for people who treated me with contempt. I felt the choke of oncoming tears and breathed hard, watching the sink water run red. I didn't want to cry in the Hodgepodge toilets. But I felt like shit. Because however bad I thought my job was, I wasn't even good at it – and I wanted to be.

That was the problem with working here: maybe I bitched and complained and said the right things to my friends, but I never skived off or coasted. I tried really hard. I'd spent years of my life trying to get a Good Grade in Jeannie! I knew the birthdays of her children, and her brother, and the date of her divorce, knew she always went for dinner with her oldest friends on the anniversary, because I booked the table. I knew her lunch order, and her drinks preferences, and what kind of wine she wanted me to buy for dinner parties; I knew she favoured a dry white, cooked with butter, got regular cravings for Kettle Chips, that she liked to holiday in France and wore a 32C bra. I knew everything, because I did everything for her. And now I was going to be fired, and it would all be for nothing. The last four years of my life had been a waste. I'd been so desperate to believe it was going to cohere, the shitty houseshares, shitty jobs, shitty mornings crying on the bus to work, into a story I could tell about my life. A story that would carry me from here to some future place where everything made sense, where all those wasted hours were somehow holy. Wasted efforts. All that work.

I blew a couple of shaky breaths from my mouth, turned off the tap. Then one of the stalls flushed, and in some funhouse mirror parody of that morning, Jeannie emerged. She froze, clearly as surprised to see me, bleeding into the sink, as I was to see her.

Were we going to agree to say nothing? Surely she couldn't sack me in a toilet, not after four years. I stared in mute horror as Jeannie came over.

'Now, Danielle,' she said, quite seriously. 'We're going to have to have a conversation. Because that poor woman was very upset, and I need to be able to trust you with important things, don't I?'

I watched as she washed her hands, two pumps of soap, dried them. What could I say? That I was sorry, and ashamed? That Suzanne was a prick, and I hadn't even made her stupid tea wrong, she'd just wanted to humiliate me, make herself big and me small, which was a waste, because I felt small most of the time anyway. I didn't know where other people got it, their big-ness, their ability to keep going and not care what anybody thought of them. I cared what everybody thought of me. Jeannie wouldn't be able to imagine that feeling, I knew – but why? What was it about her and me that made us so different? Nature or nurture? Upbringing or birthright? Then she said, 'Danielle, are you at least going to apologise?' and I burst into tears.

I generally try to keep a pretty firm grip on myself. There have only been a handful of times in adulthood when I've been unable to keep from crying, mostly hormone-related. I once burst into tears on a bus at rush hour because I thought the driver hated me. I had PMT; we hadn't spoken. This was unquestionably worse.

For a few seconds, Jeannie was stunned into silence. I suppose that was fair because in four years, I'd never shown the faintest shred of real emotion in front of her. The expression of respectful detachment and mild horror frozen on her face was quite funny, though I was too stressed to really enjoy it.

'Oh, Danielle,' she said uncomfortably. 'It's not *that* bad. There's no need to get upset.'

And for some reason, what I said was, 'Chris and I split up.'

I don't know why. I just did. Suddenly, against my will, I was telling her things. How he'd said, 'I think we both know it's over,' and I hadn't wanted to look stupid, so I had said yes, even though until then I thought things were, basically, fine? I told her that I was staying on Anita's couch, but had to leave, and didn't have anywhere to go, because Chris already had a new girlfriend, and all the time I was talking, a voice in my head was shouting, *Stop! Stop!* But I couldn't stop. It was like a floodgate had opened and it was all pouring out. How awful that, of all people, it should open in front of *Jeannie.* Who spills out the most intimate details of their personal life to a boss that's not even nice to them? I was horrified, but went on talking as if I was possessed, someone else speaking through me. I thought of spirit mediums, table rappers, people who could make it look like other voices were tearing from their mouths, and then Jeannie said, 'I'm sorry, are you saying you don't have anywhere to *live*?'

I tried to explain that this wasn't precisely true. I had a home, and all my stuff was there; I just couldn't be in it for the next couple of months. I was tempted to begin explaining about the things I'd already tried, credit cards, rental costs, so she would know I was a serious person, but then I got worried that going into all of that would sound ludicrous, like I was asking for a raise, when a minute ago, I'd thought she was going to sack me.

'I'd say you could stay with me, but Edward . . .' Jeannie said vaguely.

'No,' I interrupted. 'I wouldn't want to do that – God, I would never expect – sorry, I'll just—' I moved away, turned the taps on, started throwing cold water onto my swollen face. The cut on my hand was bleeding again. What a mess.

Jeannie glanced at the clock. 'Sorry, Danielle. I have to get back to . . .' She gestured towards the door, beyond which was the lift, the room, the panellists, all waiting for us. The thought of going back there made me feel unwell.

'Of course. I'm fine, sorry.' I was ashamed at having said so much, given myself away, held her up. I was private by nature, always embarrassed after personal disclosures, even with people I loved, but this was worse. Why? Because she was my boss? Because she was older? Maybe because it made my job easier, remaining opaque to Jeannie, and now for the first time, I had failed to do that. She knew very little about me, beyond the absolute bare minimum, while I knew everything about her, and maybe I preferred it that way, the safety of anonymity. It just felt wrong, telling her all this, letting her see these parts of me. Not my place.

'Go and get a plaster for that,' she said. 'Take a minute. Calm down. And stop worrying, okay? I'll think of something. Leave it with me.'

*

That night, I got in late from the event to find Anita waiting up for me. The flat was cold – the weather had turned and they'd agreed not to put the heating on until November – so she was wrapped in a blanket on the couch, with a hot water bottle, and she'd made an extra one for me. She handed it over, and wrapped me in the same blanket as her. I burrowed down like an animal getting ready to hibernate.

'Do you want to talk about it?' she said.

We were always in contact, texting back and forth about nonsense, but I hadn't told her about last night, calling Chris drunk from the bus, our stupid argument, or crying in front of Jeannie, or any of it. I'd just said I was having a really bad day.

'No,' I replied. 'Not tonight, if that's all right.'

She had a scented candle burning and the room smelled like oranges. The TV was on low, some kind of property programme. Someone was painting their house. *Coppice red. Biscuit yellow. Lichen green.* There was another smell in the room, a light kind of verbena, coming from Anita herself, and I remembered she'd spent too much money on posh hair oil after TikTok convinced her she had an 'undiagnosed curl pattern'. I loved her.

'Can you stay here until I fall asleep?' I said.

Anita stroked my head. 'Of course.'

I woke with a jolt, hours later, to find the room in darkness. I must have dropped off; Anita had put the lights out and covered me with a blanket. But waking in the night like this, lying on my back on the couch, made me paranoid.

I scanned the corners of the room. They were empty. I moved my arm experimentally. I wasn't having any kind of nightmare: I was just awake in the night, like a normal person. Good to know that could still happen. I sat up and stretched. I'd slept at a funny angle, had a crick in my neck, and my mouth was dry.

I got up and went into the kitchen. I'd fallen asleep without brushing my teeth and they were furry under my tongue. Horrible. I would drink some water and then go and find my toothbrush. The wall clock above the sink said it was just after 3 a.m.

I filled a glass and drank. The water was warm and slightly metallic. I spat it back into the sink and let the tap run, looking out of the window at the scrubby park, foxes skulking by the bins. My vision shifted and I saw my own face in the glass. Thick eyebrows. Dark hair sticking up at odd angles. *What are you going to do now, then?* I was standing there, letting the water run cold, when my eye was caught by movement in the reflection. My heart stuttered. I'd thought I was alone in here, that everyone was asleep, but I'd been wrong – there was someone sitting at the kitchen table.

For some reason, I didn't want to turn around. I just stood there, very still, staring at the glass of the window, searching for their face. City lights and treetops outside; behind me, a dark shape. I couldn't make out who it was.

The tap was still running. I reached down to turn it off, but it was the wrong shape under my hands. Stiff, heavy brass. The basin was wrong too. Chipped enamel that was too deep. Too full. My hands went down and down, reaching for the bottom. *I'm dreaming*, I thought. *I have to be.*

Behind me, the shadow on the chair stood up. I watched her in the window for a moment, coming closer.

*

Then I was back at my desk. It was Friday morning, quiet in the office; Femi, blitzed on free wine from the panel, had gone out with a friend after work, sent me a 2 a.m. club selfie with the caption *PULL SICK* and three cowboy emojis. She hadn't actually called in sick, but was working from home all day, and Jeannie wasn't in yet either.

'Did you have fun?' said Nick, who did our finances. He never came to the events.

'Mm,' said Mollie vaguely. Even she looked slightly green around the gills. Our fees for panellists were insultingly low, so Jeannie and Mollie always took them for dinner after, at the Italian fusion place around the corner. Clearly it had gone on late.

The office door opened, and we all turned to look. 'Morning!' Jeannie said brightly, although it was half eleven, and there was not that much of it left.

'Morning,' we replied.

Jeannie swept off her jacket, stood at the end of my desk and said, 'Danielle, could you . . . ?' She beckoned me into her office. I got up and followed her, wondering what she wanted me to do. When I shut the door, she said, 'I've had the most marvellous idea.'

I sat on the little stool as Jeannie slid her phone across the desk, like that bit in films where people write down a big number on a piece of paper. I picked it up and saw, on the screen, a photo of a blocky, sandstone house, with steps leading up to the front door and a pair of Doric pillars either side. I looked up at Jeannie.

'It's called Westerley,' she said. 'Westerley Hall. I grew up there.'

I wasn't sure why she was telling me, or how to respond. 'Right,' I said. I remembered that she'd grown up in a country house, she'd told me before – just a small one.

'My brother and I both live in London now, but we have a duty to keep the place up. Since the live-in groundsman died, we've been paying a local woman to help, but she – anyway, that doesn't matter. The point is, we could really do with somebody to stay a couple of months and take care of the place.' Jeannie raised her eyebrows and nodded. 'So . . .' she said portentously.

'Sorry,' I said, slow, stunned. 'Are you saying that . . . I should stay here?' I was still holding Jeannie's phone. Westerley looked back at me, flat roof, two rectangles of windows, like a house a child would draw. It was large and grand, but pretty, and not too imposing.

'You'd be doing us a huge favour,' she said, taking the phone back. 'I spoke to my brother this morning and he was over the moon. He worries about the place so much. It's really quite a burden.'

I pushed my hair back from my face. Outside the open window, October rain was coming down, filling the room with a fresh, clean smell. I couldn't tell if she was serious. 'Jeannie,' I said.

But she was all business. 'We wouldn't expect you to pay in for bills, although you'd need to put a bit of money into fuel if you want to run the fires, which you might do – it can get cold in Yorkshire at this time of year.'

'Yorkshire?' I repeated.

'As long as you can cover fuel and train fare, we'll take care of the rest.' She must have noticed my expression. 'Yes, it's a little way out,' she said vaguely. 'But Nigel pays the phone and internet all year round, he needs it working in the summers, so you won't be too cut off.'

Nigel must be her brother. 'But I work here,' I said stupidly.

Jeannie laughed. 'I thought it would be – you know,' she gestured towards her computer. 'Phone calls and zooms and all that. Like the lockdowns.' Of course. She'd enjoyed the pandemic in a jolly hockey sticks way that I'd found difficult to tolerate at the time, but then it had all been more fun for people with gardens.

'Jeannie, it's so kind of you. But it's so far, and—' I wasn't sure what to say. I didn't want to remind her how adamant she'd been that my work be done here, in person, and not remotely. Still, touched as I was by the offer, and desperate for a solution, living alone in a country house in Yorkshire was not what I'd imagined. If anything, I'd been expecting her to say she had a friend with a loft conversion in Belgravia, or knew someone going on holiday for a few weeks who I'd be able to cat-sit for in Peckham Rye. This was – huge, unimaginable. A different life.

'No, no, of course,' said Jeannie. She looked a little crestfallen. She'd probably expected me to be excited, and I felt guilty.

'It is amazing, it's just – far,' I said lamely. 'I can't drive.'

She smiled. 'Well, why don't you take the weekend to think about it? I can get Nigel to send you all the details in the meantime.'

*

The house had its own Wikipedia page:

Westerley Hall is a Grade II* listed country house in West Yorkshire, England.[1] It was built in the 18th century for Sir William Grant, a British Army officer and Member of Parliament[2], on the site of a much earlier hall (built 1308) about which little is known. The original hall was sacked and burned to the ground in the 17th century, with only minimal foundations remaining. Architect Sir James Newman used the foundations as a blueprint for the modern Westerley Hall.

There were a few more lines, mainly the names of men who had owned, lived in, sold or inherited the house over hundreds of years. The final owner must, I thought, be Jeannie's father. It was funny to imagine her having one of those, having been a child at all; funny to imagine her growing up in such an imposing place. Over and over again, Google showed the same image of the house I'd already seen, same pillars, same front steps. Beyond that, I could discover nothing else.

*

When I got back to Anita's, everyone was out at parties or drinks or restaurants, whatever people did on Friday nights, and the flat was empty. It was my last weekend here, four days left until I had to be off the couch. I made a stir fry, called my mum while I was eating it.

'Hello, you,' she said, answering the phone. She had a bright, warm voice and a Brummy accent ten times thicker than mine, which I'd begun to get rid of before I even left school. Her accent meant that, if everything went to shit, she could always get call centre work; there were loads of call centres in our town since some kind of study, decades earlier, had said people from the West Midlands sounded *unintimidating*.

I could hear Mum turning the TV down. 'Everything all right, love?' I felt bad about calling so irregularly that she thought something must be wrong, although obviously, she was also correct.

I kept my voice calm. 'I'm okay. But actually, Chris and I split up.'

'Oh, no,' she said. 'I'm sorry to hear that. Are you all right?'

'Yeah. Bit sad, but it's probably for the best.' The kitchen was smoky from the wok. I crossed the room to lift the window open; in the scrubby green below the block of flats, I could see some teenagers passing a joint around and laughing. I remembered when I used to do things on Friday nights.

I sat back down at the table. 'Well, you don't sound too bad,' Mum was saying. 'I'll never forget the call after you split up with Matt. You were wailing like a dog trapped down a well.'

'Yeah,' I said, spearing baby corn with my fork. I'd felt bad about that one for years. It was one of the reasons I'd waited so long to tell her about Chris. I wasn't going to worry her like that again. 'It's all right really. Except we live together, so that's a bit of a faff.' I told her about Anita's couch, Jeannie's offer.

I guess I was testing the water. If Jeannie was happy for me to work remotely, maybe I could stay with Mum after all, without having to quit my job? Maybe she would say, *Oh, don't rely on your boss, you don't even like her. Come and stay with me!* But she just said, 'Are you eating something?'

'Yeah, sorry.' I swallowed.

'What you having?'

'Stir fry.'

'Nice. Well, I'm glad to hear everything's sorted. Must have been stressful.'

'It has been, a bit.'

'Sorry I don't have a spare room at the minute. I wish you could stay with me, but this place is so small.'

I didn't want her to feel guilty about her flat. 'No, it's fine,' I said. 'Don't worry about it.'

'Nice of your boss, though?'

I agreed that, yes, it was nice of Jeannie, and changed the subject. 'How are you, anyway?'

'Bloody boiling, all the time,' she said. She'd been going through the menopause for ages, or what seemed like ages to me. I laughed.

After we got off the phone, I did the dishes, had a bath, washed my hair, and was in Anita's bed by 9 p.m. I texted to say I was sorry but it was too stressful to sleep in the living room this early, and she could move me when she came in. She said it was fine, she was on a date that had turned out to be fun, would probably be back late anyway.

In the end, she didn't come home at all, and I slept eleven hours straight through in her incredibly tidy bedroom, with its nice, posh sheets. I had vivid dreams all night, presumably brought on by Jeannie's offer: a big house, Regency ball, ladies in brocade. Colour and noise. No, not Regency, later than that. It seemed to shimmer and shift, the way dreams do, dresses growing longer, shorter, now with wide hems, crinoline, and now above the knee.

It was Christmas, a huge tree sparkling in the corner, and we moved around it, all of us dancing, ladies in dark velvet and furs, fox, ermine, men in suits and hats, little girls in red and gold. We wore bright colours and dark colours, dresses that looked like port being poured from a bottle, dresses that looked like candlelight. The room was full of greenery, sweeps of holly and ivy. It was beautiful – but something was wrong. People were whispering in the corners, they were pulling away from the dances, looking out of the windows. They said somebody was out there, someone watching the house.

So I left the party and went out into the house, into the hallways that stretched on and on. There were doors on either side, for what felt like miles, but none of them would open. I walked and walked, and still couldn't shake the paranoia of the party, the bad feeling, the sense of being observed.

Footsteps behind me. I turned, but there was nobody there. Then I realised I was the one following, that the footsteps were up ahead – and they were waiting for me, whoever they were, further into the house. They were waiting. They knew my name.

*

'You can finish this,' said Ben, leaning forwards to slide half a dosa onto my plate.

It was Saturday night, about half ten, and we'd gone to Drummond Street for a late dinner after Ben's last show. The restaurant, with its pine walls, BYOB and huge portions, was a long-standing favourite since we moved to London. I'd never managed to finish a meal here yet.

'I can't even get through mine,' I said, pushing Ben's plate away. He gave up, put it back on the table.

Usually there would be some kind of cast knees-up at the end of a long run, so it was weird that Ben was out with me instead of at a party. I'd kept checking there was nothing on tonight, and he'd kept saying no, but now he seemed distracted and was drinking quickly, not eating much.

'Hey,' he said. 'Did I tell you I know a sublet going in Bow?'

'Yes, but it has to be *free*,' I replied for the millionth time. Ben had been making unhelpful suggestions about my housing situation all night. I'd decided not to tell him about Jeannie's offer yet. I'd been thinking about it all day and couldn't really come up with a good reason to say no – except that ostensibly I didn't like her, and my friends would think I was a bitch for taking a huge favour from someone I wasn't supposed to like. 'Look, I don't want to talk about this. Tell me what you're going to do now the play's closed.'

'Ugh. I don't know. Die.'

'Back to the temp office?'

'No, I'm all right for another couple of weeks. I've got voice-over stuff on Wednesday.'

'Oh my God,' I said, delighted. 'Is Epherim back in town?'

'Epherim does indeed ride again,' he said sadly.

A couple of years ago, Ben had become the voice of an elf in a series of phone games. They kept making additional content, and new releases, and getting him back in, and now the games were surprisingly popular and some thirteen-year-olds on Twitter were obsessed with his character, Epherim the Honourable. Last summer, I'd downloaded the game, recorded the voice-over of him dying ('AARGGHHHH' [blood splatter noise]), looped it, and made it my ringtone for months. It drove Ben *insane*.

We talked about the voice-over work, and an advert he'd auditioned for, until a waiter came to take our plates. We didn't get the bill; it was quietening down and they didn't seem to mind us hanging around to finish our wine.

'So,' said Ben, when we were alone. 'Do you know what I think?'

'No, what do you think?'

'I think we should go to a party.'

I laughed in his face.

'What?' he said. 'Do we not like fun anymore?'

'Yeah, but not with strangers. Whose party is it? Someone I know?'

'Well . . .'

'Oh my God,' I said, putting two and two together at last. 'It's the cast party, isn't it? Ben, I asked if there was something you were missing.'

'It's not! It's not that, it's a friend's birthday, and I thought it would be fun to go together, that's all.'

I sighed. 'I'm really not in the mood.'

'Why not?' Goldfish-level attention span. We'd been talking only moments ago about where the hell I was going to live next week. I made a face, and he said, 'Because you just split up with Chris? Isn't that a good reason to go? Get "out of yourself"?'

'Oh sure, I'd love to spend a Saturday night meeting loads of people I don't know, and telling them I've just had my heart broken.'

Ben took a sip of wine, not looking at me. 'Hmm.'

'What?'

'Nothing, I guess. It's just interesting.'

'What is?'

'Well, the other day, I said something about you being heartbroken, and you said you weren't, so – I don't know. Which is it?'

This wasn't what I'd been expecting him to say.

'Don't look so stressed, I'm not accusing you of lying. I'm just wondering if you like . . . actually know how you actually feel?'

'Huh,' I said. I let my eyes drift over the pine and white-washed walls, big windows, other diners, hoping to see something that would justify changing the subject. There was a group of friends at the next table, one of them, thirty-one today, in a little party hat. An older man and younger woman sat the other side of the birthday group, her dark hair in a pretty braid, with ribbons woven into it. I wondered if they were father and daughter, or a couple, and whether Ben would be up for speculating about it.

'Mac?'

I sighed. 'Yeah, look, I don't know. It's hard to say, isn't it?'

'Is it?'

Was it? I wasn't sure. Somewhat against my will, I thought about Chris. We'd met between lockdowns, on the apps, dated casually for a summer. He was nice. We got on. But I remembered how surprised people (Ben) had been when I said we were moving in together after less than a year: how impulsive it had looked on the outside and how coolly practical it had been on the inside.

We'd decided when we were out for dinner at a Mexican place, me anxious about the rent going up in my house-share, because it was that era, the mid-pandemic explosion in London when every landlord pushed up prices by twenty, thirty per cent because of the mysterious 'market forces' that were really just them smelling blood in the water, and thinking, *I'm not being left out of that*. Chris lived alone in a one-bed but his rent was going up too, more than he could afford. After a bit of mutual complaining, he'd said, 'Or I guess you could move in with me? Two birds, one stone.'

In the weeks between me saying yes and moving in, I'd tried to convince myself that 'two birds' meant 'a practical solution *and* the joy of your company' – but really I'd known that one bird was his rent and the other was mine. Had Ben noticed? He often observed more than I expected. Did he remember how uncertain I'd been about it even at the time? That when he'd said, 'Wow, that's fucking quick,' I hadn't replied with, 'When you know, you know!' or whatever other romantic platitudes people trotted out when they were doing something objectively insane. I had just agreed with him. 'Yeah, pretty quick,' I remembered saying. Chris and I had both gone in with our eyes open.

Ben was still watching me, and I wondered what a normal, well-adjusted person would feel about my situation. A normal, well-adjusted person wouldn't, I supposed, be in it. They wouldn't have turned a casual relationship into a serious one by moving in with somebody just because neither of them could afford their rent. 'Look,' I said. 'Two years is a long time.'

'Yeah,' Ben said slowly. 'But don't worry about how you're *meant* to be feeling.' Irritatingly perceptive. I'd never understood how one person could simultaneously be so self-absorbed and so observant – it was like hanging out with Sherlock Holmes.

So, no. Maybe I wasn't 'heartbroken'. Fine. If I was honest with myself, Chris and I had shared a relationship of affection and convenience rather than love. Even when we were as happy as we'd ever been, even on those nights where you go out for dinner, drink too much, come home giggly and ebullient, we had never talked seriously about the future. He'd never asked if I wanted marriage, children, and I had never asked him – although if we had discussed it, I don't know what I would have said. I was now six months from thirty and my future was something I still couldn't picture at all, an untuned television set.

I said none of this out loud. 'Look,' I began, with no idea what was going to come out of my mouth. Then the singing started.

'Haaaappy birthday to you, happy birthday to you, happy birthday dear RA-CHEL!' The woman in the little hat, thirty-one today, glowed as her friends brought a cake out. It had sparklers on top. Everyone in the restaurant joined in, politely, including us. 'Haaaappy birthday to yooooou.'

We clapped, and in the quiet that followed, Ben said, 'Let's stop talking about this. I'm sorry for stressing you out.'

I waved a hand. 'It's fine.'

'But can you just . . . I mean, you are all right, aren't you? Like, if you weren't, you'd tell me?'

I smiled. Irritating as I sometimes found Ben's pushing (*stay out a bit longer, go on, say yes, have another, talk to me*), at a deeper level, I appreciated that he wasn't taken in by any of my bullshit. I liked that he saw through me. Maybe I didn't want to talk about my not-great life, or how I felt about it (not great), but I was glad he loved me enough to ask. I turned to catch the waiter's eye. 'Course,' I said. 'Let's get the bill, shall we?'

We paid up, tipped cash, went outside, and soon I was standing under the restaurant awning watching Ben light a cigarette. It was raining again, and my hands were cold, so I put them in my pockets. 'Are we going to the pub, then?'

Ben looked unsure of himself. 'Well,' he said. 'We can. But . . .'

'Oh no. Not the party.'

'Mac, come on. You're all,' he drew his shoulders up to his ears, 'clenched up, like a little crab. You need a blow-out.'

'Go without me if you want, it's fine.'

'But we're hanging out!'

'Yeah, but I'm not up for a big one. Honestly, I don't mind, you can go, I just really, really don't fancy it.'

*

We got to the party just before midnight. The man who opened the door threw his hands up in delight when he saw us. 'You came!' he said. There was something familiar about him, French and fashionable, if a little harassed, with his hair in disarray, shirt flattened damply to his chest.

'Hi Claude,' said Ben, as they hugged. 'This is my friend, Dan.'

Claude smiled. 'Nice to meet you,' he said, and ushered us both inside.

While we stood in the hallway, taking our coats off, I realised why Claude was so familiar: he'd been in the show, Ben's terrible play, he was the one in all Ben's stories from the tour. I felt a spike of irritation.

Claude was telling Ben in hurried whispers how the party was a disaster, his housemate Ellie had become too drunk, too quickly and started crying on everyone about her father, which was very sad, but didn't she know that this was supposed to be a *fun night*?

'What happened to her dad?' said Ben.

Before Claude could answer, they were interrupted by someone shouting from the hallway above. 'She's locked in the bathroom,' the shouting voice said. 'Claude? I think she's being sick.'

'Fuck's sake,' said Claude. 'Coming!' He touched Ben lightly on the arm as he went.

Ben turned to look at me, and I waited for him to explain, or apologise for pretending there was no end-of-show party, when this was clearly it. I thought of him, distracted at the restaurant, rushing me here, just because he and Claude were – well, whatever was going on there, which was clearly something, but I wasn't going to ask.

But he just said, 'Come on, then,' with half a smile. 'Let's see what we can scavenge.'

The kitchen was empty except for the two of us. It was clear the party had been going for hours already, every surface littered with paper cups, abandoned mugs half filled with wine, crunched-down Wotsits, and the tatty remnants of what had presumably, several hours ago, been paper streamers. From the living room next door came the sounds of talking, shouting, music.

I went to one of the steamed-up windows and lifted it open. The smell of smoke drifted in. People were huddled together below the lip of the building, out of the rain. Somebody doing an Arnold Schwarzenegger impression, somebody else laughing. Sure. I looked round at Ben, who was sitting on the kitchen counter with his sleeves rolled up, pushing through the bottles on the side with one hand, in a lazy, unfocused sort of way, and smoking with the other. Like every house party I'd ever been to. For a moment I felt the weight of all the years we had done this: me and Ben in a hundred anonymous kitchens, him mixing some horrible drink while I watched. Nobody had forced me to come here. It was my own fault I was so easily persuaded. He felt me looking at him, and glanced up. 'What?'

'Nothing,' I said. 'I think people are smoking outside.' I nodded towards the window.

Ben shrugged. 'Claude smokes in here, it's fine. I think I can make us a cocktail from this lot, if you want?' He gestured to the ragtag collection of half-drunk spirits and mixers abandoned on the worktop.

'Sure,' I said, leaning against the sink. He stuck the cigarette in his mouth and began unscrewing the lids off things, sniffing at them, turning them over in his hands consideringly. For a while I watched him work in silence – but I still felt I was owed some kind of explanation. 'So. Claude.'

'Yep,' said Ben. 'Grenadine okay?'

I couldn't remember what Grenadine tasted like. 'Fine.' Ben didn't look up from what he was doing, conspicuously absorbed by pouring things into paper cups, stirring them with straws. Was I breaking some unspoken rule in our friendship by pushing? Somehow, I couldn't stop myself. 'So, have you two already . . . ?' I left the sentence hanging in the air.

Ben looked up at me, waggled his eyebrows. Then he held out a drink. His cocktails were legendary, brutal but reliably drinkable. 'Once or twice,' he said. 'It's not anything. I don't know.'

As I took the cup from him, he surprised me by holding out his cigarette too. 'Look, here, can you just take it if you want it so much?'

I laughed. 'I haven't smoked in years.'

'Yeah, and you're watching me like a man who hasn't eaten in—'

'Like I eat cigarettes?'

'Just fucking take it, Jesus Christ.'

So I did. Two cigarettes in one week; this way surely lay, if not madness, at least a habit I could no longer afford. Still, I took a drag, feeling all the lovely synapses fire in my brain that would never, ever go away, no matter how long I quit for. If the billionaires really could make me a new body, they would have to make it from before I met Ben, and started smoking.

'Thanks,' I said, passing the cigarette back. I sipped my cocktail. '*Christ.*'

'Good?'

'Mm,' I said evasively, waiting for my vision to become normal again. 'Is there like, cough syrup in this?'

'Flaming Ben's,' he said, miming lighting it on fire.

'What do you mean, "It's not anything"?'

'Oh. I don't know. He just hasn't been very . . .' He trailed off. 'But I do like him. I mean, I *actually* like him, as a person, which never happens.'

I scoffed. 'Ben, you like everyone,' I said, stirring my drink with the straw.

He looked at me, genuinely surprised. 'No,' he said. 'I really don't.'

For a moment, neither of us spoke. I felt like something was happening in the room that I didn't understand, but it could have been the rush of nicotine. I wasn't cross anymore, obviously, but I wanted to ask Ben why he'd dragged me here. Because he really had been evasive. He could easily have told me whose party it was and why he wanted to come, so why hadn't he? Because I was too recently dumped to hear about his love life? Because we almost never talked about the people we were seeing?

Anita, who told me everything about the men she slept with, up to and including the shapes of their dicks, thought we were insane. I had always been more reserved than her, but perhaps she was right, the little bubble of privacy in mine and Ben's otherwise close friendship went beyond what was normal.

If he'd just told me it was Claude's birthday party, and that he wanted to go, that would have been fine. Maybe I wouldn't have come, but I should have been allowed to decide for myself instead of finding out when I arrived what a passenger I was. Fine, maybe I was still annoyed. I wanted Ben to *want* to hang out with me, not use me as a wingman, which he almost never did – and right now, when I'd just been dumped, was obviously not the best time to start.

There was something dog-like about the way Ben was looking at me from under his mop of hair, and I wondered what was going on in there; were we each rehearsing one half of an argument? The same argument, or different ones? He didn't look angry. Then he said, 'I swear, Mac, you always think that if somebody loves you, it must be general, and not specific.'

I blinked. 'What are you talking about?' I said.

'It's called a tequila sunrise.' I turned. We were no longer alone in the kitchen: a girl with pigtails was standing by the fridge, talking to a skinny, bearded guy. 'It's tequila and juice and like . . . something pink. Is there ice?'

'In the freezer, I guess,' said the man. 'Oh no way! Ben!'

Ben jumped down from the counter, roaring in an indiscriminate way that could have meant he was delighted to see this very old friend, or that he couldn't remember the man's name and this was his best disguise. Suddenly I wanted to get away. I ducked around them, out of the kitchen, and into the room next door.

I stood in the doorway of an open-plan living-dining space, unusually large for London, full of people lounging across the furniture, deep in conversations. Pot plants hung from the bookshelves. There was a poster on the wall for a French film I hadn't seen or heard of, and one of those hot-pink neon signs people seemed to have got into: 'FRIDAY'. I wondered if they changed it every day, then remembered it was actually a Saturday. It must be punishing, looking at that neon sign on a Monday morning while they ate their Shreddies. I sipped my cocktail. It needed ice, but I wasn't going back now.

'Danielle?' A woman with a swoop of dark hair and big glasses was looking up at me from the couch. I couldn't place her.

'Hi!' I said.

She must have seen the panic in my eyes, because she laughed. 'Mandip.'

Of course. She was a theatre person; we'd met through Ben. 'Shit, yes, sorry. How's it going?'

We exchanged pleasantries, and she introduced the small woman sitting beside her as Annie. I wondered if Annie was Mandip's girlfriend, wife, sister, colleague, friend, or some combination of the above. Maybe they'd just met. There were so many people here, so many ways of knowing and not knowing another person, that I felt exhausted. This, I supposed, was why people took drugs at parties: to not have to think such boring things.

'You good, mate?' said Annie.

They were both looking at me. And then I heard myself say, with all the grace of an eleven-year-old on a school trip, 'Please can I sit with you? Is that weird?'

They laughed. 'Sure,' said Mandip, and shifted up on the couch to make space.

*

We talked about everything: work, life, politics, TV. Mainly TV. We all loved the same slightly schlocky, semi-prestige American show, about a mismatched pair of detectives of the supernatural, and talked for so long about the episode set in Prague that Mandip began to look up flights on her phone.

'Cheap,' she said, and then we all did 'shots' from the bottle of whisky by Annie's leg, and then we all did shots again, and I realised I'd been worrying about nothing. I was so happy to be at this party, with my newest and best friends. I was exactly where I was supposed to be.

We were joking about the trip to Prague, and then we weren't. Annie found a highly rated but surprisingly affordable apartment, which the website informed us was *usually booked*. Maybe this was all fate? I wondered if I was up for going on a holiday with an acquaintance and someone I didn't know, and came to the conclusion that I might be.

Wasn't this why, despite everything, I still lived in London? Didn't I find these moments of connection and possibility so thrilling that it was worth everything, the chaos, the mess, the expense, to hold onto them? I was addicted to the feeling that life could still, at any moment, surprise me. I so loved the possibility that Annie and Mandip would really, one day, be my friends, that it didn't matter whether it happened or not. The point was now, the night, the moment, the feeling of throwing ourselves into whatever came next. Then I realised the conversation had moved on from Prague, and that Annie had been talking about her all-women's volleyball group for some time.

'Every Wednesday night,' she said. 'You should come, seriously.'

'Yeah, maybe,' I said, despite knowing I would never, ever do that.

It was over. The two of them went outside to smoke, and I wandered back into the kitchen. Fine, no Czech minibreak, but I felt better, loose and expansive from Annie's whisky and ready to take the party how I found it. The kitchen was busier, but Ben wasn't in here; he hadn't been in the living room either. I felt a spike of anxiety that he might have left without me, and wondered where I should look for him. Then a man standing by the crisps said, 'So how do you know Claude?'

This man, bearded and tired-looking, turned out to be called Dave, though I didn't catch the names of his friends, a gaggle of nice-seeming young dads. As I was drawn generously into their conversation, it became clear that they all worked in writer's rooms. 'But what rooms? Writing what?' I asked.

One of them waved a hand. 'Oh, you know, this and that.'

But I didn't know. 'Like for films?' I said.

'God no, just TV!' said Dave, embarrassed. I waited for further explanations, the silence stretching a beat too long before he said, 'Sorry – and what do you do?' He must have thought I was waiting for him to ask a question. I felt bad.

'I work in an office.'

Dave's friends had fallen into conversation with each other. 'Doing what?' he said.

I didn't want to talk about Ideas, so I changed the subject, and soon found out he was married, with a six-month-old daughter; we talked for a while about what a bad sleeper she was. I liked Dave enough to stay by the kitchen table, eating Twiglets and enjoying the dregs of the harmony I'd felt before. Bright streamers hanging from the ceiling. Smokers' chat still drifting through the open window. The smell of rain, and distant smoke, and spilled drinks with sticky mixers that gummed your shoes to the lino.

'Do you have kids?' Dave asked.

I laughed. 'I'm only twenty-nine!'

He looked slightly offended. 'My wife's twenty-nine,' he said neutrally.

I was stunned. I couldn't believe he'd had babies with a child – and she wasn't at the party, or didn't seem to be. But I didn't want to pass judgement. I mumbled something about having just had a break-up, actually, needing to find somewhere to live. Apparently I'd reached the stage of drunkenness where I was just *telling* people things.

'That's shit,' said Dave. 'Sorry.'

'Yeah.'

'I know a houseshare that's got a room coming free soon, 950 Balham sort of thing?'

I laughed – £950 a month was so far out of my price range that I couldn't immediately think of a nice way to reply. I began trying to explain the situation. Maybe that was what I should have been using this party for the whole time, a way to meet people with spare rooms?

Dave listened sympathetically while I talked, trying to thread all emotional context out of my story, so it would seem that I was in a ludicrous but essentially relatable scrape. 'Jeez,' he said eventually. 'I don't think you'll find anywhere free in London.' I'd been beginning to think the same thing, but it wasn't nice to hear it said out loud, especially not at a party. 'Might be time to ask the awkward question!'

I blinked. What question? Ask to stay on his couch? We didn't even know each other.

'E.T. phone home,' he went on, waggling his finger at me. 'You know, ask for help. Call your folks.'

I nodded, but suddenly I could feel my pulse beating so hard that there was a sort of rushing in my ears, like bass thudding through the wall. Was this a fight or flight response? It had occurred to me for the first time that Jeannie probably wondered the same thing, that almost everyone who knew about my situation had probably thought, *why doesn't she just ask her parents for money?* As though it was that simple. As though I didn't worry as much about my mum making rent as myself, as though that wouldn't just mean debt going onto somebody else's credit card instead of my own. These people – they couldn't even imagine. Dave, nice Dave, it wasn't his fault, but standing here with his good trainers and his private school accent and no fucking idea at all, I wanted to unhinge my jaw and swallow him whole. The complete and utter distance from my entire reality. How nice it must be if you looked at these situations and thought only: *wow, she should really ask her parents for money*. How safe you must feel. How safe you had always been. I had to get out of this conversation before I said something I'd regret. I made my excuses and left the room.

*

One of the couches had a red wine stain on the arm – not from me, it was already half dry when I sat down, but still, it would be bad in the morning. I should have been looking for Ben, but instead I was back in the living room, talking to a beautiful woman whose dark hair lay in two pigtails on her shoulders, like Wednesday Addams, and who could have been anywhere between twenty-five and forty years old. A foot away, a woman with bleached hair was dancing alone. I'd begun to suspect she was Claude's housemate, sad Ellie, because her eyes looked small from crying, and because she was the only person dancing, and it wasn't really that sort of party. She looked unsteady on her feet.

'What do you do, Dan?' said Beautiful Wednesday Addams. She spoke softly, with an accent that was hard to place, but could have been Spanish.

'Writer's rooms,' I lied. What did it matter? I was never going to see her again.

'Oh, wow. Writing what?'

I waved a hand. 'This and that. What about you?'

Wednesday smiled enigmatically. She was an artist, she said, working in experimental soundscapes and audio compositions, mainly with a man named Stephen, as part of a committed and exclusive but, as far as I could discern,

102

non-sexual artistic partnership. 'Our relationship is a kind of palimpsest,' she said. 'A feedback loop, a layering of sound, one over the other; what I create, he takes from me, and what he creates, I take from him – and then we give it back, inextricable, forever altered.'

She turned and gestured to a small man in spectacles, sitting beside her on the couch, who'd been so inert and disengaged until now that I hadn't realised they were together. I'd spotted him an hour or so earlier and assumed he was at the party alone, possibly by mistake.

'Is this . . . Stephen?' I asked, then felt embarrassed for not addressing him directly. *Is Stephen in the room with us now?*

'This,' said Wednesday, smiling, her voice like music, 'is Stephen.'

'Wow.' I didn't say *Why?* though I'd been thinking it, and perhaps Wednesday heard the question in my voice.

'He fascinates me,' she went on. 'We are consumed by one another.'

I looked at Stephen, who for some reason, was wearing a suit. Acknowledging that he was being discussed, he lifted one hand in a little half-wave, like I was on a train pulling away from him. 'Hi,' he said.

'Hi.' I'd already begun trying to commit this whole encounter to memory, so I could tell Ben about it later, but then I realised I was being a judgemental prick. So what if this beautiful, mysterious woman seemed to have projected a set of artistic ideals onto a bank manager? At least she was happy. At least she was doing something she cared about. And who said looking like a bank manager meant anything at all? Who said Stephen wasn't an incredible artist? Who said Wednesday was, just because she looked like one?

There was a little snarl of self-loathing in the pit of my stomach, which probably meant I was hungry, although it felt more serious than that. I was a monster. I squandered love. I stood up.

'Are you okay?' said Stephen.

'Yes, sorry. I need to find my friend. Good luck with the art.'

'Thanks,' said Wednesday. 'Good luck with the writer's rooms.' She was holding Stephen's hand.

I was lost until I remembered I'd lied about my job. 'Thanks,' I said. I went back to the kitchen.

I had to find Ben, get some food, go to bed. But he still wasn't in there: it was just the tequila sunrise couple from earlier, talking unbelievably intensely in one corner, and Mandip, sitting at the kitchen table alone, rolling a huge joint.

'Hey,' I said. 'Sorry, have you seen Ben anywhere? I think I need to leave.'

'Not for a while.' Pink of her tongue on the Rizla paper. 'Want some of this?'

'Oh,' I said. 'Uh. No, probably not. But thanks.'

The flat was a duplex, with a set of stairs. I went to the top floor, where there were several closed bedroom doors and a queue for the toilet. I hadn't been for ages, and maybe Ben was in there? I joined the queue, but by the time I reached the front, there was still no sign of him. I used the bathroom, went back to the ground floor and then, on instinct, out of the front door, leaving it on the latch. Then I took the communal stairs to the front lobby and stepped out into the night.

The flat was in a flash new build, several towers connected by brightly lit overpasses. I could see the awning the smokers had been huddling under when I looked out of the kitchen window. You could usually find Ben in that sort of crowd – he'd probably been told off for smoking inside after all. But they didn't seem to be out here anymore. Actually, there was nobody out here at all.

I checked my phone. Already after three in the morning, Jesus, we really needed to leave. I tried calling Ben, but it didn't ring, and I remembered his phone had died on the way here. *Don't let me forget to plug it in*, he'd said, but I had forgotten, and clearly, so had he.

Maybe the smokers had moved into the open now the rain had stopped? I set off in a slow circle around the tower to look for them. There was some green space back here, belonging to the flats, that must be more impressive by day; manicured, a picnic spot for houses-mates rather than a park for families with kids. They hadn't bothered to light it at night, and it took on a strange, slightly sombre aspect next to the lights of the buildings, a great empty nothing.

Maybe the smokers had gone out there? I squinted into the dark. There definitely was someone, a figure maybe twenty metres away, standing alone on the green.

'Ben?' I called, and they turned. No, it wasn't Ben. Whoever it was had heard the sound of my voice, but they were too tall to be Ben, a streak of deeper dark out there on the unlit grass. They began to walk towards me.

'Hello?' My voice sounded strange, uncertain. She didn't answer, only came steadily nearer.

I wondered why I was afraid. It was just a person. Soon she would move into the light and I would see her face. And I knew her. It wasn't Ben, but it was someone I knew, of course; there was something so familiar in her gait, in the speed with which she was approaching. And she knew me too. She'd been waiting for me.

'Dan?' I turned. Mandip was standing between me and the building, joint in one hand, leather jacket thrown over her shoulders. 'You okay?'

I was breathing hard. 'Yes, sorry.' I laid a hand on my chest, felt the fluttering of my heart. 'Why?'

'You were just like, walking into a dimly lit park in the middle of the night. Didn't seem super smart, no offence.'

I blinked. I hadn't been walking, had I? I'd been standing still. She'd been walking towards *me*. I turned back to the darkened green where I'd seen the figure, but nobody was there now. Mandip and I were alone.

My pulse began to settle. Nothing wrong. I was safe, I was fine. I'd just seen a stranger, probably a dog walker, freaked myself out for no reason. But I couldn't shake a feeling of wrongness. Why, when it was too dark to make them out at all, had I been so convinced I knew her? Why had I even been sure it was a woman?

'Come and sit down, mate,' said Mandip. 'You look really pale and weird.'

I followed Mandip to a low wall on the other side of the building, where we could sit out of the wind and chat. I soon felt better, the fear fading like a bad dream.

We watched a fox dig through the bins, while she smoked. 'D'you want some?'

I wasn't sure that I did. I was drunk, and tired, and clearly for some reason quite paranoid, so probably didn't need to add anything else into the mix. But it seemed rude to say no. I lifted the joint from her fingers and took a small, polite drag.

Mandip laughed. 'You can have more than that.'

There was a clatter, and we looked up. Someone had left their binbags piled on top of the waste container, and the fox was pulling one open with its teeth, spraying kitchen roll and empty food packets all over the concrete. 'I'd actually never seen a fox before I moved to London,' said Mandip. 'I remember when I first came down, I got woken up by them screaming outside my flat at five in the morning. Thought it was a banshee.'

'Yeah,' I said. 'They're very *present* here.'

'It's their city really. We just live in it.' She took the joint back; it had gone out. Her face was orange in the flare of the lighter. 'I've been offered a job in Manchester, actually.'

She hadn't said this with much excitement, so I wasn't sure how to respond. 'Oh,' I said neutrally. 'Are you going to take it?'

Mandip sighed, rubbed her eyes with the back of her hand. 'I've no idea. I only applied for practice. But then Manchester's really nice. Like, does it matter? Will it be different?'

'It'll definitely be different.'

'Yeah, but would it be different enough to uproot my whole life? Wouldn't I just end up doing the same sorts of things in the same sorts of places with the same sorts of people?'

'You want to do different things with different people?'

'No,' she said sadly, passing the joint back. 'Not really. I like my life. I don't know. It's a big decision and it's freaking me out.'

We sat in silence for a while, watching the fox. Then I said, 'I'm leaving London too, actually.' I hadn't expected to say it.

'Really? Where to?'

'Uh,' I said. Even out of the wind, it was cold outside. October. Darkness coming. I crossed my arms and folded in on myself, trying to keep the heat in, then said that I was going to stay in Yorkshire for a couple of months. I didn't say that I was going to a country pile, with a Wikipedia page, or that it belonged to my boss. It was all too weird to explain.

I hadn't known, until I said it out loud, that I'd decided to accept Jeannie's offer – but I had. I felt a strange mixture of relief and gratitude and sorrow.

The thought of going away was strange. I wasn't sure what made a life – work? The pub? The people you spent all your time with? – but for better or for worse, my life was here, and leaving for so long made me afraid. Mainly, I guess, that if I left, I wouldn't be able to come back. Living in London was like trying to make a life on a moving platform, on sand that was going out with the tide; once I stopped, I might not know why I'd ever been trying to do it, or be able to start again. I'd leapt onto the platform at twenty-one and that had been that. Maybe once I left, the spell would be broken. But I'd chosen this life. Didn't I have the right to choose? I didn't want to leave for good, not yet, and not like this, broke and ashamed, before I was ready. I didn't want to leave my city to the Daves. I felt bad thinking it because it wasn't even his fault, he seemed nice, but there were just so many of them, and they were all nice, and none of them could understand the measure it cost me in rage and shame to cling onto the side of this place every month, and only barely manage that. How sometimes I hated myself for doing it, wondering what I was trying to prove and to who. Even my friends who were broke had people they could ask for money in a pinch. I felt so alone with it sometimes: the sleepless nights, sick feeling of watching my rent swallow half my pay in an instant and having to stretch the rest out, the strain, the pull of it, month after month after month. I didn't want to be afraid anymore, but I didn't want to have failed whatever test this was by giving up, either. Not after all this time. And yet. I was so tired.

'Come on, Mac.'

I turned. Ben was standing behind us, lit cigarette hanging from his mouth, holding my jacket. He looked orange in the artificial light, and sad. I wondered how long he'd been standing there and how stoned I was. It felt like I'd been out here with Mandip for a hundred years, talking, talking, heaving my heart into my mouth. I looked at my phone: twenty minutes since I left Claude's flat. Great. I must have had more of her joint than I'd meant to.

I stood, unsteady on my feet, and Mandip did too. She and Ben exchanged some pleasantries, then she hugged me goodbye, like two old colonels at the end of a long war. 'Good luck in Yorkshire,' she said. 'Good luck in Manchester,' I said. Then she patted me on the cheek, gave me a clumsy kiss on the eyebrow, and tottered back into the building.

Ben and I were alone. The sounds of shit techno drifted from the open window. It was 3.30 a.m. and cold, the air full of fine rain, as Ben held my jacket out to me. When I didn't move, he put the cigarette in his mouth and offered me his free hand. He looked louche and scruffy, but then he always looked a little of these things, something Puckish and youthful about him, however old we got. I walked over, put my hand in his. Ben draped my jacket over my head, even though my hair was already damp. 'I'm tired,' I said.

'Me too. Come on,' he said. 'Bus goes from over there. I've got potato waffles in the freezer.'

*

110

And then I was back at my desk. Monday morning. Jeannie in her office with the door shut, on a call; I waited until it had finished before I knocked.

'Jeannie,' I said. 'Do you have a minute?'

'Of course.'

I went inside. The window was open, fresh, damp air coming in.

'Erm,' I said. I shut the door behind me. 'Can we talk about – about what you said last week? About the house.'

Over the hours of my interminable Sunday hangover, I'd managed to convince myself that I'd been insane not to accept her offer right away, that by waiting the weekend out, I would have offended her, missed my chance.

'Great,' Jeannie said. She gestured to my usual stool, and I slid onto it. My legs were shaking. 'Have you made up your mind?'

'Yes. I'd like to go, please. If that's still – if it's okay with you?'

Jeannie smiled. 'I'm so glad to hear you say that,' she said.

I needn't have worried. My whole body was warm with relief. Everything was going to be okay.

'Wow,' I said, voice cracking. 'Thank you so much. That's really – that is amazing news.'

Things moved very quickly after that.

II.
Quiet

I MADE THE 10.33 A.M. TRAIN with minutes to spare, dragging my huge suitcase through King's Cross Station, red-faced and puffing. It wasn't what I fancied on a hangover, though perhaps that wasn't the only reason I felt queasy. It had all happened so fast, organising and booking and agreeing things, and now I was away, leaving everything behind – for a little while at least.

As we pulled out of the station, I picked up my phone. There must be people I needed to tell. I would be staying at Westerley Hall for nearly seven weeks.

I looked through my WhatsApp groups. Sex Cases, a group of university friends I no longer saw; Trojan Sex Cases, a smaller group of the same people from a production of *The Trojan Women*; Witless Girls, a bunch of colleagues from Witley Café, where I'd waitressed for a few months in my early twenties. I'd seen less and less of so many people, contacting them now would be weird. Old house group. Old house group. Old colleagues. The detritus of my life. I liked all these people, but I could go and come back without any of them even noticing. I put my phone down and looked out of the window.

We were leaving London, the city centre turning to suburbs, ragged outskirts, fields. And then it was all behind us: my friends, my desk, my flat. It was midweek, but I'd booked a day of annual leave to travel, so I had nothing to do but watch as the green rolled in, the sun came out and the towns got further apart. No one needed me.

I had a slight but lingering headache; I'd stayed out longer than intended last night, with Ben. For good reason. We'd had a fight about nothing after Claude's party on Saturday, and things had been stilted between us for days – lots of weird, polite texts – so I'd needed to clear the air before I left. I wasn't entirely sure I'd succeeded. But now I would be away for almost two months, and surely when I got home, everything would just go back to normal? Long friendships had that elastic quality, they could contain things, complicated things, and snap back into place. That was how it would be with us, I was certain.

I had to change trains in Leeds to get to Jeannie's house. I hadn't been back since graduating, so I'd arranged a long layover, to look around. The station had been redeveloped, but the experience of pulling in on the train, something about the light, was almost unbearably familiar.

I paid a fiver to put my suitcase in a locker, then went for a walk. It was immediately clear that the ninety minutes I had wasn't long enough to get anywhere interesting to me: the old bus route up to the university from the station, the brutalist self-catered halls out towards Headingley where I'd met Anita, the falling-down terraced house we'd shared a few streets from the Brudenell, where three different ceilings had caved in. The place by Woodhouse Moor, where the toilet kept leaking into the kitchen because, as it turned out, the landlord was just putting a bucket under the leak, inside the floorboards, so it would start coming through the plaster again whenever the bucket filled up. All those crap bars and biohazard bedrooms and freezing cold kitchens where I'd made pasta and pesto and more pasta and pesto and sometimes, for a change, chicken nuggets and chips.

It was term time, October, so there were students everywhere, spilling out of Primark and shuffling around town, under-slept in their branded hoodies. Everyone said young people were different now, more online, didn't drink, but they looked the same as I remembered, except less afflicted by the hideous fashions of the 2010s (all those fucking dolly shoes), and of course, more impossibly young than we had ever been.

I wandered the city centre, past some of the bars. I hadn't spent much time on the main strip, our crowd were keener on house parties than clubbing, but I recognised some places. Vodka Revs. Spoons. The big, multi-floor club I'd visited a few times, until an email circulated warning us about a drink-spiking epidemic. A cheesy pop place Anita had dragged us to for her twenty-first. I'd had to *beg* the taxi driver to take us home after, promising him again and again that she wouldn't be sick, and guiltily stuffing two £20 notes into his hand when she proved me wrong; a lot of money to me at the time. Actually, to be honest, it was still a lot of money to me.

I bought a sandwich from a Pret that hadn't been there when I was a student, walked around a shopping centre. The thing I'd loved about living here, and missed when

I moved to London, was the way you could hardly cross the city without bumping into somebody you knew. But I didn't know anyone here anymore. I thought about all the people I'd lost touch with: Nina, Ben's old housemate, who kept chinchillas for some reason; Doyle, from the photography club I'd joined at the fresher's fair, in a panic, and only gone once because I didn't actually own a camera; Tab, the friend I made in lectures, who'd been very funny and deeply pretentious, smoking Gauloises and drinking brandy at nineteen. How desperate we all were to work out who we were going to be and how we were going to live, asking each other implicitly, in every interaction: do I seem like the kind of person who keeps chinchillas? Am I going to make that a corner-stone of my personality? Does that seem right to you? Anyway, all over now. It was somebody else's turn to be young.

I walked back to the station, regretting having come at all. It had all felt so important at the time, so alive, so technicolour; coming back was no comparison. I didn't want the past to have so much power over me, but of course it did, over me and everyone else. It had happened, it was fixed, all its meanings made sense. The story was so clear. How could the mysterious, translucent present hope to compare to that? As for the future – no, of course not. It was no competition at all.

I got my suitcase back, found the platform for my train, just two carriages long, one of those small, rattly, local services. They hadn't turned the heating on yet and I huddled down in my seat. It was still jacket weather in London; clearly I'd been in the south too long. I was going to need a bigger coat.

*

Jeannie had given me the number for Mrs Waddingham in case she wasn't there when I arrived, but it was a landline, not a mobile, and I'd been worried about the whole thing, like I might end up waiting alone in a car park for three or four hours. I needn't have been – when my train pulled in, Mrs Waddingham was already outside in a little, dark blue car.

'Hello!' she said, climbing out of the driver's seat. 'You must be Danielle.' She was late middle-aged, heavy-set and strong-looking, with a thick Yorkshire accent and the energy of somebody who ate a cooked breakfast every morning and then walked for fifteen miles. I liked her immediately.

'That's me,' I said, though it was obvious: nobody else had got off the train at this stop. It was a small, old-fashioned station, the forecourt quiet and tree-lined. Though we were still a few hours from sunset, it was darker than I expected, the day overcast.

We put my suitcase in the boot and set off, making small talk about my journey (fine) and how long Mrs Waddingham had been waiting (not long). The winding country roads were very picturesque, but made me feel queasy. I wondered how far we were from the house.

'Are you hiring a car once you're settled?' asked Mrs Waddingham.

'Oh,' I said, embarrassed, as I always was when I had to tell older people that I couldn't drive. Lessons were so expensive. I'd been broke as a teenager, and then in London it had seemed time-consuming and unnecessary, and also I had still been broke. It rarely came up. But as soon as I went anywhere rural, I felt stupid. 'No,' I said evasively. 'I'll have to get the bus.'

She looked surprised. 'Is there a bus?'

I felt a jolt of anxiety.

'Didn't used to be,' she went on. 'But that's okay, we can sort you out with something. Just a couple of months, isn't it? My husband's a mechanic, I'm sure we can lend you some old banger for getting around. Let me ask him later and I'll let you know.'

Now I was doubly embarrassed. 'Oh, no, it's fine. I don't – I mean – I can't actually drive.' I laughed awkwardly. Mrs Waddingham didn't join in.

'Gosh.' She looked genuinely concerned.

'It'll be fine, though,' I said, despite not knowing if this was true.

'Westerley's very remote. I'm surprised Jeannie suggested you stay there without a car.'

'Oh, well,' I said vaguely. Had I told Jeannie I couldn't drive? I thought so, but I wasn't sure. Maybe she'd just assumed I could – unsurprising, given I was an adult woman of nearly thirty. I was terrified at the thought of having to go back to London with my tail between my legs. But there would be ways to manage, of course there would. Online shopping. Deliveries. It was an old house, but it must be part of the modern world.

Mrs Waddingham, clearly embarrassed for me, changed the subject, asking about the work Jeannie and I did together. Never my favourite topic, but I had a good crack at making it all sound fun, careful to speak about Jeannie with absolute neutrality, as I wasn't sure of their exact relationship. Jeannie said Mrs Waddingham had looked after the house for her and her brother for years, since the groundsman left. When I asked what *looking after* entailed, Jeannie had trotted out a set of vague phrases that were hard to parse, about how Mrs Waddingham *looked in on the place sometimes*, kept an eye, made sure things were maintained. She'd implied that Mrs Waddingham couldn't get around as well these days, but she looked perfectly mobile to me. I wondered whether my coming had put her out of a job, or if she'd been looking after the house as a favour and was relieved to have it off her hands.

It was Westerley that made this weird, of course. Like, was she a friend of the family? Or was she, as the person who looked after Jeannie's *stately home*, actually sort of a servant? I didn't know if people even had servants these days. Perhaps, after all, we were the same – both just Jeannie's employees.

Anyway, I was careful not to imply that I either did or didn't get on with Jeannie, that we either were or weren't friends. I might be a twenty-nine-year-old woman without several basic life skills, including an operational mode of transport, but I'd survived in the world long enough to know one thing: if I had to live alone, in the middle of nowhere, with no way of getting around or meeting anyone other than Mrs Waddingham, I bloody well wanted her to like me.

'Here we are,' she said. The car had stopped outside a wrought iron gate. A real one, like in films. I laughed, thinking she was making some kind of joke, that Jeannie's house would be around the corner, but Mrs Waddingham was already climbing out of the car. I scrabbled out to give her a hand.

'We don't lock these,' she said, lifting the heavy gate with some effort. I took some of the weight. 'There. We can leave them open for now, the road's quiet anyway.'

We got back in the car and were soon travelling down a tree-lined drive, gravel crunching under the wheels. I don't know what I'd been expecting, but it wasn't this. Phrases like *explore the grounds* came to mind, things I'd read in books but never had reason to actually say out loud. Then I spotted the house through the trees, looking like the one photograph I'd seen online: the sandstone frontage, pillars either side of the door, the set of steps. It was blocky, square, but taller and broader than I'd been able to tell from the photos. A huge place to live alone.

'Danielle, meet Westerley!' said Mrs Waddingham. She pulled up out front and killed the engine.

I didn't reply. For once in my life, I was stunned into silence. She was looking at me expectantly, like the house was something she'd built herself, a child with a sand-castle. 'Well?'

'Yeah,' I managed. 'Big.' She laughed at me.

We climbed out of the car and she unlocked the boot. 'How do we get inside?' I asked, lifting my suitcase out.

Mrs Waddingham gestured to the huge front door, and looked at me like I was a moron. 'Right,' I said, laughing, 'Obviously.' I was embarrassed but couldn't shake the feeling of wrongness, as if this wasn't, somehow, the correct entrance for us to use. It was so huge and old and osten-tatious – wasn't there another, more normal door somewhere? Around the back, maybe?

I followed Mrs Waddingham up the front steps while she began explaining how the keys worked. There were three locks, one ancient-looking, and she handed me the set and got me to do it all myself. 'Better than you getting locked out when I'm not here to help,' she said. After some jiggling around, the front door opened with a push.

The house was quiet. Light from the dying day fell across the flagstone floor, which stretched away into dark-ness. I could see a staircase, a couple of closed doors. I looked back at Mrs Waddingham. 'Is somebody here already?'

She frowned, and I realised this was a strange thing to have said. The house was empty: that was why I had come. To keep it company.

'No,' Mrs Waddingham said slowly. 'Why do you ask?'

I didn't know what to say, or how to explain the certainty I'd felt, stepping over the threshold for the first time, that someone was already inside, waiting for me. I shook my head. 'Nothing. Sorry.'

'Come on then,' she said, pushing the door the rest of the way and stepping around me, into the house. 'Do you want the tour?'

*

The tour turned out to be extensive. It was, indeed, a very large house. We started in the basement: there was a shut-up room which Mrs Waddingham said was used for storage, but most of the level was taken up by a huge kitchen, with a long, scrubbed, farmhouse-style table in the centre. Around the walls were rows and rows of cupboards, a chest freezer, and one of those big enamel sinks that comes up to your elbows with tall, brass taps. There was even an Aga, which I'd seen on Instagram but never in real life, although it was cold to the touch. 'Yeah,' said Mrs Waddingham. 'It's a faff. I'd just use the normal cooker over there.'

We went back to the ground floor. First, I was shown an echoey dining room with dark blue walls, a long mahogany table, and imposing Victorian portraits of (presumably) dead people. There were cabinets along one wall full of odd things, empty glass decanters and silver bowls of various sizes, none of which I could imagine finding a use for.

Next came a drawing room, with big bay doors that opened out into the garden. What were drawing rooms for? I had no idea. But this one was like a stage set, with huge, wall-to-wall bookshelves full of dusty, unused-looking nineteenth-century hardbacks, a few uncomfortable-seeming sofas, a low table, and other odd, mismatched pieces of furniture. Between the bay windows and the shelves, there was only one bare wall, and it was full of paintings, giving the room a slightly cramped feeling, like it was somewhere to store things you inherited, which was a problem I couldn't really imagine having.

The next door was locked. 'What's in here?'

Mrs Waddingham shrugged. 'Before my time. Used to be the billiards room, apparently.' I managed not to say, *Like Cluedo?* 'I think the pipes burst and it got ruined, but they've never got round to sorting it, so for now it's just closed.'

We moved on. A storage space, a bathroom, and then the 'snug' at the back of the house, which felt like a living room: warm colours, a couple of framed art prints, watercolour landscapes rather than oil paintings of dead relatives, plus a couple of low, squashy, comfortable-looking couches and a pine cabinet that turned out to contain a television. This was more like a room people actually used, the bookshelves full of romance novels, Penguin Classics, a set of Wilbur Smiths.

After that, we climbed the stairs to the first floor. At the top was a study that looked quite nineties, with a big desktop computer and filing cabinets. Mrs Waddingham said it had been a nursery once. 'Nigel had it converted. He still comes up and works from Westerley in the summers sometimes.' Jeannie's brother, I remembered.

Several rooms on this floor were closed: not locked, like the billiards room, just dust-sheeted. 'Since the kids grew up, they don't come here very often,' Mrs Waddingham said. 'They don't tend to use more than a few rooms at a time.'

There was a large but unimposing bedroom with pale blue walls, the bed stripped, but the furniture uncovered and ready for use, so I assumed I'd be sleeping here. Then Mrs Waddingham led us into the master, with a large, sumptuous sleigh bed and thick, deeply patterned curtains, all done in the kind of deep reds that feel somehow expensive.

'I made the bed up for you. All the linens and towels and things are here.' She gestured to a cabinet. 'Of course, if you'd prefer a different room, you're welcome to change. The blue room wouldn't take long to set up. But most of the dust-sheeted ones would need a good airing.'

'No, this is great,' I said quickly. I felt bad that she'd done all this for me before I came, even offering to make up another room, like I was the lady of the house. 'It's amazing,' I added. 'Beautiful.'

Mrs Waddingham beamed. 'Well, it gets good light,' she said. There was a dressing table in one corner, a couple of low chairs by the window, a moody portrait of a Victorian woman holding a small dog. She showed me the small adjoining room, a sort of walk-in wardrobe you could actually get dressed in, and I felt a bubble of hysterical laughter rise in my chest. I had a brief mental image of the broken Ikea chest of drawers where Chris and I had tried to cram most of our clothes, the rattle-rattle-rattle of the stuck drawer waking me when he got up early. Maybe if we'd had a dressing room we'd have argued less.

There were two bathrooms on this floor, one just a toilet, the other very large, with a roll-top bath. 'Oh my God,' I said involuntarily. It looked like a hotel. Mrs Waddingham laughed at me.

Then there was only one door left, at the end of the hall. 'Just the attic. But I can take you up if you want to see?'

We climbed the stairs together, Mrs Waddingham leading and me following. The attic contained another locked-up storage space, and through a final door, a small bedroom. Twin beds, a chest of drawers, some forgotten toys in a box in the corner. It had a scrubbed wooden floor and looked plain and sensible compared to the rest of the house, which to put it kindly was not otherwise restrained, with all the gilt and velvet and Regency people looking sternly out of paintings. I took a few steps into the room, peered through the window.

'I think the children would sleep up here sometimes, when they were young,' said Mrs Waddingham.

'Jeannie's children?'

'Or her brother's.'

There were two windows, one new, a Velux built into the slope of the roof, and one smaller, old-looking, built into the wall, which was probably original. It must have been very dark in here, back in the day. It wouldn't have been a room for children then – Nigel's office used to be the nursery, she'd already told me that.

'All grown up now, but they've kept this room in good order for nostalgia's sake. The family still uses it sometimes.' Of course – no dust sheets. 'No grandchildren yet, but that's your generation, isn't it? My sons are like you, down in London, paying through the nose to rent some box off a banker – no wonder you lot can't afford kids, eh? It's a bloody scandal. Would you rather stay up here?'

'I'm sorry?'

She was looking at me strangely. 'Just,' she said slowly. 'The way you sat down. Like you're stopping.'

Without meaning to, I had sunk onto one of the beds while she was talking. I stood up quickly. 'No, sorry,' I said. 'Just tired.'

We went out of the attic and down the main staircase, to the ground floor. It was early evening, sunset, and the windows above the front door were full of golden light. It looked spectacular, and I said so.

'West-facing,' said Mrs Waddingham. 'We thought that might be where the house gets its name? But who knows.'

As we came down into the entrance hall, I wondered if I should ask her to stay for tea, although I had nothing to offer, and perhaps that was presumptuous anyway. She knew the house, I didn't; it was more hers than mine; if she wanted to stay, maybe she would offer *me* tea? This whole thing was uncharted waters, socially.

But she said, 'Well! It was lovely to meet you, Danielle,' holding a hand out. I shook it.

'Thanks for everything.'

'It's no bother. Jeannie gave you my number, I think, but it's pinned up in the kitchen cupboard as well, by the phone – call if you need anything. And I've a spare key if you get locked out. I mean, don't get locked out, I live bloody miles away, but – you know. In an emergency, don't panic.'

I thanked her and then, before I knew it, I was watching her little blue car head back down the drive. I waved until she was out of sight, and shut the heavy door behind me, startlingly loud. Then nothing. The sounds of the building settling. I was listening keenly, in an animal sort of way, though I don't know what for.

I took a few steps towards the staircase. The windows above me were still golden, light falling on the bannister, and the tasteful carpet of the entrance hall, and the backs of my hands, which I held up in front of me, like I was trying to prove I was really here. But I was. Somewhere deep in the house, a clock ticked. I was here, and alone. I was alone at Westerley.

*

That evening, drinking a glass of wine at The Hart's Salvation, I decided these were going to be the best two months of my life.

The Hart was my new local – an old, cramped, winding country pub, with small doorways and gnarled tables, an atmospheric little rabbit warren of a place, but modernised, with bottles of sambuca behind the bar, a pool table and a TV mounted on the wall. Its existence had been a great relief to me. After Mrs Waddingham left, I'd double-checked the local buses online and found that, as predicted, there wasn't one – or rather, a single bus seemed to pass Westerley once a day, at 10.13 a.m., which wasn't going to be much use. I hadn't brought anything for dinner.

Alone in the house, I'd gone down to the kitchen, rummaged in the cupboards: plates, bowls, oil, salt, vinegar, but the cupboards were bare, except a few tins of kidney beans and stock cubes, and some old breakfast cereal. The freezer contained half a Viennetta (I'd always *known* it was posh) and an unopened bag of frozen peas. None of this was enough to scrape a meal together. I was on the verge of panic when I remembered pubs existed, and checked maps on my phone, finding The Hart's Salvation only twenty minutes' walk across the fields, at the edge of the nearest village.

British food and real ales abound in this pub with open fires and beer garden, the internet had promised. I wasn't disappointed.

'Bangers and mash?' said the barman. He was standing over me with a steaming, piled-up plate.

'Yes, please,' I said.

'There you go. Condiments over there.' He pointed, turned to leave.

'Sorry, just quickly, is there a Wi-Fi password?'

'Not for customers,' the barman said, but not unkindly. 'We encourage people to talk to each other. We're old-fashioned like that.' He was a tall, laconic man in his sixties, with a thick Yorkshire accent and a thatch of grey hair.

'Oh, yeah, sorry, of course,' I said.

But I must have looked put-out because he asked if it was an emergency. 'Not lost, are thee? Lot of people get lost walking round here, with the nights cutting in.'

'No, I'm not lost,' I said. 'I'm staying at Westerley.'

His eyebrows shot up. 'Westerley Hall?' He looked like he was reassessing everything he'd thought about me and I didn't like it.

'It's not mine,' I said quickly, spilling out useless information: that it was my boss's house, and I couldn't drive, and didn't have any food, and there was no signal here, and I needed to do an online shop or I would have to live under the bar at The Hart's Salvation.

He whistled. 'You are in a pickle, aren't you?' he said. 'I'm Ted – the landlord here.'

'Danielle.'

'Danielle. Well, the password's *salvation1756*, all one word. Can't have thee dying of hunger up in that big house, can we?'

It worked: I was online. I thanked Ted and then, while I ate, did my online shop, putting eggs and bread and beans and booze and tangerines into the little box on my phone. I hadn't done a proper food shop for weeks, living itinerantly on supermarket sandwiches, late-night takeaways and Anita's kindness. I sent her a picture of my dinner: *Living my best life.*

I thought about texting Ben, too, drafted a few messages, deleted them all. I'd sent a nice goodbye from the bus that morning, and he'd replied with several heart emojis but no actual words; maybe I should wait until he sent a full sentence before I said anything else. He wouldn't still be cross, I was sure, but still. I should wait.

Four sausages?! Anita replied. We texted back and forth a while, which wasn't quite like eating with a friend, but wasn't exactly like being alone, either. It was funny how often, in London, I'd felt that my phone was my enemy, a psy-ops prick of a Pandora's box that had been put into my life expressly to ruin my attention span, self-esteem and bank balance – and yet up here, alone, it was already my best friend. Everyone I loved was in there.

I went back to my online shop. Rice, pasta, chicken, onions, mushrooms. I rarely did this and it always felt like playing one of those pre-school board games, putting little cardboard squares of butter, jelly and sweets into a cardboard trolley. Strange that all these pictures meant real things, real bags of lentils, tins, a real orange I'd be able to hold in my fist, digging crescents into the peel with my fingernails. Stranger still that all these things would come to Westerley, just because I wanted them to. It felt like being able to make things happen. I thought about the huge, silent basement kitchen, the cold Aga, the row of copper pans above the cooker. I was going to cook in there. Ridiculous.

'All right?' said Ted. I'd finished eating, and he took my plate.

'That was so good,' I said. 'Thank you. You're a lifesaver.'

'Got your shopping sorted? Not gonna starve to death?'

'No, I'll live. It's coming tomorrow afternoon.'

'What are you going to do for breakfast, then?'

'Oh,' I waved a hand. 'There's teabags. Viennetta. I'll be fine.'

Ted looked at me, narrowed his eyes. 'Hang on a sec,' he said. He left with the plate and then a moment later he was back, holding a takeaway coffee cup. 'Some milk. So you can have a cup of tea before the cavalry arrives.'

I thought it was the kindest thing a stranger had ever done for me, and said so. 'Naw,' said Ted, but he looked pleased.

Perhaps he'd sensed that he would have, in me, a good and regular customer. He was not wrong.

*

First night at Westerley. Jeannie had been right, the house was cold, but I didn't mind. I slipped a hot water bottle between the sheets of the huge double bed as I finished unpacking.

The dressing room just off my bedroom had a truly insane amount of storage: even if I'd brought all the clothes I'd ever owned, the teddy bear toddler nighties and grungy, teenaged long-sleeve tops, I wouldn't have been able to fill it. I folded and piled up my jeans, dungarees, leggings, slipped my Primark multipack pants into one of the drawers. It all looked very underwhelming. I wished I'd brought whatever the lady of the house was meant to wear. Silks, and satin undergarments, and . . . what? Linen? I wasn't sure I was picturing the right things, some combination of half-remembered period dramas and Instagram trad wives.

I turned the light off in the dressing room, closed the door and went to pull the last bits from my suitcase. I'd decided in the end that I couldn't face seeing Chris, so I'd sent kind Anita to my flat with a list, to smash-and-grab. Mainly jumpers and books. Now I piled them up on my bedside table, ready to reread: *Brideshead Revisited*, *Howards End*, *Jane Eyre*, *The Secret Garden*, *Pride and Prejudice*, *Rebecca* . . . Stories I'd loved as a teenager, and which had seemed somehow necessary to bring. Though I don't know what a girl like me, pinging from terraced two-up two-downs to flats and back again, had got from all those books about rich people.

Escapism, I suppose. Grandeur. They had been like fantasy novels, full of strange, distant worlds: balls and hillsides and buttered crumpets – but better, more believable than elves and witches, because you knew that it was kind of real. The familiar, peaceful rhythms of them, with their baths, breakfasts, afternoon teas. Mainly I guess they'd filled me with warm, comforting nostalgia, even though it was nostalgia for a life I'd never known – and even though I wasn't sure that sort of life should actually exist.

Looking at them piled up together, it occurred to me that I had brought these books because, in one way or another, they were all about a house. Brideshead, Thornfield, Pemberley, Manderley. Houses that had to be loved or protected or saved, mythic, beautiful. The House. And now here I was, a guest in the kind of story I'd grown up loving.

Climbing into bed, I felt a rush of something that was not quite excitement, not as dizzy or overstimulating, but quieter, more whole. Something like joy.

*

'Goooood morning!' said Jeannie, tinny and excited.

It was 9.30 a.m., our catch-up, and I was keeping the laptop very close to my face, so she wouldn't be able to see that I was working from bed. The kitchen was the warmest room, but the Wi-Fi was patchy, so I was going to have to work from bed until I figured out the heating. Funny to be in a house with a million rooms and live like I had in my old flat, moving between the bedroom and the kitchen, the kitchen and the bedroom.

'I bet you slept well. I always sleep so soundly at Westerley,' she said. I had: a deep and dreamless sleep. I'd been relieved, after some of the long, bad nights I'd had on Anita's couch, nightmares and sleep paralysis. I felt rested.

'Yes,' I said. 'Great.'

'And you're settling in okay?'

There was something uncanny about Jeannie's face inside the screen, reminding me of lockdown, hours and hours on video calls together. I'd been in a houseshare before I moved in with Chris, no space, we all had to work in our bedrooms. I remembered pushing my bed up against the window, keeping it open all the time, trying to pretend I was sitting outside.

'It's beautiful here,' I said, meaning it. 'Thank you so much for letting me stay.'

'The hot water's all right? I know those old immersion heaters can be a pain.'

'Oh, yes—'

'And it can feel like a long wait for that bath to fill when you're used to showers!'

'No,' I said. 'Honestly, the bath is – great. It's like something from a hotel. Shall I run through my list?' I was keen to prove that I could work as well from here as anywhere, that I didn't need to rush back to London, to the office.

'I wonder how the gardens are,' Jeannie went on, not listening. 'We've let them run to wrack and ruin really. Mrs Waddingham wasn't up to it even when we hired her, and she's certainly not now. She's retiring, did I say that?'

'Is she?'

'Terrible shame, we've been wondering what to do about it ever since she told us. Did she meet you all right from the station?'

'Fine, yeah.'

'She's reliable, but not very strong. A housekeeper, not a gardener, if you see my meaning. In my grandfather's day, there were staff for inside and outside, and she's more of an inside person, you know.'

'Right,' I said vaguely.

'The problem is, if you just bring somebody in a couple of times a year to clear the weeds, that isn't nearly enough. A garden like that needs constant care and attention. So whoever we find to replace her will really need to be able to do both. Did she talk to you about all this?'

'Not really.'

'But you *are* getting on all right?'

Jeannie clearly loved the house, wished she was here. Not surprising – it was where she'd grown up – and it was kind of her to let me stay somewhere so important. But what could I tell her? What could I say that would be enough? All my concerns so far had been boringly practical; storage, shopping, settling in. And I could hardly tell her I'd been here sixteen hours and already gone to the pub. She was still my boss.

'I'm going to try and get out for a proper walk later, before it gets dark,' I said. 'Shall I take some pictures and send them to you?'

'Oh, yes *please*.' She looked delighted. 'So, what's on your list?'

*

Everything was hushed in the last of the day's light. It was a misty dusk, with a haze of pink and the smell of wood-smoke drifting across from somewhere. I stood for a moment admiring the view. Then I pulled the front door closed, and set off across the grounds.

I'd already seen the drive, so I followed a path around the house, to the back. Jeannie was right: even to my completely untrained eye, it was clear the grounds needed love and attention. I found a kitchen garden with some plants dead or dying, others running wild, including a gigantic, sprawling patch of what I soon realised, from the smell, was mint. I picked a few leaves, stuffed them into my jeans pocket. My food had finally arrived late afternoon, after several irritated phone calls from the delivery guy, who couldn't find the house, and who I had been precisely no help to. Strange to realise how little sense I had of where I actually, geographically was. Anyway, I had lamb in the fridge for Sunday lunch, so maybe I could make some kind of mint sauce. I laughed. Fresh herbs from *the grounds*, who did I think I was?

I followed the path towards a tangle of hedges, over-grown flowerbeds, perhaps the remnants of a walled garden. I closed my eyes for a moment, tried to picture it as it had been, but I lacked the imagination and, frankly, the knowledge. All the dead plants and choking weeds were depressing. I wished I understood these things, at least enough to help while I was here, but I'd never had a garden as an adult, not so much as a window box. Even my cactuses died. I kept walking.

Beyond the hedgerows, the grounds banked up steeply into forest; it was probably still part of Jeannie's land, there wasn't a fence, but I didn't know for sure and didn't want to find out by being shot by a farmer. I walked up to the treeline, peered inside. It was only early evening, but already dark inside the copse, and I couldn't see much.

I looked back at the house. Somehow, Westerley seemed bigger from this angle, more imposing. I could see the windows of the dining room, the back bedroom, the study, the attic at the top of the house. And I wondered about the man – because surely, given Westerley's age, it had been a man – who first saw this patch of land and imagined a house.

Why here? What made him call this building into being? Money, obviously, but it had to be more than that, reaching for a kind of immortality.

I tried to remember what I'd read about the house online. Built in the eighteenth century, but there had been another Westerley, destroyed the century before. Could be natural causes, an accident – but I thought probably, with those dates, the English Civil War? Lots of big houses were destroyed. It was a bit of history I'd found interesting ever since I'd been told, as a kid, that the nursery rhyme 'Goosey Goosey Gander' was really about Cromwell's men searching for priests. *Whither shall I wander? Upstairs and downstairs, And in my lady's chamber.* I tried to imagine how it had looked: fire, panic, the grounds crawling with roundhead soldiers. Foundations lying like bleached bones the next day, smoke still hanging in the air. It must have felt like the world was ending. Then it didn't. Less than a hundred years later, the new house: Westerley, as I knew it, rising from the ashes.

How many days had it stood here since then? How many mornings, slate roofs grazing the sky? On the day I was born, it was already ancient, and it would still be here long after I died. No wonder Jeannie was weird.

I tried to imagine what it must be like to grow up here, inside a piece of history that was yours to own, your inheritance. Making crayon marks on the same nursery walls your ancestors scratched at with chalk. Had it hurt Jeannie to think the place might go to her brother, not her? Had she ever been unsettled by the scale of it, big rooms, dark corners, too frightened to run down the hall to her parents' bed? And what a place to be a teenager: I pictured her reading under trees, evading her governess, longing for escape ... Although really, of course, those images were straight from books I'd read, and were bollocks. Jeannie boarded, she'd told me how much she hated it; that was why her sons were *day boys*, meaning, like her, they'd gone to a posh school, but unlike her, they hadn't lived in it.

I tried to picture Jeannie at fourteen, coming back to Westerley, home for Christmas, long summers, walking the grounds, teas on the lawn. Then I thought of myself at the same age, rattling around our flat and longing to get away somewhere, anywhere. Hours at the top of the high street, standing around in tartan skirts and Doc Martens until my knees got cold. Jeannie was decades older than me, but it may as well have been hundreds of years: our childhoods were worlds apart. To grow up belonging to Westerley, Westerley belonging to her, was to have lived inside the past, inside the evidence of its immutability in the present, in a way I could barely imagine.

But then, that wasn't true, was it? I could imagine Jeannie's childhood easily, the meals, the staff, the rhythms of an English countryside life that were preserved in all the books I'd brought with me. Hunts. Dances. Port being passed to the left. It was *my* childhood, *my* origins that were impossible to imagine, invisible. I could understand Jeannie; she made sense to me. But I would never make sense to her.

Still. Here I was.

Mum said her father's family had been servants in the Midlands, teenage maids polishing spoons, and I tried to picture them now: my face, surly even when I tried to look pleasant, hair like mine that wouldn't lie flat under their caps. Probably not working anywhere this grand, but still – from servant to master of the house, in four generations. Even if it was only temporary, you had to admit that it was progress, of a kind.

I set off in the direction I'd come, down the slope, away from the treeline. It was getting cold; time to go inside. Another bath, perhaps – why not? For now, even if only temporarily, Westerley was mine.

*

I woke in bed to sunlight streaming through the windows.

There was a cup of tea cooling on the bedside table; the girl had brought it to me. I looked up and saw her

141

standing, pale and plaited, asking if I wanted anything else. I told her to draw me a bath. While she did, I sat up on all my pillows to drink my tea and gaze out of the open windows.

It was high summer, and already the day was warm and bright, which meant I'd slept later than planned. Oh well. I lay there, listening to the birds, and a moment later I was sitting in the chair while the maid helped me dress. She brushed my hair. I skipped through time as easily as a flat stone on water, and was constrained by nothing; the bed, the chair, the hallways, and then time changed again, and I was moving through the house alone.

Everything was different in the summer light. Westerley as I had never seen it: all the doors on the landing open; all the shut-up, dust-sheeted rooms full of light. Walking down the great staircase, I saw blue sky in the entrance hall windows. The carpet was soft and familiar beneath my feet.

I stood in the dining room. The table had been laid for several people, and on the sideboard were breakfast foods, toast and jam and bacon sitting on a hotplate, and special things, because it was summer: a plate of freshly cut strawberries shining like the inside of a mouth, thinly sliced melon, a bowl of peaches wet from being washed. I could hear laughter coming from higher in the house. And when I went to the window, the garden outside was the greenest I'd ever seen, alive with insects.

'Did you want anything else, ma'am?' The maid was waiting, standing at the door behind me. But I didn't want to turn around yet. I wanted to enjoy the light on the garden, the warmth on my face, a moment longer. I heard her walk over, closer to me, concerned I hadn't heard. She was standing right at my shoulder. 'Ma'am?'

I jolted awake in my borrowed bed at Westerley. 'Jesus,' I said. My heart was beating like a train, and I held a hand to my chest as I sat up in bed, looking around. It was too dark to see anything, so I flicked the lamp on.

I was alone. Of course I was. Someone had spoken in my dream, that was all: there was nobody in the room with me.

As my heart rate began to settle, I picked up my phone and checked the time. 4 a.m.: I should go back to sleep, but I still felt too wired. Not that it had been a bad dream, exactly, it had just been – what? It was already slipping away. I lay on my side reading a series of texts from Anita that had come while I was sleeping. She was out at a bar and thought an actor from *Hustle* was there. I didn't remember the actor. I barely remembered *Hustle*. I scrolled down to see a blurry photo, taken from a distance, which could have been of literally any man, and then another message two hours later which simply read, *wasn't him* ☹

It was a disorientating thought, the bar, the noise, the crush of people – very distant from where I was. I hadn't even remembered it was Friday night.

I flicked the light off, lay in the dark, and as soon as I did, images from the dream began to surface, like they'd been waiting for me. Sunlight. Blue skies. And so much green. Of course – I had dreamed about Westerley, the garden, how it must have looked when lots of people lived here. Even though it had just been my imagination, it was melancholy how different the real Westerley was, so still and dust-sheeted and quiet. Like the house was dying.

*

On Sunday afternoon, I realised I hadn't spoken a word out loud since our Friday staff meeting, well over forty-eight hours ago. An occupational hazard of living alone, of course, unless you got your shit together to call people, or see them, or they called you – but I'd never lived alone before, because it was too expensive and I was too codependent, so I wasn't good at it. Not that I was lonely. It was just strange. Anita had been busy all weekend, a date, a ceramics course, a party, and Ben was barely answering my texts. He was always bad at keeping in touch – but usually he was the one off on tour, while I was back home, busy, barely noticing that it took him two days to reply to a meme with nothing more illuminating than 'haha love it'. I'd thought he might make more of an effort, knowing I was so isolated up here. Although things had been weird with us before I left. What if he wasn't being haphazard and forgetful in a normal Ben way – what if he was actively avoiding me? I didn't want to think about it.

I'd been reading in the snug, but now I put my book down and picked up my phone. No messages. I opened Instagram and watched a host of chaotic stories from

Saturday night: a girl from college, who I hadn't seen for a decade, on a hen do; an older woman I'd met only once, in a club toilet, 'getting on the greej'; my friend Ria's birthday. She'd posted a photo of herself in a short pink dress and platforms, holding two gold foil balloons, a three and a zero. Later, some friends, a kebab. Fuck, I hadn't even texted her.

I opened our message thread. What could I say? It was a big birthday. I should have got the coach down, asked Mrs Waddingham for a lift to the station, I wasn't a prisoner here – but I'd completely forgotten it was happening.

Strange how easy it had been to get used to my new life. I was living like a monk, no booze, long baths, sleeping eight or nine hours a night, reading a lot. The fact was, even if I'd remembered Ria's birthday, I wouldn't have gone. My life in London seemed, from this vantage point, a little silly. I was always drunk and broke and living in people's pockets. Maybe, at Westerley, I'd finally grown up.

I opened Instagram again. Ria had uploaded a photo with Anita in – that was the party she'd been at, I'd forgotten. And there was Ben. Of course, Ria was one of the few uni friends all three of us had in common.

For the first time, I felt a little wriggle in my chest, a small squeezing of my internal organs. All my friends had been at a party without me and I hadn't even remembered. And they hadn't remembered either! Nobody had texted to say they were missing me, there were no bathroom selfies in my messages, no stupid, drunken voice notes. It suddenly seemed bizarre that I'd gone forty-eight hours without speaking to anyone. They all looked so beautiful and fun and alive in the photos. I'd spent my Saturday night making a cassoulet. My biggest news was that I'd finally given up trying to stream films on the Wi-Fi, accepted that, for reasons beyond my understanding, it could deal with video calls but not Netflix, and committed to a new long-term relationship with the television in the snug – though I couldn't find the remote, could only turn the TV on and off by pressing the button underneath the set, so it looked like I was going to be stuck with just BBC1 for the next couple of months.

Months. God. Months of being alone. The weight of it settled on my shoulders. I flicked through more Instagram stories, which of course, as we all know, is a great way to stave off any low moods. Alia from my last bar job doing 'date night'. My old housemate Vic at a gig. Femi at a rave, wearing an insane neon fishnet top, looking amazing. All these Saturday nights. I was about to message Femi when I remembered she was kind of annoyed at me. She'd texted the day before,

Jeannie just asked me to make coffees for a meeting lol cheers babe, guess I'm the new you!!!

Our jobs were nothing alike, but she was the other young-ish person; I should have realised Jeannie would do this. I'd sent a laughing face with an apology, then thought maybe she was actually annoyed? So I'd deleted my message, taken the laughing face out, made the apology more sincere. She hadn't answered my texts since. Maybe she was just busy, raving. Or maybe everyone was cross with me. Femi, Ben, even Ria would probably be cross with me if she stopped long enough to remember what a shitty friend I'd been. Was I having a bad time here? Was I lonely? Then I remembered the pub existed.

'Thank God,' I said, and went to put my shoes on.

*

'Ghosts leaving you alone?' asked Ted.

It was a relief to be back at The Hart, its hubbub of families eating Sunday dinners and teenagers from the village playing pool. I laughed. 'Don't mention ghosts, Ted, you know I'm all alone up there.'

'Ah, I'm only winding thee up,' Ted grinned, passing my pint over the taps. He was missing one of his front teeth. '£3.60.' While I was counting out the change, he said, 'This place is haunted though.'

'The pub?'

'Supposed to be, any road. Fella I bought it from six years ago said there's a woman in a white dress in the bar some nights.'

'That's Mary Stopes,' called another man, sitting on a stool further down the bar. He looked about my mum's age, early fifties, but more worn, presumably from being a regular at The Hart's Salvation. 'Killed herself, Mary Stopes, right where I'm sat.'

'Jesus,' I said. 'On her wedding day?'

They looked at me. 'What?' said Ted.

'You said she was in a white dress. I thought—'

'Yeah, but it's just a normal white dress, isn't it, Mitch?'

'Actually, I heard it's not white,' said Mitch. He stood up and came towards us, settling on a closer bar stool where he wouldn't have to shout. 'I heard it's dun.'

'How the bloody hell'd you know the girl I meant then?' Ted snapped, irritated. 'All I said was, woman in a white dress. *Aye*, tha said, *that's Mary*. Now apparently she's in some other colour.'

'Well, how many ghosts do you want to have, Ted? There's only one here, isn't there?'

'And the cellar. There's a cold spot in the cellar.' Ted looked at me. 'Bloody old, The Hart. Been a pub on this spot since the 1600s.'

'No way,' I said.

'Cellars are always haunted,' Mitch added wisely. 'Lot of pub landlords die like that. Late night, on the piss, changing a barrel . . . You watch your step, Teddy boy.'

Ted laughed, and went to serve somebody else. They seemed busy with hikers today, lots of thin young people in Lycra and expensive shoes, like the girls at university. I was touched that I was being treated like a local instead of one of them; for whatever reason, Ted seemed happy to adopt me. Gratifying that after eight years in London, I was still able to get on with the sort of old men who, according to the internet, hated me and everything my generation stood for. Which I guess meant . . . coffees? Did I really stand for expensive little coffees? Either way,

I struggled to believe anyone hated anyone as much as the internet made out.

'So who was Mary Stopes?' I asked Mitch.

'Didn't know her,' he said with a shrug. 'Before my time. But the story was, she ran this place with her husband. When he died in the war, she couldn't bear to live without him, hung herself from the rafters. That's what they say, anyway.'

'What war? First? Second?'

'Civil.'

'The *English Civil War*?' I said incredulously. 'Yeah, I'd think that was before your time, Mitch.'

'Well, only just,' he grinned.

Ted came back from serving the walkers, and introduced us formally: Mitch, Danielle, Danielle, Mitch.

'Nice to meet you,' said Mitch.

'Danielle's staying up at Westerley for the autumn,' Ted added, and I saw Mitch tense, like Ted had done when I told him.

'It's my boss's house,' I said quickly.

Mitch visibly relaxed. 'Blimey. Friends in high places. You've landed on your feet, haven't you?'

'It's nuts,' I said honestly.

'She can give us the tour sometime,' Ted winked, and I realised I was on the verge of saying, *God, anytime, tonight, right now, come for dinner?* I managed to keep quiet. I'd got a bit lonely earlier, but inviting men I barely knew to visit me in the middle of nowhere was probably not – nice as the two of them seemed – a completely normal or sensible thing to do. People always said nobody in the countryside locked their doors, and Ted had laughed at me for asking him to watch my stuff while I went to the toilet ('so *London*'), but surely a small amount of caution was sensible everywhere.

'I'm trying to remember what I've heard about Westerley,' said Mitch.

'You mean ghost stories?' I asked.

'Mmm.'

'Too modern,' said Ted, dismissively. Built in the eighteenth century and too modern? I began to wonder if he and Mitch really could remember the Civil War first-hand.

Mitch made a funny noise. 'We-ell,' he said. 'Actually, I heard—'

Ted shot him a look, and he stopped talking. 'What?' I said.

'Nowt. Eating with us, or what?' Ted handed us both a menu, and that was the end of the conversation.

*

Ted and Mitch were bad influences. I'd stayed later and at least one pint longer than planned, and hadn't, in the end, eaten. Though the pub wasn't far from Westerley, twenty minutes across the fields, it seemed further and darker than last time, when there had been a very bright moon. Tonight was cloudy, and I stumbled over my footsteps, the beam of torchlight from my

150

phone waving around so everything looked like *Blair Witch* shaky-cam.

At least I couldn't get lost: it was a straight-ish line from The Hart, at the edge of the village, to the house, with public right of way the whole route. Lucky – though perhaps more design than luck? Perhaps they'd decided to build the house near a village for staffing reasons, or the village had thrived because of the work. What came first, rich people or the people they employed? I wasn't sure, though I'd seen enough *Upstairs Downstairs* with my nan to know a house like that took serious running. I was walking the same route as generations of village kids who'd trudged across this field to Westerley to muck out horses, sweep fireplaces, peel potatoes. How nervous they must have been. I was glad I'd be sleeping in the master bedroom tonight.

I stopped because I could no longer see. The dark was so thick, it was like a physical presence, an object blocking my path.

My phone had died. I'd forgotten it did this in cold weather, dropped suddenly from twenty per cent to nothing. I shook it, for some reason, maybe because I remembered my mum shaking our old torch when the batteries went out? Pointless. I put it in my pocket.

Without torchlight, the night seemed dark and somehow colder. I shuddered – I still didn't have a big enough coat for this weather – and waited for my eyesight to adjust. But I could already see the shape of the house through the trees. Closer to home than I'd thought, and Westerley was waiting.

I set off again, slow and careful through the treeline, where the leaves crunched underfoot, and down to the edge of the grounds. Maybe it was nicer without my phone torch, walking through pitch black like this, alone – more atmospheric. Now that I was getting used to the dark, it wasn't too hard to see where I was going. The torchlight had focused all my attention on my footsteps; without it, I had an appreciation for the vastness surrounding me. Big field, big sky, big house. And there it was.

I stood a moment, looking at the picture Westerley made in the sliver of moonlight. I rarely came outside at night, too scared of locking myself out, but it was so peaceful. From this side of the house, there was nothing to suggest the modern world: no cars, satellite dishes, no electric lights burning in the windows, because I'd been well-behaved and turned everything off before I left. If I'd stood here a hundred years ago, perhaps even two hundred years, Westerley would have looked exactly as it did now. Although of course, it wouldn't have been empty.

And it was empty. I did know that. Except—

I shuddered. Sometimes I could still feel it, the tail end of my certainty, stepping over the threshold with Mrs Waddingham, that somebody was inside. Not in a frightening way. Ghosts, or whatever. It was more like the emptiness of the house made no sense. Standing here in the dark, I could almost believe they were all asleep inside, a family, staff, servants, full house, living house – like all the years of the new, bad century could drop away, slough off like snakeskin, and the house would live again. What would that make me? Not a guest, standing out here, breath fogging, watching the windows. A trespasser, maybe. Roundhead soldier.

Goosebumps rose on my forearms. Stupid, unsettling myself when I was staying in a big place like this. All that reading and time alone was giving me an overactive imagin-ation. I walked round to the front and up the steps, thinking that next time I went out at night, maybe I wouldn't turn all the lights off. The place was imposing in the dark, and Jeannie could afford to run a few bulbs.

I unlocked the door and stepped inside. Silence, of course. The grandfather clock in the hall ticked. Just after 8 p.m., and here I was, creeping around like it was midnight.

I locked up, headed for the basement kitchen, where I turned the oven on. I didn't know what I was going to make for dinner but the electric whirr and orange light were comforting. I plugged my phone in, flicked the radio on, and soon the room was bright and warm and full of Ed Sheeran, which wasn't really my thing, but was at least loud and familiar. Anita had been stressed when I told her I was coming to Westerley, she said I watched too many films to stay in a place like this by myself, but look at me: I was fine. Fine! I wasn't indulging my imagination. I was literally listening to 'Shape of You'.

The house key was still in my pocket, so I went back to the entrance hall, to hang it up. But as I passed the dining room, door slightly ajar, I stopped.

There was a bowl on the sideboard that hadn't been there before.

Or had it? It must have been – I was just jumpy, unsettled by the dark walk home. But I had to look, or I would only feel worse.

I pushed the dining room door. Yes, there it was, unmistakeable: a bowl of peaches. I felt strange, jangled, like I was seeing something I wasn't meant to, which was stupid, obviously, it was only fruit. Although I hadn't bought them, or put them there. And I was the only person living here.

I never used the dining room; as I crossed the floor, the creak of the boards beneath my feet was unfamiliar. The peaches looked wet, like somebody had washed them before laying them out. I picked one up: soft to the touch, moist, heavier than I'd expected. The smell of summer. Without really deciding to, I took a bite.

It was delicious. I wished I'd known they were here. My first morning in the house, before the supermarket delivery, I'd been starving, ended up eating frozen peas from a mug with a stock cube, trying to convince myself I'd created 'a broth'. I'd only maintained my dignity and resisted the Viennetta because the house was so cold. But of course, I'd explored every room the night I arrived, and again the next day, taking pictures for Mum, and if the bowl had been here all that time, why hadn't I noticed?

Well – because it hadn't been. I knew that. It hadn't been here that night and it hadn't been here when I left earlier today. Someone had been in the house.

Oddly, I didn't feel any panic. I was calm, methodical. I hung up the keys, put down my half-eaten peach, and began to move from room to room. I checked wardrobes. I checked under beds. The more I looked, the more obvious it became that there was nobody here and nothing out of place.

It took twenty minutes to search everywhere in the house a person could feasibly hide. Of course there was nobody: whoever heard of a thief that steals nothing and leaves you fruit?

The only room I couldn't check was the billiards room, on the ground floor, the one Mrs Waddingham said had flooded, because it was locked. I pressed my ear to the door and listened. For a moment I remembered those stories about – was it a woman in Japan, who'd had food disappear for years and years, found a man living in the crawlspace above her apartment? I shuddered. The thought of someone staying locked in the billiards room, letting themselves out to move around the house when I was away, was very unsettling. But it also didn't make any sense at all, and was clearly bollocks. Yes, Anita, sorry. Too many films.

There was nothing more to do. I went down to the kitchen – where the radio was still on, inexplicably playing 'Mr Brightside' – and filled the kettle to make pasta. I was alone at Westerley. I knew I was. I must be wrong about the bowl, or – or . . .

And then it came to me. I'd been stupid. Hadn't Mrs Waddingham told me she had a spare key? She must have been passing, come to check on me and then, finding the house empty, let herself in and left the peaches. She probably had extra from somewhere, a friend with a greenhouse or whatever, and with her sturdy, neighbourly manner, wasn't that just the kind of thing she would do? She probably worried about me, a young-ish woman, all alone in this big house, thought I was the kind of impractical person who would give herself scurvy with too many chicken dippers and not enough fruit. Fair enough.

To think, I'd searched under every bed in the house. I would tell Mrs Waddingham about it. She would laugh.

Not yet, though. I wouldn't call and tell her, just in case. In case she said she hadn't been out to the house at all. Because if that happened, I had no idea what I would do.

*

I was standing on the first-floor landing, in front of the master bedroom. Music and voices drifted from downstairs, indecipherable and strangely echoing, like people speaking in a church. With the logic of dreams, I knew I had to go towards the echo. The party was waiting for me.

As I walked downstairs, I saw that the entrance hall was brightly lit and decorated. There were candles everywhere, holly, bunches of mistletoe – the whole room was full of greenery, strung up prettily in every window. It was snowing outside, and I could hear a band playing. A Christmas party.

'Ma'am?' somebody said. I saw the maid at the bottom of the staircase, looking up at me, in her black dress, plaits under a white cap.

'Yes?' I said. But she wasn't talking to me. She was looking over my shoulder.

I turned to see who she was speaking to, and found I couldn't: the top of the stairs, behind me, was in darkness. But there was definitely someone there. I could hear their footsteps getting closer, coming towards me. And the dark was getting closer too, each step of the stairs vanishing one by one, like a spotlight going out. Step by step – right up to where I stood, frozen to the spot.

*

When I woke, tired from a night of too-vivid dreams, I knew it was time to surrender. The weather had grown bitterly cold over the last few days, an abrupt turn from the part of autumn that was almost summer to the part of autumn that was almost winter, and now I couldn't feel my own nose, even in bed. I was going to die at Westerley if I couldn't get the heating working.

I went to work first. But by 4 p.m., I'd reached the bottom of my email inbox, reorganised my digital filing system, reconciled all Jeannie's expenses, and decidedly run out of things to do. My job was weird up here – never quite busy enough. This was why Jeannie had never wanted me to work remotely, of course, so much of my job was running around, and it was getting rarer that I could scrape enough tasks together to last all day. Technically it should have been nice, the free time, but somehow it wasn't. It made me feel pointless. Still, today I had a job to do.

The boiler was in a cupboard in the kitchen. I'd looked at it when I arrived, flicked a few switches and then, when nothing worked, given up; now it was sufficiently cold that I had given up on my own giving up. The boiler must be made to work. I brought my laptop down to the kitchen, sat at the one seat that got okay Wi-Fi, and tried googling the make and model. Nothing came up. It was either too old or too weird.

After a while, I called my mum, figuring that boilers were the sort of things mums knew about. I sent her a photo and she laughed.

'Is that an antique?' she said. Then she got worried about carbon monoxide. 'Is there an alarm? Do you want me to send you one?'

'I don't think there's any carbon anything,' I said. 'It doesn't work.'

We talked for a while, but it was no use. I tried some more searching online, then poured a big glass of wine, to warm myself up, and tried Anita. She was the most practical person I knew, so if she couldn't help me, nobody could. I texted her the photo with the caption, *Please tell me you understand central heating I am freezing to death*, and was surprised when my phone started ringing almost instantly.

'Wow,' I said, answering. 'Can you actually help?' I wondered if she'd done a plumbing course I'd forgotten about; seemed plausible.

'No, I was just bored and fancied a chat, and it seemed like you weren't busy. Are you busy?'

I was never busy, these days, but that seemed too needy to say out loud, or somehow unkind. 'No! Hi! I'm free!'

Anita suggested we switch to video call so she could get a tour. I picked up my glass of wine and took her through the whole house, room by room. She was a good audience, ooh-ing and aah-ing at everything, asking lots of questions. I left the ground floor with all the best rooms to last. She couldn't get over the drawing room, which I'd thought ugly and over-full. 'Do you have, like, afternoon tea in here?' she said.

'Course not. I drink instant coffee in front of the telly, like everyone else.'

Anita sighed. 'This is wasted on you. You need to get a job lot of cheap ballgowns from eBay and start living the high life. Elbows off the table, candlelit dinners, be your own butler, all that stuff.' I laughed, and she said, 'I'm serious!'

She was right. There was more I could be doing to make the most of Westerley. But I was so tired; sometimes I woke up feeling like I hadn't slept at all. And the cold was oppressive. I wished Anita was with me. Everything would be different.

'Are you okay?' she said.

'I miss you, that's all. It's good to hear your voice.'

Her grainy face was sad inside my phone. 'Sorry it's taken so long to call.'

I waved a hand. 'I've only been here like, a week.'

She frowned. 'Two.'

Two? That didn't seem right. I tried to remember how many days – how many mornings – tried to count them out in my head, but it all just blended into one.

'Dan?'

'Yeah,' I said. 'Sorry, I'm here, I was just – thinking. Anyway, how are you? How's work? How's that guy you're gonna murder?'

'Oh, I'm over him,' said Anita. 'I hate someone else now.' I sat on the couch in the snug, drinking my wine, as she explained how she'd bonded with Fish Colleague Greg over their new, shared hatred of Sara, a woman from HR who had recently paid £260 to get a 'seasonal colour analysis' that she would not stop talking about.

Apparently, Sara had discovered she personified the season of spring. 'It's exhausting. I can't bear her. Who needs to pay that kind of money to be told they look good in coral? Can't you just *wear* coral and work out yourself if you look good? Or look shit like the rest of us, and shut up.'

Anita dressed very well, usually in warm, autumn tones, but obviously her colleague had spent a lot of money on something stupid, and sounded annoying. 'She sounds very annoying,' I said. Anita was pleased.

'Oh shit,' I said. 'The grounds. You want to see the grounds?'

'Yeah!'

It was dusk, so I wasn't sure how much would be visible on my phone camera, but I left my empty glass on the table, threw my jacket on and headed down the front steps. I took a slow circle around the house, to give her a sense of it.

'Lovely,' she said, and then, faux casually, 'So have you spoken to Ben lately?'

I was surprised by the question. 'Er, I don't know. Not much? You know how he is – not great when you're not, like, actually in front of him. Why?'

'Oh, hmm.' Her voice was strange. 'I bumped into him at Ria's birthday thing and he didn't seem himself. I don't know.'

'What do you mean?'

'I'm not trying to worry you.'

'You're not worrying me,' I lied.

'I mean, I don't think it's a big deal, I don't know. He was really drunk though. Not in a fun way – like, too much.'

'Ah,' I said. I knew that Ben. He was a more reliably fun drunk than anyone I knew, but even he overshot, sometimes. Who didn't? I'd seen it over the years, tipped him out of enough pubs and onto enough buses. 'What did he do?'

'Nothing,' Anita said quickly. 'Nothing bad. But, you know.' I did know. 'And also, he said he wanted to talk to me, like he made a whole thing about it, so I figured maybe he wanted to talk about you.'

'Why?'

'We always talk about you. You're like, the main thing we have in common.'

'Oh,' I said, wondering what I thought about this.

'Not in a bad way, just, you know. And I thought he was worried, maybe? Anyway, the next thing I knew he was gone. I texted, but he hasn't replied, and he's seen it, so, I don't know. Maybe it's nothing. Or maybe you want to just . . . check in?'

It was unusual for Anita to worry about Ben, and I could feel my unease growing into real anxiety – not just about him, but having to call him. What if things were still weird between us? I was so far away.

'Okay,' I said slowly. 'Yeah, I'll check in. Thanks.'

'Dan?'

'Yeah?'

'He doesn't need to be, does he?'

'Doesn't need to be what?'

'Worried about you.'

The sky was growing dark over Westerley; the stars had begun to come out. I couldn't believe how many there were. Had they been there the whole time, and I just couldn't see them? How ridiculous that was. No stars in London. But then, London had so many other things to recommend it.

'No,' I said, trying to put a smile into my voice. 'Of course not.'

After I'd hung up the phone to Anita, I circled the grounds one last time before heading in. It was really dark now, and I spent a while trying to get a good picture of the sky. I thought I might send it to Ben. *Watch out, Richard Attenborough!* I could say, although actually he was a dead actor, wasn't he? And David Attenborough was animals. Richard Wilson? Eventually I googled 'TV astronomer', opened my message thread with Ben: *Watch out, Sir Patrick Moore.*

I didn't send it in the end. None of the photos looked like anything at all.

*

It had all gone wrong after the party at Claude's. I'd slept on Ben's shoulder on the night bus, and by the walk back to his, I was unsettled, disorientated. We got to his shitty studio flat at about 5 a.m., Ben throwing the front door open, going inside without hitting the lights. I rolled my eyes and flicked the switch myself, but nothing happened.

'Bulb's gone,' he said, already bustling around, throwing his coat onto the peg and kicking his trainers off. 'Could you shut the door?'

'But it'll be dark.'

'It's fine. That streetlight's bright.' He gestured to the window.

I sighed, shut the door and leaned against it, trying to get my bearings: everything was shadows after the slick, fluorescent hallway light. 'When did your bulb go?'

'Dunno. Couple of months.'

'A couple of *months*? Jesus, Ben, change it.'

'I will! I don't know how. It's one of those funny ones with the – look, the fixture's screwed in, can you see?' He'd put his phone torch on, shone it towards the ceiling. 'So I can't get at it. And I don't want to remind Jonathan I'm alive in case he puts the rent up.' Jonathan was his landlord. 'One or two?'

'Of what?'

Ben shone his phone torch at the box he was holding: potato waffles from the freezer.

'No, I'm fine,' I said.

'You should eat. You'll feel better tomorrow.'

'One, then.'

Ben went back into the kitchen, here meaning that he took three steps to the strip of lino in the corner of the single room he lived in, where there was a small fridge-freezer, a cupboard, and a plank of wood with a kettle and toaster balanced on top. There was a double-hob under the plank, but he almost never used it. He almost never cooked. Of all my friends, Ben seemed most likely to die of scurvy. Did scurvy kill you or did it just make your teeth drop out? Whatever. One way or another, his teeth always seemed to be in peril.

The rest of the room was dominated by the messy, unmade double bed. No chairs, table, not much storage – there wasn't space. There were only two doors, one leading out into the corridor, the other looking like it held a cupboard, though it actually led to a bathroom the *size* of a cupboard. There wasn't even a sink, I remembered miserably, you had to run the shower to wash your hands. Oh well. I was only staying one night.

I threw my wet coat over the radiator, kicked my shoes off, hung my socks on the heater to dry. None of this was easy to do in total darkness, and I felt irritated with Ben, with the childish way he lived, even though his carefree attitude was one of the things I liked most about him.

'This is ridiculous,' I said.

I went to the kitchen strip, where Ben was putting frozen potato waffles into a toaster by the light from his phone torch. 'Yeah, look, I mean, it was summer, so it was never that dark, and then I was on tour, and . . .' He made a *blah blah blah* gesture with his hand.

'It's October. I can't believe—' I stopped just in time.

'What?' said Ben.

'Nothing.'

'No, go on.' There was an edge to his voice that surprised me. 'What were you gonna say? You can't believe what?'

'No, it's just,' I sighed. 'I don't know, I mean, we're nearly thirty, change your fucking bulbs.'

There was a beat of tension. 'Right,' he said.

I heard him turn away from me, run the tap, pour a glass of water, and felt irritated. An unfamiliar urge to get a rise. Why? What was I so angry about? Then I heard myself say, 'Did you drag me to that party just so you could hook up with the guy from your show?'

Ah.

Ben had left his torch on, facing up, lighting a patch of kitchen ceiling. I could barely see him, but I heard the tap go off. 'Why are you trying to pick a fight with me, Mac?' he said levelly. 'I'm toasting you a waffle.'

'I'm not,' I said, although clearly, I was. 'It's just like, you didn't even tell me whose house it was, or why you wanted to go. We were meant to be hanging out. But you sprang the party on me, took me all the way there and ditched me.'

'I didn't ditch you.'

'Well, I couldn't find you anywhere, so yeah, you did.'

'*You* ditched *me*,' he said, voice rising. 'We were in the kitchen, and I bumped into some guy I didn't even want to talk to, and when I turned around, you were gone!'

'No,' I stammered, but I was wrong-footed. Had I done that? Maybe. I had a dim memory of leaving Ben in the kitchen and couldn't remember why. Because I was cross? Because I thought he'd dragged me there to be his wingman? I'd been his wingman before, we'd scraped each other off the floor after all our break-ups, we were The Twins, none of that mattered. But that night, for some reason, it had made me feel – shit. Used. Or something else, something worse and weirder and harder to name. Something like jealous. Of Claude?

'Ben,' I said, but I'd got what I had wanted before, drawn him out, made him angry. He came out of the kitchen and stood facing me in the dark.

'You're the one who left me there. You're the one who wandered off. And you're the one who lied.'

I blinked. 'What?'

'I *heard* you. I heard what you said to Mand. You're moving away.'

'No,' I said, mystified. 'No, I'm not?'

'And I didn't want to do this tonight because we're drunk, but it was horrible, it was horrible to hear you telling someone you barely know this huge thing, when I'm meant to be your best friend, and—'

'Oh God, no. Ben. No,' I interrupted, realising: he'd heard me telling Mandip about Jeannie's house. 'I'm going to stay out of town, that's all. For like, two months. It's just – it's the flat thing.'

My eyes had adjusted to the dark. I saw Ben put his hand over his forehead. 'Well,' he said, voice faltering. 'Okay, but why lie? We talked about the flat thing all through dinner.'

My heart was pounding. Ten years of friendship and we'd never had a real fight before. I hated how wobbly and petulant I sounded when I said, 'Why are you so angry with me?'

'I'm not angry, I'm upset! Why are *you* angry with *me*?'

'I'm not, I'm not,' I shouted. 'I was just embarrassed, because – it's Jeannie – I'm going to stay in her massive house, I didn't want you to think I was being a bitch.'

Ben looked like I'd hit him. 'Jesus,' he said slowly. 'Why would I think that about you?'

'No, but—'

'You act like I hate you. Like at some level you think I hate you.'

'What are you talking about?'

'Do you know how annoying it is that you're so fucking private? When you don't say what you're thinking, and I have to guess, it makes me feel like a monster. You say I'm your best friend, but you won't tell me anything, you don't confide in me, I always have to fucking wonder—'

'Stop, shut up,' I shouted. I was shaking. 'I'm not saying you'd think I was a bitch because you're *horrible* and you *hate me*, I'm saying it because factually, objectively, I am being one. I'm taking this huge favour from someone I hate, it's—' Ben laughed. 'What?'

'Oh, come on,' he said. 'You don't hate Jeannie. I wish you did.' We stood for a moment, staring at each other. I was too stunned to speak. 'Go on, Mac – if you hate her so much, why haven't you quit?'

'I – I'm applying for stuff,' I said. Strange, brittle tone. 'I can't quit with nothing to go to, I can't afford it.'

'Yeah, but you're not in *prison*. Why not go back to bar work?'

'I . . .' My face was hot. 'I just can't.' Because it would be a step back. Because then, none of it would have meant anything. Four years of my life. I was too drunk and tired and overwhelmed to put any of this into words.

'This is what I'm saying,' he sighed. At least we weren't shouting anymore. 'You should hate your job, but you don't, because when Jeannie treats you like a big piece of shit, you think that's what you deserve.'

'Ben.' I sank onto the bed, heard it creak under my weight. God, I was tired.

'No, you do. You love chasing around after her, worrying about what she wants and what she likes and what wine she drinks, because then you never have to think about what *you* want. When I asked if you were sad about Chris, you had no idea. Sometimes I worry you're so private because *you* don't know what you're thinking. Like, what do you want, Mac? What do you actually want?'

I covered my face with my hands so I wouldn't have to look at him. 'Stop, please, stop talking.' He did. I drew a shaky breath. 'Please don't make me fight with you at five in the morning about my stupid job.'

Quiet. I heard the bed creak as Ben sat down next to me and touched the top of my arm. I looked at him. 'Sorry,' he said.

'No, it's fine.' I pushed my fingertips hard against the bridge of my nose. I was hot with embarrassment and stress, but I wasn't going to let myself cry. 'I should have told you about the house. Ben, of course I don't think you *hate* me.'

'I know, I was just being . . . I was upset. I'm drunk. We shouldn't have talked about it tonight.' We sat in silence for a little while, Ben's hand warm on my shoulder, his thumb stroking a small circle. 'I didn't mean to have a go,' he said at length. 'Really. I just wish you felt you were worth more than cleaning up after Jeannie. You're so . . .' He trailed off. We were still looking at each other. In the darkness, he was so close that I could feel his breath on my face.

'Ben?' I said.

Then the toaster popped in the kitchen. We both jumped.

'Okay,' he said quickly, standing up, moving away. 'Well! Waffle time.'

I stayed sitting there as he went into the kitchen, banging plates around, opening the fridge. My heart was racing: we never fought. And maybe a little part of me was still angry, because Ben didn't know what he was talking about: I was trying to leave Hodgepodge, of course I was. Maybe I didn't apply for as many jobs as I used to, but I was allowed not to want to go back to bar work. I was allowed to want what Ben had, a job I would love. Because let's be honest, I'd never have the money to retire, and I didn't want to spend the rest of my life wishing away all the time I was at work; hours and hours and hours that were my life, and would not come back.

*

'Morning!' said Jeannie. 9.30 a.m., our catch-up. I was working from bed again, the house still freezing. I was also nursing a slight but noticeable hangover: even in this gigantic, posh sleigh bed, it was hard to get warm enough to fall asleep without a glass or two of wine in the evenings. Maybe three.

'How are you?' I asked, trying to smooth the gravel from my voice.

Jeannie rolled her eyes. 'On the verge of getting a noise complaint.' Her son Edward was still staying, playing electronic music well into the night, sleeping late, then disappearing for hours without a word. 'And all these parcels. I told him, the neighbours are cross enough about the music as it is – asking them to take in three, four packages a day, he's going to get me in *trouble*. He doesn't care! I said, if he wants to order things so badly, he can jolly well wait in for them himself.'

'Right,' I said, and my breath fogged. Inside. 'Jeannie, I actually wondered if you could help me with something.' She looked surprised to be interrupted, but it was urgent. 'It's just, the heating. I can't work it out. And the house is getting really cold now.'

Jeannie frowned.

'The central heating,' I went on. 'I've found the boiler, but it doesn't seem to do anything. So I wondered . . .'

'Oh, well, no, of course not. It wouldn't, not unless you've had the crude oil refilled.'

'Crude oil?'

'The heating's run from a tank in the garden. How did you think it worked?'

I had never given it much thought. Heating, like water, was just one of those things: you turned a tap, pushed a button, and whoosh. 'Right. How do I do that?'

'Oh, we never do, these days. It's a terrible faff and quite expensive. It isn't worth it, unless you're staying a long time.' I *was* staying a long time. How could I point that out without seeming rude? 'You're better off getting some firewood – I thought I said that?'

'Right, sorry. Yes.'

'Mrs Waddingham can help. Has she been in to check on you at all?'

I thought of the peaches in the bowl. 'Kind of.'

'Because I didn't want to ask when you'd just arrived, but she did show you, didn't she, where all the cleaning things are?'

I must have looked blank, because Jeannie went on, slowly, like I was dense, 'The polishes. Oils. Things like that. Those bannisters are particularly important, the wood needs to be kept in good order. She showed you everything?'

'Yeah. I mean, I can work it out.'

'I thought she'd have shown you. Because,' her voice light, careful, 'because we did ask you there to look after the house, didn't we?'

I opened my mouth to reply, my cheeks warm. She'd asked me here because I was desperate. Because I had nowhere else to go. Then I remembered sitting in Jeannie's office, dusky lilac and the fresh, clean smell of rain outside the open window. 'We could do with somebody to take care of the place,' she'd said. 'You'd be doing us a huge favour.'

God. Had I been stupid?

Yes. I had. For weeks, I'd been acting like I was family, or a guest, when Jeannie had quite explicitly asked me to come and look after the house – to take over from Mrs Waddingham while they found a replacement. I felt a rush of embarrassment at the lack of caretaking I'd done, cleaning in only the most cursory ways for weeks. This was the price of staying here, and I had not been paying it.

'Of course,' I said. 'No problem, Jeannie.'

That afternoon, when I'd reached the bottom of my inbox, I went downstairs to the kitchen cupboards, where the cleaning supplies lived, and began pulling things out. Sprays, polishes, Brasso and shammy leathers, everything higher-end than the supermarket own-brand stuff I used at home, which left strange smears on my worksurfaces. I felt defeated looking at all those bottles, defeated by my lack of knowledge. It seemed embarrassing to have to call Mrs Waddingham and admit I needed help with such a basic task, but then I thought that I would be more embarrassed if I accidentally melted Jeannie's special bannisters. Could you be sued for that sort of thing? You could probably at least be sacked.

Not that this was my job. Yes, I was being asked to clean Jeannie's house, but it wasn't the same as when she asked me to do her food shopping or collect her dry cleaning or wrap her friends' birthday presents before she met them for dinner. I wasn't cleaning the house because I was her assistant, I was doing it because I was staying here. And perhaps I could do it badly, or just the bare minimum, and get away with it, but why? I had little else to fill my time. There were so few work emails to answer these days; it was nice to be needed by someone, or rather, something. It was nice to be needed by the house.

I opened the cupboard under the kitchen stairs. Inside was a landline phone on a little table, a corkboard nailed up inside the door, with numbers for local taxi services, a takeaway, and others, handwritten, old and peeling.

Mrs Waddingham's number was there in neat biro. She answered in three rings.

'Hello?'

'Mrs Waddingham? Hi, it's Danielle, from Westerley. I mean – staying at Westerley.'

'Oh, hello!' She sounded pleased. 'What can I do for you?'

I explained, without going into detail, that I had some questions about looking after the house, and wondered if she could help. We fixed a time for her to come over at the weekend. 'Looking forward to it,' she said kindly.

'Me too,' I replied.

But I didn't want her to think I was a complete moron. After I'd hung up, I hauled the vacuum cleaner out of the cupboard and upstairs. If nothing else, hoovering would warm me up.

There were a lot of rooms. At first I thought I'd simply clean the ones I used, but then I remembered Mrs Waddingham had been coming round to clean without using *any* of the rooms, so presumably that was a bad idea. I didn't mind. What else was I going to do?

As I rolled the rattling, old-fashioned vacuum cleaner back and forth, lugged it up each set of stairs and down again, I thought how strange it was that Westerley had sat here, unlived-in, for most of my adult life – all the time I'd spent in single beds, paying through the nose for box rooms and death traps. The year I'd lived in a room where the damp was so bad the walls actually ran with water. The houseshare Anita and I had moved into, in a converted office that hadn't really been converted, and still felt strangely industrial. My room had one of those weird office skylights, and a month after we'd arrived, a pigeon died on top of it, cracking the glass with its beak. The landlord ignored all my texts, so I woke every morning for weeks to the sight of a bird slowly decomposing above my bed.

When the hoovering was done, I was warm enough to feel the tips of my fingers. I walked from room to room, looking at the floors that had been dirty, and now were clean, because of me. It was good to be able to affect a change in the world, even a small one; good to see such clear, undeniable evidence that I was here.

*

I sat at the dressing table in the master bedroom while the girl brushed my hair. I looked up at her, pale in her dark dress and apron, plaits emerging from under her cap. She smiled at me, a kind, almost maternal smile. The silver-backed brush looked heavy, but her movements were fluid, regular, and she kept a palm against my scalp to stop it pulling.

It wasn't sunny outside, this time. The curtains were drawn, everything safe and quiet.

'Turn around,' she said. I did, so she could reach the back of my hair, and met my own eyes in the dressing table mirror. Strangely, I seemed to be wearing the same clothes she was: dark dress, apron. I reached out to the cap that lay abandoned on the dressing table, and it felt right in my hand. It was mine.

'What is it?' said the girl.

I looked up, met her eyes in the mirror, and my face was full of fear. 'We're not meant to be doing this.'

Then the door opened, and the lady stood there, skinny shoulders and a furious expression below her great crest of hair. I wasn't the lady. I was a maid.

'What are you girls doing in my room?' she said, and on the last word, everything sank.

The colours. The furniture. The pitch of her voice. Everything sank down and down into the earth until there was nothing. And I sank too, of course, a nauseous feeling and a tug in my ribcage, a plunge into nothing but darkness and the low, awful hum of dread.

I was lying in bed. I couldn't move. And I wasn't alone.

It had been different before – half-light in Anita's living room, from streetlights, or being close to morning – but the nights at Westerley were something else. As I lay, watching the shadow unpeel itself from the deeper darkness of the bedroom, the shape of it like dread made flesh, I felt true horror. The sleep paralysis was back. It was back, and now I would lie for hours while the shadow watched, unable to move, unable to speak, panic clawing at every nerve-ending in my body.

I wanted to scream. Was that what the sound was, filling the room, my own voice caught in my throat?

Then the shadow stepped forwards – and it wasn't a shadow at all. One of the curtains was rumpled, letting a shaft of moonlight in, and as the figure moved through it, I saw pale elbows. Fabric. I still couldn't move, but it had never been like this before, had it? It had always been a shadow. And yet there she was: dark dress, pale apron, standing by the dressing room table, just like in my dream. She had followed me. Somehow, she had followed me here, out, out into the world, and the wrongness of it was a pressure in my throat, a trapped voice trying to escape.

But this was a dream too. Sleep paralysis. I knew that. And as she walked towards me, that was what I tried to focus on: that I would soon wake up, because I had to. Wake up. Wake up. Wake up.

*

'Happy Halloweeeeeen!' said Femi, tinny inside my laptop. I was working from bed again. I blinked: Halloween, already? Or was she joking? She'd really committed to the bit if so, blood streaks, eyeliner, some kind of cloak.

'Are you in costume?'

'Yeth,' she said, tongue catching on her vampire teeth. 'Bleugh. Maybe I thould take thethe out.'

She disappeared a moment, and I checked the date on my phone. 31 October. I was staggered. If it was Halloween, I'd been here three weeks. How could it possibly have been that long?

Femi popped up, wiping the spit from her chin, and said, 'That's better. I've had those in all day.'

I tried to laugh in the way a person would laugh – easy, carefree – who definitely knew what day it was. 'How were you talking?'

'Well, you're the first person I've spoken to. I thought Mollie might notice, but no. I sat next to her for an hour and a half, dressed as a vampire, and she said *nothing*. Like being on the Tube.'

Femi was a teenage goth, and Halloween was still her Christmas. Every year, she and her housemates would take a half-day of annual leave and make a thing of it. The Halloween before last, she'd come to work dressed as Rochelle from *The Craft*, with the braces and the little skirt, and Jeannie had said, 'Good morning, Femi, what a lovely outfit. An usherette!'

'So what's the plan this year?'

'Well, the theme is vampires—'

'No shit.'

'So we're going for a triple bill: Bela Lugosi, Gary Oldman, Christopher Lee.'

'You're going to watch three *Dracula* films?' I said. 'That's insane.'

'I thought the same, but Dee's curating, so . . .' Femi kept talking, joking about the *Craft* year, witch-themed, when she'd had a whitey in front of *Suspiria*. I remembered the story well enough that I could scroll while she talked.

The BBC front page said 31 October. The *Guardian* front page said 31 October. Fine. I was glad I'd checked, obviously, but: yes. November tomorrow. Sure.

I knew it was only an illusion caused by the emptiness of my days at Westerley, which crawled by so slowly, in a haze of hoovering and baths, that really, they were speeding away from me. I knew time did that. Things were slow, and then all at once they were over. It was the first day of the holiday, and then you were on the flight home. I had lost track of time – that was all. There was even a phrase for it. But it didn't feel like that. As I sat there, listening to Femi talk, it felt more like the time had been stolen from me.

*

Mrs Waddingham arrived on Saturday morning. It was nice to see her, nicer still to have a real, flesh-and-blood person inside the house for the first time in weeks. We headed to the kitchen, then I made tea as she pulled cleaning fluids from the cupboard, pointing at them. 'Silver. Brass. Hardwood. Softwood.'

'This is great,' I said guiltily, taking milk from the fridge. 'But I'm afraid you're going to have to show me which bits of the house are made of those things.'

Mrs Waddingham drank her tea in a few hot gulps, then we spent twenty minutes wandering from room to room, me carrying the box of sprays and polishes, as she pointed out what went with which tables, or wainscotting, or bannisters. We were in the blue bedroom upstairs, talking about the brass wall sconces, when she said, 'Is it freezing in here, or is it me?'

I laughed. 'Yeah. No, it's not you.'

'The whole house is baltic.'

'Well, the heating doesn't work. Jeannie said to light the fires, but . . .' I trailed off, too embarrassed to say that

I hadn't known what to buy, or where from, or what I would do with it if it came, so I'd been enduring the cold, first bravely and then by drinking through it, putting myself to sleep with a few glasses of wine most nights, and now, actually, my sleep paralysis was back, so that clearly hadn't been one of my better ideas, thanks.

Mrs Waddingham looked at me. 'Right,' she said, heading back into the hallway. 'Come on.'

I followed her. 'Come on where?'

*

The garden centre was overwhelming after so many days at Westerley. It had everything: rooms of artisanal foods, remaindered books, greetings cards, candles, even a much-too-early room of gaudy Christmas decorations, where I sped up and Mrs Waddingham slowed down, to contemplate a wicker reindeer.

'It's November,' I said.

'Wait till you're my age. You've got to start Christmas early or it's gone before you know it.'

This was so close to my recent experiences, everything gone before I knew it, that I winced. Mrs Waddingham didn't notice. She shook her head at the reindeer and we headed through the sliding doors to the outside area.

On the patio around the door were sheds, love seats, arbours, and now it was her turn to speed up. I followed, pushing my empty trolley, past the hedgerow starters. 'Here we are,' she said. Under her direction, I filled the trolley with huge bags of firewood, ovoids, boxes of fire-lighters. 'That'll see you right.'

I was ready to pay and get going, but Mrs Waddingham lingered, looking at large outdoor pots. Then she was tempted by some hellebores, picking up different ones, scrutinising them, putting them down again. It was a bitterly cold day and I'd forgotten, in the excitement, to put on the sixteen or so jumpers that made my jacket bearable. I stamped my feet, folded my arms across my chest, trying to keep warm without looking impatient.

'I'm terrible for coming out with things I don't need,' Mrs Waddingham said, putting the flowers down. 'But the garden's all dying off and it looks so miserable.' She glanced at me. 'You're not sickening for something, are you? You look nithered.'

I laughed. 'My coat's a bit thin, that's all.'

'That's not a coat,' she said, scandalised. 'Is that all you've got?'

So after I'd paid for the firewood (extortionate) and we'd loaded it all into her car, Mrs Waddingham insisted on driving me back via a string of village shops. 'We've got to get you something proper to wear.' I tried to protest, but not much: I was truly sick of being cold all the time.

I offered to buy Mrs Waddingham a coffee while she waited, but she said she missed shopping with her kids, so after we'd parked up, she came round with me. I hadn't been to town with my mum since I left home, but there was something familiar about the experience, trying on a succession of dead people's charity shop coats while Mrs Waddingham said things like, 'Not practical enough. Haven't you seen the weather forecasts? This is going to be the wettest autumn since 1870-something!' The most underwhelming catwalk of my life. It wasn't the Saturday I'd been expecting, but at least I was out of the house.

In the third place, I tried on one of those really good, thick raincoats that come from posh walking shops. It cost more than I'd wanted to spend, but Mrs Waddingham made me turn from one side to the other saying, 'There, that's more like it.' Next to her, I felt like an essentially impractical person who would die young. I couldn't drive or start fires and I didn't know what all the polishes did. At least buying the coat was a step in the right direction. I paid and we headed back to the car.

'Now,' said Mrs Waddingham, side-eyeing me from the driver's seat. 'Have you lit a fire before? Do you know what you're doing?'

'No,' I said. Truth at all costs from now on. 'I'm useless. Please help me.' She laughed.

Back at the house, in the drawing room, Mrs Waddingham showed me how to make a fire with kindling and scrunched-up newspaper. How to lay the wood, and make sure you didn't give it too much attention, which was fatal, or too little, which was also fatal. How to use the fire-lighters when it got stuck. She was a good teacher, kind and patient, and made me have a go instead of just watch and nod. Before long, the room was bright, flames crackling in the grate.

'Good job, Danielle.'

I was genuinely delighted.

She had to head off – dinner with her husband – and I walked her to the door, thanking her for all the help she'd given me.

She waved a hand. 'It was nice,' she said. 'I had a nice day.'

'Me too,' I said. From where I was standing in the entrance hall, I could see the dining room door, slightly ajar. The edge of the sideboard. 'Hey, can I ask you something?' She nodded. 'Is . . . this the first time you've been back to the house since you brought me here?'

Mrs Waddingham looked apprehensive. 'Yes. Why?'

'You didn't come another time, drop anything off?'

'No, love. I would've given you a bell if I was driving all the way out here. Why?'

I'd known it. Deep down, really, I think I'd known. I shook my head, smiled. 'No reason.'

After we said goodbye, I closed the door behind her and went back to the dining room. I flicked on the light, but I could already see the sideboard was empty. No bowl. No rotten peaches. There was nothing there at all.

'Right,' I said, out loud. 'Okay then.' My voice echoed in the empty room.

*

I stayed in the drawing room for a long time that night, sitting on one of the low, uncomfortable sofas and watching the fire. All the sounds of Westerley, the creaking walls, the rattle of the pipes settling, had become so familiar to me over the last few weeks – but tonight, I was hyper-aware of each one. I'd closed the curtains, but it was hard to shake the feeling of faces looking in through the windows. Not that I was really scared of anyone out there; it was the thought of someone being inside the house with me that was frightening.

I racked my brain: had other stuff moved around, gone missing, since I arrived? Nothing I could think of, but then I'd always been a lax housekeeper, putting things down and losing them. Yes, probably I had misplaced a few things, but that was nothing out of the ordinary; it didn't mean someone was breaking into the house and fiddling with my stuff. Although I'd never gained or lost a bowl of fruit before.

The possibilities, it seemed to me, were limited. Firstly, a peach-loving psychopath was hiding somewhere in the house, moving things just so I knew they could. I'd heard on a podcast once that was something the Mafia did, so you knew they were watching you, that they could get you anytime. But I wasn't a criminal, I was a PA, and anyway, why would anyone bother? I'd been here weeks already, alone, in the middle of nowhere. Anyone who wanted to murder me had had ample opportunity.

So, second option: I'd imagined the whole thing, or dreamed it. An unpleasant thought, but maybe the best of a bad bunch, because it meant that soon, I would get better, and it would all stop. Like getting over a cold.

My sleep had been weird since Chris and I split up, the episodes of sleep paralysis, the bad dreams – I'd been under a lot of pressure. But I was resting more now, so surely the dreams would stop, soon, and I would start sleeping better, keeping track of time again.

Although of course, there was a third option. The possibility that there was nothing wrong with me, and everything wrong with the house.

I rubbed my face, topped up my wine glass, glad I'd remembered to buy a bottle when Mrs Waddingham and I were in town. What was I suggesting here? Haunted fruit? Not necessarily. I wondered if it might be something to do with physics, with the way time worked in the house, slippages, things where they shouldn't be. A wormhole? God, I wished I'd listened in science classes, and knew what anything was.

Options three and four, then: a natural explanation that I didn't understand; or an unnatural one.

There were bits of wood on the carpet in front of the fireplace, they'd flaked off when we piled the logs up, and I moved to kneel there, flicking big splinters into the flames. I had a desperate urge to call Ben. I wanted to say all this out loud to someone, and not just anyone, but Ben, who would laugh at me, but also take me seriously. Anita would back option two, I knew that, be ready to parachute my mother in, a care package, some strong medication – but Ben was an actor, with an actor's highly developed sense of the dramatic. If anyone was going to be up for discussing haunted fruit, it was him.

The fire was beginning to die and I wondered whether I should build it back up. I had a caveman's urge not to let it go out, but it trapped me in the huge, uncomfortable drawing room, a place I did not particularly like. The snug was my favourite room in the house, but it was modern, with no fireplace. So I could go there and be comfortable, but cold, or stay here and be warm, but uncomfortable – or go down to the kitchens and have dinner, but be uncomfortable *and* cold. What a choice.

I drained my glass. Maybe I would just sit here and drink. Maybe I would sit here and call Ben. Why shouldn't I?

Yes, things had been weird before I left. Yes, I'd been trying not to think about it. And yes, in all this time, we'd barely spoken, which wasn't like us – he could be useless, distracted, but he'd never left me hanging so long without a proper phone call or voice note, something to let me know he was thinking of me. So maybe he was pissed off, but Christ, we'd been friends a third of our lives. What would all that weird stuff matter if I called and told him I needed him? It wouldn't. Of course it wouldn't.

Unless it did. Unless he really didn't want to talk to me after what happened. That would be unbearable.

*

I'd stayed at Ben's the night before my train to Westerley, dragging my suitcase to work, then down on the bus to a pub a few streets from his place in New Cross. I could probably have begged Nice Pete to let me stop on Anita's couch one night longer than planned, but I wasn't about to leave London for two months without clearing the air with Ben.

We should have talked the day after the party, hungover and apologetic, but I'd woken that morning (fine, early afternoon) to find Ben already dressed and heading out to work at The Prince, a shabby old-man pub at the end of his street, where he pulled shifts when the acting dried up. 'I'm not leaving in a bad way,' he'd said, and I'd said of course, no problem, and then our texts had been weird and stilted and try-hard all week.

It was my last night in London. I was anxious, dragging my suitcase through the busy pub and out into the garden, but I needn't have been: Ben got up as soon as he saw me, just like normal, and pulled me into a hug. He was wearing a scruffy leather jacket and a T-shirt with a line-drawn group of Victorian mourners that said LIVE LAUGH LAMENT. Face close to my ear, he muttered, 'Sorry, in advance, about everyone.'

The table was a blur of people I might have met before, but wasn't sure. All of them had cool, one-syllable names, like Jay, an actor, and Shay, a comedian, and Jazz, a chore-ographer, except for one guy I thought might be called Biscuit, though I could have misheard. I ended up sat next to Biscuit (?) and his heavily pregnant girlfriend. They both worked in accountancy and I couldn't get to the bottom of how they'd ended up with this lot. The girlfriend was drinking a J2O and looked bored by how drunk everyone was. With a nod of apology, I began drinking quickly to catch them up, leaving her behind, alone, on the island of the sober.

I couldn't do enough, though, to not find the evening boring. A lot of them were network-y people, who looked over your shoulder while they were talking to you in case somebody more important was there. The only member of the group I knew and liked, other than Ben, was Jo, the birthday-haver – but you never really see the person whose party it is, and actually, I couldn't see Jo at all. I wondered if they'd ditched their own birthday drinks, and felt a wave of respect and jealousy.

After the pub shut the beer garden, the last hour inside was hot and noisy. I ended up trapped with my suitcase, pinned to the wall by a guy called Booth who worked in visual effects and seemed to think I worked in graphic design. He kept saying things about Photoshop that I didn't understand. I figured he must be mixing me up with somebody else, but couldn't be bothered to put him right. In the end, Ben must have spotted the look of desperation on my face, because he appeared at my shoulder and said, 'Okay, time to go.'

It was only half ten. I felt guilty for dragging him away. 'Do you want to say goodbye to everyone?'

'No, no.' He waved a hand. 'I don't even know where Jo is. Come on, I want to see you before you go.'

Somehow, in the crush of the evening, I'd forgotten I was leaving. Something in my chest clenched. 'Yeah,' I said, and followed Ben out of the bar.

It was cold outside, in a nice way. I carried my jacket under my arm, enjoying the feeling of heat rising from my skin. We were only fifteen minutes from Ben's flat, so we walked, him pulling my suitcase with one hand and smoking with the other. 'Sorry again,' he said. 'I know they're a lot.'

I said it was fine, but took the mickey out of some of the people I'd got stuck with, while Ben laughed. 'Wonder who Booth thought you were.' Then the rain started, absurdly abrupt and heavy as it had seemed to be all month, setting a car alarm off down the road.

We ducked under a bus stop, out of the downpour. Neither of us had an umbrella, so we agreed to wait here until the worst of it was over. We sat on the bench. Ben lit another cigarette off the first. We were on a main road, and it wasn't late, but there was nobody around, like they'd somehow known the weather was going to turn. Buses passed, but we didn't put our hands out, so they didn't stop.

Somewhere behind us, the sound of voices drifted down into the street. A couple arguing loudly in their flat. 'I never even said I wanted a baby,' she shouted. 'You're the one who told your mum we were gonna have kids, and now she keeps texting me, and you're acting like *I'm* pushing you, pushing, pushing, pushing, pushing, even though . . .' The rain got heavier and I missed the rest of the sentence. There was something intimate and embarrassing about hearing this argument. Maybe because it reminded me that Ben and I had shouted at each other like that on Saturday night, and I didn't completely remember what we'd said.

'Do you want some?' Ben asked, holding his cigarette out to me. I did, but shook my head. His shoulder was warm against mine through our T-shirts. He tipped his head back against the bus shelter, closed his eyes. I wanted to ask if we were still in a fight, but I didn't know how. 'Hey,' he said. 'Did you see Johnny Christie tonight?'

'I don't know who that is.'

'No, you do,' said Ben. 'He was at uni with Leanne.' Leanne was a musician, one of Ben's few serious exes, though that was years ago, and she'd since moved to Bristol. I'd never liked her much, not for any real reason. I'd felt guilty about it, tried to cover up by being scrupulously nice.

'What about Johnny Christie?' I said.

'He's been away two or three years, in America. He has that cabaret act, you remember? Leanne used to do the music. You said they were like an evil version of us.'

'Did I?' I couldn't remember ever seeing Johnny Christie's cabaret act. Why would I have called them that? I couldn't get a handle on this conversation.

'Yeah, he moved to New York, trying to get into *showbiz*, but the winters were too cold apparently, so then he went to LA. He drove across the country in a rental car and tweeted about it, it was this whole thing, do you seriously not remember? Just – incredibly annoying. Anyway. He did the live circuit in LA for a couple of years, but the only thing that happened was like, two viral tweets, and now he's just . . . back. It's like, what is this, the sixties? I mean, why did he go? What was he looking for? What the fuck did he think was going to happen?'

I realised then that Ben was drunker than I was. There seemed to be some deeper meaning in his story that I couldn't grasp. It wasn't like him to say this kind of thing, to say essentially that it was better not to try, in case you failed. 'Ben,' I said carefully, and he turned to look at me, eyes so large and dark in the night that it was like looking at a woodland animal.

The rain was easing off now, enough that I could hear the couple arguing in the flat behind us, her voice clear as a bell. 'Fuck off, Adam! Just fuck off!'

'What?' said Ben.

Again I felt the desperate, childish words rising in my throat: *Are you cross with me? Are we still fighting?* I didn't ask: I was too scared he'd say yes. What if we had another row? I was going away tomorrow for months – and yes, I'd come to clear the air, but I wanted to do that in the normal way, by *not* talking about things, and everything just being how it was supposed to be. 'Nothing. Come on, shall we go?'

Ben didn't bring up Johnny Christie again. Back at his flat, I realised he'd changed the bulb since my last visit. 'Wow,' I said.

'Yeah, well, guests.' He shrugged. 'Didn't want you taking the piss again. Or breaking your neck. Tea or nightcap?'

We had both, talked for a while about nothing, his shift at The Prince on Sunday, all the old men there, who loved him, getting him to pick their horses before they left for the bookies. Then I put my pyjamas on in the bathroom, and when I came out, Ben seemed to have fallen asleep already.

I was relieved. Victory! The night was over and we had been so, so normal. I turned out the lights, and we lay side by side in the dark. It was rare that I stayed over without being drunk enough to immediately pass out. Next to me, Ben fidgeted, and I realised he wasn't asleep after all, even though he'd had enough beer to knock out a small horse, or a large pony.

He sighed, and rolled onto his back, looking up at the ceiling. On my side of the bed, I did the same. It was one of those textured ceilings everyone liked so much in the eighties. I looked at the patterns, orange from the street-light outside Ben's window, bright even through his curtains. Maybe it wasn't weird that it had taken him so long to change his bulb.

'I'm sorry about Saturday,' Ben said, into the dark.

I tensed. 'You already said that. You don't need to be.'

'I am, though.'

'Yeah, look, me too. Don't worry about it.'

'I can't believe I don't have a couch for you to stay on.'

Whatever I'd expected, it wasn't that. I laughed. 'Why does that matter?'

'Because you're going away for months.' He lifted his arms, covered his face. Voice muffled, he went on, 'You don't even want to go and I wish I could help.'

'Ben, it's fine. You already offered to let me stay!'

'Yeah, but look at this place. It's a shithole, and tiny, of course you can't stay here. I barely fit in this flat. But if I lived somewhere normal—'

'Ben.'

'No, if I did something normal with my life, then I would have money, and I'd have a spare room. You're my best friend, and I can't help you, because I'm always fucking broke, because I'm – selfish.'

I didn't want to laugh anymore. 'What are you talking about?'

'Nothing. I don't know.' He'd taken his arms away from his face, but his speech was slightly slurred, accent thicker than usual, like it always was when he was drunk, or close to sleep, or both. 'Did you think things would turn out like this?'

'What things?'

I felt him shrug beside me, shoulder rising and falling against my own. I wanted to say that *turn out* implied something finished, some kind of ending, and I didn't think that was true, or anyway, I didn't want it to be. 'I don't know why I live in this stupid way, in one horrible room, just so I can act.'

The phrase was familiar. Had I said that? Had I said something like it when we were fighting, when we were drunk? 'There's nothing wrong with how you live.'

'I should get a proper job. We're not even young anymore.'

'We're only twenty-nine!' I shrieked. I must have sounded ridiculous because Ben laughed, a thin, bright sound in the dark.

'Okay,' he said. 'I'm being a twat.'

I laughed too. 'No.'

'I just wish you weren't going. And what if – I don't know, what if you don't come back?'

'Are you saying I'm going to die in rural Yorkshire?'

'No.'

'What of? Dysentery?'

'Well—'

'Aren't you, like, from there?'

'Bradford's not rural.' We were laughing. When we stopped, the room was too quiet. 'I'm being weird. Sorry.'

Ben rolled over so that we were facing one another, his pupils large in the half-light. Small nose. Hal. Puck. He always seemed so free; I hated to think he was trapped in the same miserable labyrinth I was, behind and broke and tired and not good enough. He had the thing I didn't, the thing I'd always wanted: he'd found something he loved, and was good at, and now he just needed to do it. But even he thought he was wasting his life. 'Ben,' I said. 'I don't care that you never change your bulbs.' I wanted to say that it was somehow stupid and brave at the same time, the way he lived, and that I wished I could be as brave as him, that there was something I wanted enough. But I couldn't work out how to arrange the words. So I just said, 'I don't want to live in a world where you have a proper job.'

Ben smiled, pushed my hair back from my face. 'Well, lucky you, because I doubt I can get one now. Looks like we're stuck with the – one bulb, no sink, vacuum-packing everything I own when someone comes over.'

'I like it here,' I lied.

Ben laughed, breath warm on my face. 'No you don't.'

'No, I don't.'

'But if you did want to stay, you know it would be okay, right? Like it would be crazy but we'd make it work.' His hand was still in my hair.

'We'd go mad,' I said, but something caught in my voice. 'You'd throw me out of that window by the middle of next week.'

'I really don't think that's true.'

We were quiet, looking at each other. He moved his hand, stroking my cheek absent-mindedly with a thumb, fingers curling at the nape of my neck, and something happened in my stomach. In nearly a decade, we'd touched each other hundreds of times, shared beds, held hands – of course we had, we were The Twins. But something about this was different. A weird gesture, the wrong kind of intimacy. *Oh my God*, I thought, *is Ben going to kiss me?* 'Mac,' he said, quiet, and I felt the weight of his eyes in the darkness.

And then it was over, gone, quick as the thought had arrived. I don't know who pulled away, only that, next thing, I was lying on my back in the dark, face warm where Ben's hand had been, heart thudding with panic, and something else. Something that wasn't panic. A lorry drove past, making the window casements rattle.

I tried to review what had happened. Nothing, maybe. Me being weird, imagining things. I'd had a funny feeling lately, like I couldn't trust myself. It was an unbearable thought, that Ben had touched me, normal, the way we always did, and seen something longing in my face; I felt like I'd given something away that I barely even understood.

'Sorry,' he said, voice thin. I didn't know what he was apologising for. Sorry for doing nothing, or doing something? For making me wonder – crazily, like the part of your brain that thinks about throwing your keys off a bridge – about smashing another part of my life up, now, when I could least afford to do it. I wished I knew what Ben was thinking. What had he seen in my face when he touched me?

I don't know how long we lay there, side by side on our backs, in the dark, watching the ceiling. But I remember thinking I would never get to sleep, that sooner or later I would have to say something, ask something, or he would.

Then it was early morning, and I was being woken by my alarm.

I turned it off quickly, and sat up. Ben was still asleep, face-down on the other side of the bed. I should wake him to say goodbye, was reaching for his shoulder when I stopped. It would be better to get ready first, dress, pack, let him sleep until I was done fiddling around.

So I did these things. I dressed. I packed. I brushed my teeth. And I found that I was doing them as quietly as possible. At some point, zipping my suitcase up so, so carefully, I accepted that I was actively trying not to wake Ben, because I was not going to wake him at all. I was too afraid to revisit the night before, see in his face what he'd thought of me. Disdain. Repulsion. Whatever it was, I didn't have to see it, and I wasn't going to.

I slipped silently out of the door, texted goodbye from the bus. I said I hadn't wanted to wake him, without saying why. Just thanks, and sorry, and nothing real.

*

When I woke the next morning, the fields below my window were thick with fog, sunlight struggling to break through the clouds and making the whole view sickly. Shatter-backed trees in the distance curling against the sky. It was like a painting where all the colours had been taken out with turpentine, white spirits – something bleached.

I worked by the fire in the drawing room, curled up on the floor in a blanket. The other rooms were very cold, but I could hardly light fires all over the house with just me here.

My emails didn't take long. There were fewer and fewer of them these days. After I'd finished, I went to the kitchen to get the cleaning things. Wood polish. Brasso. I hoovered every room, then took a cloth to the bannisters. It was easy now that I knew how.

At three o'clock, there was a staff meeting. I got back to my laptop just in time, clicked the link to join, and watched the wheel tick round and round. And round. And round.

I waited nearly twenty minutes, watching, before I gave up. They'd forgotten I was meant to be there at all. They'd forgotten me.

*

'So how are you?' said Anita.

She'd called while I was making dinner. It was nice to be thought of, though I was tired, not really in the mood to talk. 'Yeah,' I said. I wondered what to tell her. Ceiling light. Peaches. Mist on the fields. Strange dreams. 'Yeah, I'm – fine. Just working, quiet. How are you?'

'Oh, yeah, you know,' she said, rattling into a funny set of complaints about Fish Colleague Greg and Seasonal Colour Sara and her new enemy, Silent Luke. 'I'm working like a dog, trying to get him to chat in meetings. I feel like a court jester.' She'd called me from one of her posh wine bars, I could hear the muzak tinkling underneath. Small plates. She must be waiting for a date.

'Dan, how actually are you? You've been weird on texts.'

'Have I?'

'Not in a – not in a bad way. Just quiet. You don't sound like yourself.'

I turned the heat off on my chilli, stepped away from the cooker. I wasn't hungry anyway.

I'd been letting it all get on top of me. The quiet. The strangeness. Being alone, day after day, and waking at night unable to move. The figure by my bed. The figure by my bed that was no longer a shadow. And worrying about Ben, that he hated me, that we weren't friends anymore. Things moving in the house. Nobody to tell that things were moving in the house. But it must be me, in my head, because I could no longer trust myself, so what was I supposed to tell people? Family, friends – how could

I talk to them when I didn't know what to say? So I said less and less, and they said less and less to me, which made the quiet worse. The strangeness. But here was Anita, still thinking of me.

'I'm sorry,' I made myself say. 'Everything got a bit . . . I'm just lonely up here, I think. I miss you. I'll be fine when I get back.'

'Oh. So it's nothing to do with . . .'

'With what?'

'I don't know,' she sounded evasive. 'I just, you know, wanted to ask how Ben was.' I said nothing, heart in my mouth. 'When you called him. Was he okay? He never texted.'

'Oh.' It hadn't occurred to me that Anita might follow up. 'Well. I haven't spoken to him.'

'Dan.'

'I know, I just, I don't know, it was weird, before I left, and I couldn't – I mean, I didn't want to—'

I was relieved when Anita put me out of my misery. 'Oh wow,' she said, and I stopped talking. 'No way. You guys *fucked*.'

I wasn't relieved anymore. 'Jesus Christ. No. What are you talking about?'

'Shit,' she said. 'I thought – when you said it was weird, I thought—'

I was furious. I couldn't believe that after weeks of anxiety, I was finally about to tell her everything, and now it wouldn't even sound like it *was* anything. She thought Ben and I had *had sex* immediately before I went to Yorkshire for *two months*? Jesus. I would have had to call her from the train station. I would have died from anxiety.

Then Anita started laughing. I felt a flash of irritation before I accepted that the whole thing was, to be honest, quite funny. The nothing of it. How scared I was. Then we were both laughing, on opposite sides of the country, like I hadn't laughed in weeks. It was an exorcism. I was weak with relief. Anita, my life, it was all still there, waiting for me. I would be home in a few weeks. Everything was going to be fine.

I sat at the kitchen table and ate crisps while I told her what happened with Ben before I left. Claude's birthday party, the fight, how weird I'd felt, like maybe I was jealous? Then going to stay at Ben's, to clear the air. The storm, his weird mood, and the moment I'd thought he was going to kiss me. Nothing seemed that bad now I was saying it out loud. Why did I always have to be so weird and secretive about everything that mattered? Why hadn't I talked to Anita before? Although I still couldn't bring myself to say that in the moment of it – Ben's hand on my face, in my hair, thinking he was going to kiss me – that in the moment, I had wanted him to.

'So, yeah. Nothing really happened, but it was weird, and I feel weird now. Like I don't know what he's thinking, or what he thinks I'm thinking, and it's just – I don't know. Bizarre.'

Anita sighed. 'Oh well. Inevitable, I guess.'

'What do you mean?'

'Just like – I don't know. You guys. You've always been a bit like that.'

This was news to me. 'Like what?'

'Well, you know, I mean, Ben had that crush on you for ages, it was a whole will-they-won't-they thing, wasn't it?'

White noise in my brain. 'Anita, what are you talking about?'

'Duh,' she said. Then, quieter, presumably to a waiter: 'Yes please, one more, the same.' I heard her laugh slightly flirtatiously, the roil of a restaurant in the background, rumble of a man's voice. 'Yeah, well, he's late, what can you do?' The waiter laughing.

'Anita,' I said again, through gritted teeth.

'Sorry, I was saying – yeah, don't you remember after you guys met, in first year, and then he was like, always there? And you started dressing the same . . .'

'Yeah,' I said. 'But—'

'Because I was basically a single parent after Matt chucked you, if you remember. And then you met Ben, and just – disappeared. It was actually a bit shit. But mainly I was worried you were just going to jump into a new relationship with this guy I didn't know, and he would do the same thing maybe, and then all my good work would be undone and you'd just be a big bomb crater instead of a person. So, yeah. I had to give him The Talk.'

'What talk?'

'You know, *what are your intentions towards my friend, blah blah*. I've told you this.'

'You have never told me this.'

She laughed. 'So – remember the foam party on our block for that guy – what was his name? Amit? That mature student who was turning twenty-five or something, some age we thought was really ancient, so everyone covered his kitchen in clingfilm and got that foam cannon from eBay—'

I didn't want to get bogged down in details. 'Yeah, yes, I remember.' Did I? I had a vague feeling that had been a bad night for me.

'I'll be amazed if you do. You were twatted.'

Ah.

'We had to get you back to your room, me and Ben, then we had a drink in the kitchen and I did that thing, you know: *If you hurt her, I'll have to murder you.* And Ben was like, *Oh yeah, I like her but she's clearly still sad and blah blah blah, maybe we should just be friends.* I said, do whatever, but you guys were getting into this weird thing, like you were doing everything *but* having sex, you know?

I didn't reply. I was too busy thinking. Yes, I remembered the foam party, early summer, nearly exams. Ben and I got really close and then he just disappeared. I'd freaked out to Anita about it. And then he'd turned back up, like nothing had ever happened, dating a boring guy with a moustache whose name I could no longer remember.

I remembered the horror of that time, wondering if I had a crush on Ben, if he could tell, if I'd scared him off, not knowing myself or what I thought. And hadn't I just gone through all of that again, now, ten years later, like a fucking idiot? God. I was too restless to stay still, took the stairs up from the kitchen so I had somewhere to pace, thinking so hard I could barely see.

'Dan, are you still there?'

'Yeah,' I said. 'Just – give me a minute.'

Anita did, and in the quiet, I walked a loop of the ground floor. She'd definitely never told me any of this. If Ben had really said that stuff to her, then the funny seam of *whatever* in our friendship hadn't just been me, hadn't all been in my head. Maybe he really had wanted to kiss me. Maybe, as far as he was concerned, I'd panicked, run off to Yorkshire, never called.

I walked blindly from the back staircase, past the snug, the locked-up billiards room, the drawing room, around to the front staircase in the entrance hall, and then I heard the sound. It was muffled, a low and repetitive *thud, thud, thud* coming down the line.

'Anita?' I said. No answer.

I strained to listen. No, it wasn't on the phone. It was here, in the house, with me. Getting louder. Thud. Thud. Someone throwing themselves at a door? Strangely, I wasn't afraid. I turned back. I knew where the sound was coming from now.

I stood outside the locked door of the billiards room. Thud. Thud. Thud. I wondered if the chimney hadn't been sealed properly. Could there be a bird in there? An animal, trapped? But really I knew that was nonsense. The rhythmic, focused way she beat against the wood, over and over again – only a person would do that. I put my phone away.

'Hello?' I called. I don't know why. 'Hello?'

And then the answer came: 'Hello? Hello?'

I'd been wrong. It wasn't a person at all, couldn't be anything but an echo. That was my own voice behind the door.

'Hello? Is somebody out there? Please.'

I touched my throat. I hadn't said a word. But I knew my voice, knew that it was mine.

'Hello?' It came again, muffled by the door between us. 'Hello? Help. Please help.'

And I was in the hallway, holding the handle, and I was in bed, with dawn light on the ceiling, and she stood in the corner, watching me. The girl. The maid. Every muscle in my body thrummed with the urge to run, but I couldn't move. I couldn't move at all.

*

'Danielle! We were getting worried.' Ted grinned wide enough that I could see the gap where he'd lost a tooth. 'Where have tha been all this time?'

Sunday afternoon at The Hart. I'd had to get out of the house. That morning, I'd woken on top of the covers, freezing, with my phone in my hand, after a night of vivid dreams. And Anita . . .

We'd spoken, I was sure we had, I remembered the beginning of our conversation clearly enough: her colleagues, the wine bar, me standing in the kitchen, all far too banal to be a dream. But I couldn't remember what came next. I had no memory of going to bed: blank space until I woke on top of the covers, like a film with half the reel snipped out.

Obviously, there would be a normal explanation. I'd drunk more than I thought, maybe, or been ill in the night, a fever – maybe it was all just stress. Didn't the sleep paralysis, how real it felt, prove that stress could do bizarre, incredibly *physical* things? But I could hardly call Anita up and ask. She'd worry. Better to move on, and to do that, I needed to feel normal again. I needed company, and noise. I needed the pub.

'Just work,' I said vaguely. 'Nothing exciting. Is Mitch around?' I had half a mind to ask him about Westerley, whatever story it was he hadn't told me before.

Ted checked his watch. 'Be in later, maybe.' It was just after one in the afternoon. This was usually their prime time, packed with hikers, families eating Sunday lunch, but the place was empty. There was an old woman in the corner eating roasted peanuts and reading the paper, but nobody else. Just me and Ted. I looked around, confused.

'Is everything all right?' he said. 'We don't usually see you on a Monday.'

I laughed. It wasn't a Monday. But then where were the people? The old woman looked up from her paper, watching us through rheumy, disinterested eyes. 'Right,' I said. If it wasn't a Sunday, I had lost a whole day. Had

I slept for that long? For a day? I couldn't have. I was exhausted.

'Danielle?'

I rubbed my face, tried to look normal. 'Yeah, I just – I was on a walk. Thought I'd call in and say hello.'

Ted smiled again. 'That's nice. Anything to drink?'

Monday afternoon. I was meant to be at work. 'No. I should . . . I mean, I can't stop. But you're well? You're good?'

'Oh aye, all the same here,' he said, but I was already turning, rudely, back to the door, heading off. 'Come again soon,' he called after me.

I walked quickly, almost ran back over the fields I'd just crossed. I'd done nothing all morning, hadn't even checked my emails. Anything could be happening! I tried loading them on my phone, but the signal was bad and they wouldn't refresh. I had visions of an apoplectic Jeannie pacing in her lilac office. I was for it. Worse, I might have to explain myself. What could I possibly tell her?

Inside, I took my laptop up to bed, got under the covers and loaded my emails. There were only two, and one of them was spam. Nobody had noticed that I'd been away all morning.

I should have felt free, like I could do whatever I liked, work when I wanted, go back to the pub, but I actually felt depressed. What was the point, if nobody even noticed? What was the point of any of it?

*

I was in the kitchen when the rain started. It was Wednesday morning and I'd gone downstairs to wash my breakfast things. Tired, already on my third coffee, I was lifting wet hands from the water to rub my face when I realised the windows were dark. I looked at the wall clock, wondering with horror if I'd lost time again – but no, it was definitely still morning. Then it began to rain, heavy and sudden, throwing itself against the high, basement windows.

Heavy enough that I wanted to see. I went upstairs, into the snug, and looked out. The gardens were wind-blown in the storm, thornbushes tearing themselves apart. Too heavy to last, I thought, as I went back to work. But I was wrong.

The rain got lighter, but it didn't stop. That night, as I lay in bed, I could hear it on the walls of the house, strangely comforting – and when I woke the next day, it was still raining. The day after, too.

The supermarket emailed to cancel my order. They had to suspend deliveries in the area, because a lot of the country roads were flooded. This was the first time I actually felt worried. I knew I'd be okay – I had a tendency to cook too much, over-order, and there were plenty of meals in the freezer, ends of bread I hadn't been able to finish, living alone, and had frozen. Still, I began to ration, thinking things might get worse before they got better.

There wasn't much work to do, but that was okay. I had plenty to think about. Like the clagging, sticking sound of the pipes when they drained water from the kitchen sink; I wondered if something was stuck in there that I ought to try and remove. Or the birds at the bottom of the garden, who'd made a nest in a tree near the drawing room window, and left when the rain started. I wondered where they were. I thought about the hoovering, and the dusting, and how to make my food stretch. I was very tired still, too tired to be unhappy, and I slept a lot, but there were no more dreams. The days were strange, unreal, a kind of suspended animation, like I was waiting for something. Maybe I was just waiting for the rain to stop.

It kept going all Saturday. No emails. I had fresh fruit in the fridge from my last shop, apples, some blackberries from the kitchen garden, but they were on the turn, so I decided to make a crumble and freeze it. While I was doing this, weighing out flour and sugar, spooning everything into one of the dishes, I wondered how many times people had done these exact things in the spot where I was standing. Even the weighing scales looked older than me. I thought about how permanent the house was, and felt temporary. I checked my phone. No messages.

Sunday was the fifth day of rain.

I didn't get out of bed, because what was the point? I had nowhere to go and nobody to see. I scrolled Instagram on my phone. An acquaintance was at a thirtieth birthday party; a girl from uni, who I hadn't seen in years, was on her honeymoon in the Maldives; a guy from college, who I hadn't seen in even longer, had recorded a video of the rain from his window in Manchester, soundtracked it with Radiohead. I watched all the videos from people I knew, every one, until they were finished. I'd never completed Instagram before. Luckily, the algorithm had lots of videos of strangers to offer me. I kept watching.

A woman crying into the camera because she'd been stood up on a date. Someone posting a graph about globally declining birth rates, followed eerily quickly by another video, a woman with a baby on her chest, talking intensely to camera about how motherhood was the only fulfilment she had ever known. The comments on the video said that she was deranged, a truth-teller, speaking out, being silenced, brainwashed by patriarchy, free from capital. There were so many people talking into their phone cameras, and the internet wanted me to listen, telling the world about their bad jobs, dead grandmothers, promotions, SPF, pets, Kegels, climate anxiety. At some point I realised well over an hour had passed since I woke up, and I felt queasy, the way you do after eating only crisps for dinner. An hour of my life, and I'd just sat here, filling up on junk food. I could have been doing anything else. I felt disgusted at myself, and then, on impulse, turned off my phone.

Why not? It wasn't like my friends were clamouring to reach me. I hadn't heard from Ben for ages, Femi never texted on weekends, even Anita was too busy. Although I'd dreamed about her calling. The kitchen. A wine bar. Something. It had felt so real, but then the details faded, like a dream, so it couldn't have been. Anita wouldn't call. No one did.

My phone looked so small and innocent now that it had been switched off, a little black rectangle. I slipped it into the drawer of my bedside table and the ancient room seemed to sigh around me, like it approved. Stupid to be somewhere this beautiful and waste time on my phone. I lay back down, listening to the rain, wondering what to do next. Breakfast, probably, though I'd run out of milk. That was okay. I could eat the fruit crumble. It wasn't like anyone was going to know.

*

By late afternoon, I'd begun to worry about the house. BBC news had images of flooding, sandbags, people in villages with inflatable dinghies and wellington boots; it had been raining for days. What if the water was getting in somewhere? Obviously, Westerley was old, and had survived a lot, but I was here to look after the place.

I went to the attic room at the top of the house and stood, wondering how I'd know if something was wrong. I looked at the twin beds, the children's books. The rain sounded different in here, beating cosily on the roof, like being in a tent. For a moment, in my perpetual exhaustion, I thought about lying down on one of the beds and going to sleep. But I had stuff to do.

I scanned the corners of the room, edges of the windows, places rain might get in. The bedroom looked fine, and smelled like clean, dry linen, no damp. I peered out of the window at the drains, which also looked . . . normal? I didn't know much about houses. I'd had images of water pooling in rooms I wasn't using, bursting out, like the lift doors in *The Shining*, but everything seemed fine.

I took the stairs down and lapped the top floor, standing in all the empty spaces one by one, the blue room, the study, the dust-sheeted bedrooms, until I was certain I couldn't hear or see or smell anything amiss. The carpets were all dry and the windows looked shut, and that was about the limit of my qualifications. If the constant rain was damaging the house at all, at least it wasn't doing it in any obvious way that someone could be angry with me for missing.

The ground floor seemed fine as well – except the billiards room, which I couldn't check because, of course, it was locked. Standing outside the door, I remembered Mrs Waddingham saying it had been shut up because of a leak. What if the rain was making it worse? I wondered if I should call her, if the key was somewhere in the house. Then it started. Thud. Thud. Thud.

'Oh God,' I said, without meaning to, but it didn't stop. It was like someone pounding with their fists on the other side of the door, a rhythmic, brutal, relentless sound, and I'd heard it before, hadn't I? Or had I only dreamed it?

I had to do something, find out what was going on in there. Shaking, I went to the entrance hall and pulled on my trainers. The knocking, pounding sound was ceaseless as I threw open the front door and ran out into the rain.

I was soaked in an instant, like stepping into a shower, hair flattened against my face, clothes against my skin, but I was too panicked to notice. All I could think about was the locked room. It was impossible to hear anything over the rain, but the sound had been so rhythmic that my brain filled it in, *thud, thud, thud,* as I circled the house at a run, counting windows.

The dining room: one, two, three. And there, the next window, that must be it. The billiards room.

There was no longer any fear in my body, only adrenaline, as I threw myself across the flowerbeds, nearly slipping. I gripped the wall, pressed my face against the glass. It was grimy, layered with years of dust, and I rubbed at it, but of course it made no difference – the outsides had been cleaned. I was straining to see or hear something when a hand slammed against the window from the inside, right by my face.

I screamed. I skidded back, sliding in wet mud and landing hard on the ground. I had never known fear like it, animal fear. And I stayed there, in the dirt, watching the window, waiting to see her, it, something, a face, someone watching me, something in there. But there was nothing. Nothing happened.

I must have lain there quite a while. Eventually, I realised I was shivering too hard to keep still. My bones ached when I clambered to my feet, but my eyes stayed fixed on the window. Part of me wanted to run, but where would I go? I had to see. I had to know for sure.

Gripping the wall again, I levered myself back over the flowerbeds and peered into the billiards room. As my eyes adjusted to the light, and to the grime, I could see quite clearly: a small, square room. Stripped, bare pine floorboards. Pale green walls. Blank. No paintings, no other windows, not so much as a candlestick on the mantelpiece. There was nothing in there. Nobody. It was just an empty room.

I went back into the house and closed the front door behind me. In the entrance hall, I took my clothes and shoes and socks off, everything, wrapped myself in the coat I stupidly hadn't worn outside, not that it would have helped much. The house was eerily quiet after the tumult of the rain. I regretted turning my phone off, and how far away it was. I wanted noise, comforting noise.

Naked and freezing under my coat, I made myself pass the locked room, silent now, to the snug at the back of the house, where I turned the television on. *Antiques Roadshow.* I put the volume up as high as it could go. This was the soundtrack to which I padded around the house, focused on whatever task came next. I shoved my muddy clothes into the washing machine. Mopped the entrance hall, where I'd left puddles of dirty water. I ran a bath, found clean pyjamas, left them folded on the bathroom stool.

I lay in the bath a long time, watching the steam rise to the ceiling. I kept adding more hot water, stewing and reading, until I felt better, could almost convince myself nothing had happened. Except I knew that it had. I didn't know what, but something, something I didn't understand, couldn't explain. And not for the first time. My stomach roiled with horror as I let myself remember it: things moving around, lost time, dreams that felt real, days that felt like a dream, and that terrible pounding – mud under my feet – a hand on the window … Or something else. Of course it couldn't really have been a hand, because the room was empty. Just like things didn't move by themselves, and days didn't actually get away from you, unless you let them. Yes, I knew there must be an explanation for all of it: I was rational. I lived in the world. The thing was, whatever the explanation, I no longer cared. I'd had enough.

It was Sunday night, too late to do anything now, but tomorrow I would call Mrs Waddingham, ask her to drive me to the station, and leave. I wasn't trapped here, I was looking after a house, and Jeannie could find someone else. If she sacked me, I would get a new job. I would stay at Mum's. Whatever. Anything but go through another day like this one. Then I heard the sound of the front door opening downstairs.

I sat up, listening. I could be wrong, I was still tense, strung out. But as I listened, I heard another sound, definite this time: the door closing. Somebody was in the house with me.

I climbed quickly and quietly out of the bath, dried myself and pulled on the only clothes I had in here, a set of pyjamas, then eased back the lock on the bathroom door. There were voices, too far away to make out, though I could tell one of them was a man. I'd half hoped it was Mrs Waddingham – but no.

Thief? Murderer? It sounded like they were going down to the basement. Was there anything valuable in the kitchen? Nothing came to mind, though the locked storeroom could be full of family heirlooms for all I knew or cared. I wasn't about to be killed protecting the family silverware.

I crept along the corridor and down the main staircase. As I reached the brightly lit entrance hall, I realised I was very frightened. Had I left these lights on myself, or had somebody else turned them on? I couldn't remember. I could definitely hear voices from the kitchen, the man's low rumble and another, quieter, harder to make out. Two people, at least. Could be more.

I stood for a few moments, wondering what to do. I could run. I looked at my boots in a muddy pile by the door. My coat. Laughter from downstairs. I should go, now, slip out of the door before they heard me. I would be across the fields and in the pub before they knew anyone was even here. They probably thought the house was empty. They wouldn't chase me. Shoes on. Go. But before I could move, I heard light, quick footsteps, coming up the kitchen stairs towards me.

Run, I thought, *run*, but I did nothing. I was frozen to the spot.

The figure reached the top of the stairs, came out into the hall, and stood, looking straight at me. A man I didn't recognise, with dark, curly hair. He frowned. He didn't look much like a thief, in his expensive shirt, corduroy trousers, desert boots. Then he laughed, maybe at the expression on my face. That was when I realised I was wrong: I *did* recognise him. We'd met before, of course we had.

'Mum?' he called. 'She's up here.'

It was Edward. Jeannie's son.

III.

Other Masters

I SAT AT THE KITCHEN TABLE, pressing my hands down hard on the woodgrain to stop them shaking. 'She looked at me like I was a ghost,' Edward was saying. 'I've heard people say that, but I'd never actually *seen* it before.'

Jeannie was bent over, lighting the Aga, and the kitchen felt bright, warm and safe. Obviously, it wasn't great to see my boss while I was wearing my most embarrassing pyjamas, covered with little paint-splodge ducks in little hats, but I was deeply relieved – even if they were both taking the piss.

'Gosh, I'm so sorry, Danielle,' Jeannie said, standing and wiping her eyes with a forefinger. She'd been crying with laughter. 'We did try to call, but you weren't answering your phone.'

My phone. Of course: it was still switched off in the drawer. I wasn't really sure how to explain that one. I could hardly say that the thought of spending another day flicking through the better lives of strangers, while I waited to hear from friends who seemed to have forgotten me, was too depressing to bear. I managed to mutter something about a digital detox, spending more time reading.

Edward looked impressed. 'Man, I'm jealous,' he said. 'I'm addicted to my phone, it's killing my attention span. You're gonna have to share your secrets.'

It had been almost funny, the social ambiguity of coming down here to find Jeannie standing at the counter. Her house, my tea, and of course I'd never actually seen her boil a kettle before; I wondered whether to take over. In the end, I'd been pressed into a seat, while Edward did it. He passed the mugs out now, Jeannie slipping into the seat next to mine, while Edward leaned against the counter with his arms folded, watching us both.

'We really are sorry to crash in on you,' she said. 'We've had the most unbelievable couple of days. This weather, good lord! It's as bad up here as it is in London.'

'Is everything all right?' I asked.

'You won't believe it,' said Jeannie. 'You honestly are not going to *believe* me when I tell you.'

'What happened?'

'It's been – oh, Danielle.' She shook her head. 'It's been just *dreadful*.'

'Our roof fell in,' said Edward, cutting to the chase, which I appreciated. Jeannie had a flair for the dramatic.

My eyes flicked to the ceiling, thinking of the walk I'd taken round the house that morning, looking for leaks. 'Our roof in London,' Jeannie added, and I realised she was really upset, the laughter masking a brittle, more general hysteria. She drew a shaking breath. 'The upper floor's a complete mess, of course. But that's Hugo all over. Such a *bodger*. We had trouble with that roof in 1998, but would he get a man in? No, he would not.'

'Dad hasn't lived with us for sixteen years,' Edward said. 'At some point, we might have to take the blame ourselves.'

Jeannie was a pain in the arse, but I felt awful for her. 'I hope it's not too bad?'

Her eyes were full of tears. 'We have insurance. And it's fixable. But it's been such an ordeal.'

'I'm so sorry.'

'No, no,' she waved me away. 'These things happen. We've got an expert in, there's a tarpaulin up, it'll all be fine.'

'That's the spirit,' said Edward.

'I'm sorry we gave you a fright. I just couldn't think where else to go.'

'Of course,' I said. It made sense: this was Jeannie's home. 'You've been so kind, letting me stay.'

'Well, you've been wonderful, clearly. Hasn't she been wonderful, Edward? It's all so clean, and feels so loved – *so* much nicer than dashing up here to find the place dark and empty.'

'I can't believe you didn't know we were coming,' Edward said, shaking his head. 'If it was me, the house would've been a fucking state.'

Always interesting, seeing people swear in front of their parents. I glanced at Jeannie to see if she minded, but she was laughing. 'Underpants all over the dining room table,' she said.

I smiled. Yes, I'd kept things nice. Nobody could have asked me to do more. And now it was over.

I was glad. With the house full of people, the fear I'd felt earlier was easier to rationalise, but I still didn't want to stay. And now Jeannie was here, I could leave in good conscience, without looking strange or leaving her in the lurch. Thank God.

'You've been so kind,' I repeated. Only a few weeks till I could move back into my flat; I would go to Mum's, work something out from there. My chair scraped as I stood. 'I should pack, get out of your way.'

Jeannie looked surprised. 'Gosh,' she said. 'You don't have to do that.'

'Well, I probably can't go tonight.' I looked at the clock on the wall; after 9 p.m. already. The chances of getting a train to Leeds and another connecting to London seemed slim. 'But if you can run me to the station in the morning . . .' I let the sentence hang.

'No, no,' said Jeannie. 'We're not going to be here that long. A week, if that, and this place is more than big enough. Please don't feel we expect you to go.'

'It's really no problem.' I would look up train times in the morning, work everything out after a night's sleep. 'Wait,' I said, embarrassed. 'Mrs Waddingham made up the master room for me. Let me just take my things out.'

'Oh, no,' said Jeannie vaguely, but of course, it was her house. It would be absurd for me to stay there while she slept somewhere else. Edward was watching us in silence and, slightly against my will, I wondered what he was thinking.

'No,' I said firmly. 'It's fine. Won't take a moment.'

*

I took all my clothes out of the dressing room in the master, tossed them pell-mell into my suitcase, and stripped the bed. After a moment's hesitation, I made it up again, for Jeannie. She could have done it herself, but it felt more polite to do it for her. After all, she had let me stay here all this time, and I appreciated it.

There were a lot of bedrooms, but most were dust-sheeted and needed airing, which seemed a lot of work. The other open one on this floor, the blue room Mrs Waddingham had offered when I first came, would be for Edward. So I dragged my suitcase upstairs, to the children's room.

Jeannie caught me in the middle of moving my things. 'We can't shut you in the attic, like Bertha Mason,' she said, looking guilty, but I laughed.

'It's fine!' I said. It wouldn't be for long, after all: I was going back to London in the morning.

The door was rickety, without a proper handle; there was a latch, instead, which you had to lift into a catch on the wall. A breeze was blowing in from somewhere, and the door rattled gently on its hinges when closed, making the room seem colder than it really was.

I tried both beds, but they seemed much the same, so I picked one at random and made it up with sheets from the linen cupboard. There was something unnerving about sleeping in a room with another empty bed. After a moment's hesitation, I dragged the unused blankets off it and threw them over the weird, old-fashioned toys in the corner, to stop their beady eyes watching me while I slept.

I went to the bathroom to clean my teeth, then realised I should probably say goodnight. Downstairs, I heard voices coming from the snug, so I knocked, and found Jeannie and Edward sprawled on the sofas, drinking what looked like brandy.

'Oh, hello,' said Jeannie. I felt awkward, like I'd walked into their living room. I guess I had. They glanced at one another, and I realised they weren't sure whether they should ask me to join them. 'Sorry, Danielle. Do you . . . ?'

I waved a hand. 'Oh, no, no, I'm knackered. Sunday. Just wanted to say goodnight.' Did they look relieved, or was I imagining things?

I went back to the attic room and climbed into bed. In the dark, the rain was startlingly loud on the roof. I suddenly felt very awake.

I let my mind wander to a drink I'd had with Femi before I left London. 'Are you joking?' she'd said, when I told her I was going to Westerley. 'You're going to live with Jeannie? Lady Actual Di?'

And I'd laughed, Femi's purple fingernails digging into my forearm, shielding my face with my pint. We were both laughing. 'No, Christ, she won't *be* there, I'll just be in her *house*.'

I wondered if I should have seen this coming. But it had been a freak accident, of course, Jeannie's roof falling in.

'You're going to turn into her,' Femi said. 'You seem normal now, but when you come back it'll be all chiffon scarves and reading the *Telegraph*, doing yoga, *can't get the staff these days, not like you could in Grandmama's time . . .'*

*

When I came into the kitchen the next day, Jeannie was already at the table, drinking coffee.

'Morning, Danielle,' she said. She looked more well-rested and put-together than I did, even though she'd been up, drinking brandy, when I went to bed. There was no justice in the world. We exchanged pleasantries and she apologised for Edward, who was going to miss breakfast. 'He's always been a late sleeper,' she said.

They'd brought a lot of food up with them, the sides laden with jam, bowls of fruit, a farmhouse loaf. She must have seen me looking, because she said, 'Help yourself. We brought enough to feed the five thousand. I packed in such a panic!'

I felt bad, but also hungry; I'd been living on freezer food since the supermarket cancelled my delivery. 'If you're sure that's all right?'

She made an expansive gesture with her hand, which I took to mean yes, so I thanked her, made myself toast and coffee.

'Sleep all right?'

'Yes, thanks,' I said. I actually had. No nightmares, no paralysis, just a long, deep sleep. Maybe it was having other people in the house, or knowing I'd be leaving soon, but I felt better, more like myself. 'Did you?'

'I always sleep like a baby at Westerley,' said Jeannie with a smile. She'd finished her own breakfast and was reading a Sunday supplement, turning the pages slowly, thoughtfully, with a forefinger. I wished I had a physical paper to read, so much classier.

Instead, I sat down at the table with my toast, turned my phone back on and began to search for trains to London. But the webpage was covered with red alerts: the line between here and Leeds was flooded. Of course it was. There would be no trains today, perhaps none tomorrow, either; I scrolled through the ranting on social media, people complaining about flood defences and public infrastructure. My appetite was gone. I had no way to leave – unless I asked somebody to drive me all the way to Leeds, a thought that made me prickle with embarrassment. Why had I never learned to drive? Though it might not have helped; so many roads around here were flooded. I felt a spike of claustrophobia, but told myself I was being stupid. It would only mean staying a day or two longer – and being at Westerley was already better, easier, with other people here.

'Jeannie,' I said. She looked at me. 'I'm really sorry, but the trains are cancelled because of the weather. So it looks like I will have to stay here with you guys for a little while. Is that okay?'

She seemed sincerely unbothered. 'Of course. We really don't want to throw you out. We're only going to be here a week or so anyway.'

'Thanks,' I said. The trains couldn't stay down forever. I would be gone soon. I pushed my queasy feeling down, made myself eat the rest of my toast.

'Anyway,' Jeannie went on. 'Won't it be nicer and cosier, working like this and not on the horrible screens?'

'Yes,' I said vaguely. 'Of course.'

'Speaking of which!' She pushed her newspaper aside. 'Shall we start? If you've finished breakfast.'

'Oh,' I said. It was only 8.30 in the morning, earlier than we'd usually start in London, but it seemed silly to point this out, because she must know. What could I say? Pretend I had something to do, sit here playing on my phone? It would look absurd.

It wasn't the end of the world to start early. It would be nice to finish before five – maybe the trains would be working again by then.

'Just need to fetch my laptop,' I said, standing up.

When I got back, Jeannie was still at the table, drawing rings with her finger. 'Now, Danielle, I have a little confession to make, but you have to *promise* you won't be cross.'

I looked at her, apprehensive. 'What is it?'

'Promise!' she trilled whimsically.

'Okay. Sure. I promise.'

'Now, in all the excitement, I *completely* forgot to bring my laptop. It was at work and I should have called in, but it was a Sunday, and ra-ra-ra . . .'

'Oh, I'm sure Mollie can post it up to you.'

Jeannie waved a hand. 'Hardly worth her doing that, is it, when we won't be here long? I thought perhaps we could share yours for now . . . ?'

'Oh,' I said.

'If that's all right?'

I blinked. It would be weird, ungenerous, to say no. 'Yes. Of course. I'll just log you in.'

I knew all her passwords, obviously. I loaded Jeannie's emails and slid the laptop across. She thanked me, and then, without taking her eyes off the screen, said, 'Perhaps a green tea?'

I hesitated. Something about the way she had asked, not even looking at me . . . But I was just being sensitive. I was out of sorts after weeks by myself. 'Of course,' I said.

I put the kettle on and stood waiting for it to boil. She'd brought her usual brand of green tea, it was on the side with the breakfast things. I filled a small pot with the leaves, poured hot water on top. There was something faintly surreal about going through these motions again after the last few weeks. I was so used to being alone at Westerley.

Jeannie was reading her emails when I put the mug down beside her, but seemed to be struggling. 'Is everything all right?'

'It's loading so slowly,' she said, waggling her hands over the mousepad. I wondered, too late, if there was anything on my computer that I didn't want her to see. It was like letting a toddler drive a car; she could bring up anything, delete anything, God knows what would happen. I remembered with a jolt that Chris had liked us to watch pornography together sometimes. Would it still be . . . on there, somehow? What if she clicked something and it all came up?

'Oh – bad signal,' I realised. 'The Wi-Fi doesn't stretch down here very well.' That was why I'd spent so many hours working in bed, or at least, that was ostensibly why.

'Hmm,' said Jeannie. 'Perhaps we should go to the study? Though most of the desk's taken up by that old machine of Nigel's . . .'

She must mean the desktop computer I'd seen up there. I wondered if she could use that, instead. 'Does it work?'

'God no, not for years.' She laughed.

I was being paranoid. I was pretty sure we'd always used Chris's laptop anyway. I pointed out the chair that usually picked up Wi-Fi better. 'Try this one.'

'Well,' she said. 'Why don't we stay down here for now, and I'll have Edward sort the study for tomorrow?'

As she dragged the laptop across the table, sat in the Wi-Fi seat, I wondered what 'we' were going to do, today or tomorrow, with only one laptop. If Jeannie was answering emails, what could I contribute? Pep talks? But I nodded, and then, because she was working and I was at a loose end, washed up both our breakfast things. When that was done, Jeannie was still bent over my laptop, typing with two fingers and a look of fierce concentration. So I cleaned the kitchen, and began to organise the food; I was putting punnets of fruit into the fridge when Edward came downstairs, bleary-eyed and hungover.

'Here's the dirty stop-out,' Jeannie said affectionately. He waved without speaking, and began moving around the kitchen, making coffee, tearing a chunk off the bread and ripping into it with his teeth, unbuttered. He was shirtless. Awkward, given that one of the people in the room was his mother and the other was his mother's PA, but whatever.

'Hot in here,' he said.

'Mmm, this room always was the warmest,' Jeannie smiled. 'I used to come down here as a child and sit under the table when my toes got cold. Cook would always keep little sweets back for me.'

Edward didn't seem to be listening, he was looking through the piles of food. 'Where's the eggs?' he said.

Jeannie looked at him a moment, then seemed struck by something. 'Oh, blast,' she said. 'I left them on the side, at home. How silly of me.'

'Mum, fuck's sake, they'll be rotten when we get back.'

Jeannie laughed, and I thought that I would have been murdered if I'd spoken to my mum like that as a kid. Not that he was a kid, obviously, but still. Their relationship made Edward seem strangely teenaged.

'Don't worry, I'll text Mel, ask her to clear them away when she's hoovering. And we can . . .' Jeannie got up, went to her leather handbag, on the floor by the chair she'd been sitting in last night. 'Give me twenty minutes, darling.'

Edward sloped back upstairs.

Jeannie brought the bag to the table and began rifling through, pulling out pieces of paper, her keys, her purse. Was she going to drive out straight away, in a storm, just to buy eggs? Man, this guy was spoiled.

'Danielle,' she said. 'I wonder if you could do a little job for me.' Was I going to have to remind her that I couldn't drive? 'If you go right out of the house, instead of left towards the village, there's a route through the treeline that will take you down to a stile. Climb over it, go through two fields, and you'll find a gravel path. Follow it, then take a left, and there's a lovely farm with some chickens where they have an honesty box and lots of nice, fresh eggs. Would you be an angel and buy some?'

I looked out of the windows, at the weather, and back at Jeannie, who gave no sign of noticing that it was battering down with rain. But I'd walked that way before, stopped at the stile. 'It says no right of way through the fields.'

'Oh, don't worry about that,' she said, waving a hand. 'Those signs are for other people – it's our land.' She shook a handful of coins from her purse and held them out to me, palm flat, like I was a horse she was feeding.

I wavered a moment, wondering if I could say no. If I was waiting for her to acknowledge that this was outside my job description, I was obviously going to be waiting some time. Was it, though? Maybe when I first started at Hodgepodge. But over the last four years I'd been in this situation a hundred times, saying *uh sure I guess* while Jeannie handed me a twenty-pound note or a credit card and sent me off to get the Waitrose-own biscuits she was craving, or hayfever tablets, or a pair of stockings because hers had laddered and we had an event that night, or whatever. I took the money. 'Sure,' I said.

'Oh, thank you, Danielle. I'd go, but I'm working, and there's so much to do!'

I caught sight of the laptop screen, Jeannie's half-written email:

Tamara such a JOY to hear from you after all these years!! of course we wwould love to come and stay next summer. I haven't seen your beautiful gardens since the boys were in short trousers. You always did have green fingers!

*

The rain was still hammering down as I made my way across the fields. I was glad to have my good raincoat, but my knees were wet inside my leggings within seconds of leaving the house.

I followed Jeannie's directions, right turn towards the treeline. The sky was dark and heavy with clouds even though it had been raining for days. I would have to buy vitamin D supplements. Could you go crazy from lack of sunlight? From the weather being the same, day after day? It was deeply oppressive. No wonder I was in a bad mood.

Because I had to admit that this did feel different, worse, than doing things for Jeannie back in London.

Why, though? Because I was staying in her house? Surely that should make it more okay, I'd spent a decade in houseshares doing favours for people I lived with, picking up toothpaste on the understanding that they would get it next time, letting them use my pasta and replace it . . . Why did it matter that I was the one going out for eggs? Was I really so petty?

Maybe the power dynamic was just too different: because Jeannie was my boss, not my housemate; because it was her house, and, more than that, her land I was walking across now. Everything as far as the eye could see belonged to her. It made her power over me feel, frankly, less benign than it had in London, and more ancient.

The stile was wet and cold under my palms, like the hull of a shipwreck dragged up after hundreds of years underwater. I scrambled over it and started across the fields, trying not to think about how Jeannie owned this, all of this, all of it. It was a drumbeat in my ears. I wished it didn't matter: after all, I'd seen the house weeks ago, I knew what she was. But to own everything, all this, even the grass, the trees, made me wonder how far her family's reach extended. And here I was, part of the house, staying in the attic, running errands. Part of the furniture. Staff.

'All right?' There was a man watching me up ahead, at the edge of the farm, bearded and light-eyed. He looked even more rain-soaked than I felt, water dripping from the brim of his hat. He was holding a hen under one arm. There were no fences dividing his land from Jeannie's and I wondered where one started and the other ended, or if they were the same. Maybe she'd just given me the change out of politeness, and really, if I told him I was from the big house, he'd have let me take the eggs, no questions asked – like a tithe.

'Hi. I'm from . . .' I gestured vaguely. 'I'm staying at Westerley. They sent me for eggs.'

He nodded approval. 'Good eggs, these.'

Just as Jeannie had said, there was a little cupboard with an honesty box attached. A dirt road ran away from me, and for half a second, I thought about following it. Throwing myself on the farmer's mercy, asking him to drive me somewhere. It was a strange, absurd thought; I might not always like Jeannie, but I was her guest, not her prisoner. I bought the eggs.

The farmer didn't so much as glance at me as I put the money in. He kept his back turned, picking the hens up and doing something with them that I couldn't see. He didn't have to chase them. They all just came, one by one, like they were waiting their turn. I put the eggbox under my arm and called, 'Bye then. Thanks.'

He turned and nodded. 'You give my regards to the lady,' he said.

I figured he meant Jeannie. 'Will do.' I headed back to the house.

I got back a little after ten, dripping, and decided to go up and change before I did anything else. I left the eggbox in the entrance hall, hung my sopping coat over the radiator, muddy boots by the door, and hopped upstairs. There was loud, discordant techno coming from behind the closed door of the blue room; Edward must be in there, doing what passed for his job, while I did what passed for mine.

Soaked again, the second day in a row. Up in the attic, I peeled off all my layers, skin pale and thick with water, trying to stop my teeth chattering. I was soaked down to my bra. I wrapped myself in a towel while I searched my suitcase for clean, dry clothes.

I'd dressed and hung my wet clothes up to dry, when I noticed the other bed was different. Or was it? I sat on my own bed and looked at it. I had a dim memory of dragging the blankets off it last night, to cover – something. Kids' toys? I remembered Mrs Waddingham saying the children slept here. But that must have been years ago, because there were no toys in here now, and no pile of blankets either. The other bed was intact, neatly made, eiderdown and pillowcases. I had only put sheets on my own, hadn't I? Why would I make up two beds just to sleep in one? I had a headache. I rubbed the bridge of my nose, which did absolutely nothing, and then, on some strange impulse, reached out to draw back the sheets. The gap between the two beds was about an arm's length, so I had to stretch to do it.

There it was. A slight divot in the mattress, like the other bed had been slept in, too. I drew my hand down it. Distantly, I thought: *oh. It's warm.*

A knocking, pounding sound had started downstairs. Thud, thud, thud. Edward's techno, it must be, and underneath that, a low, insistent buzzing. But that wasn't the music, I realised. My phone was ringing.

I scrambled to answer in time. 'Hello?'

'Mate, oh my God, best day ever.' It was Femi. 'Guess. Sorry to call, but I had to. You'll literally never guess.'

'I might.' Femi was younger than me, an inveterate voice noter, but I was beginning to suspect I understood why she'd called.

'So get this, right? Lady Di's house is flooded, and she has to work remotely. *Remotely*. I can't believe you're not here. I haven't felt this good since, like, 2009, when it snowed so much they shut my school!'

'Femi, she's here,' I said.

'She's what?'

'She's here. Up here, with me.'

There was a pause on the line – then an explosion of something like laughter and something like horror. 'You *what*?' Femi shouted. Somewhere behind her voice, I could hear the echo of the corridor outside our office, the familiar pitch and tang of it. Funny to be able to picture exactly where she was standing. So far away.

'I know,' I said.

'She's moved into that big house with you?'

'Well, it doesn't seem so big now. But yes. She has.'

'Oh my days. Holy shit.'

'I know.'

'But that's crazy. She said this might go on for weeks.'

Weeks? She'd said *a* week to me, hadn't she? She'd said – barely any time at all. Wasn't even worth getting Mollie to post her laptop up.

Femi asked what had happened and I told her, briefly. The bath. Missing their calls. Finding them downstairs. While I did, I listened to the familiar, ambient noise of our building, as Femi left the hall outside our office and walked downstairs, past reception, onto the street. I knew it all by sound alone: the beep of her card on the door, the receptionist talking on the phone, the sliding doors, the city.

'So now she's there, are you gonna come home?'

I opened my mouth to say, Yes. To say I was leaving as soon as the trains worked again, that I would be home tomorrow, or the day after that. I could picture what it would be like today, the Tube damp and passive-aggressive after so much rain, people dripping on each other, and for a moment I let myself imagine none of this had happened. I'd be standing in the street with Femi, celebrating. We could knock off early, go to the pub, *ding dong the witch is dead*, I'd probably be texting Ben to join us, and tonight I would go home late and drunk on the bus. How many nights had I spent like that since I moved to London? All those hours of my life, hours that added up to days or even weeks, sprawled on top decks, waiting at bus stops, late nights that were almost early mornings, all those travel-beers and bags of chips and falling-asleep-by-accidents, waking up in fucking Penge. I'd been to Penge so many times and never on purpose. How vital it had all felt at the time, and how distant it seemed now, how far away.

'Dan?'

'Yeah,' I said. 'Sorry, I'm still here. Where are you?'

'Our park,' said Femi. She meant the place we used to eat lunch, the scrub of green space between office buildings that had belonged to us. Was ours. Was *still* ours. I felt stuck in past tense, but it didn't feel wrong, either. 'So are you coming home?'

I didn't know how to answer. 'Oh shit, sorry, someone's calling,' I lied. 'Got to go. Text you later.'

'Good luck,' said Femi. I hung up.

The house was quiet, blankets on the other bed rumpled where I'd pulled them back. I could still see the divot. I stood, tugged the sheets back into place. I had tried to leave. It wasn't like I hadn't tried. But the dreams. Light on the ceiling. Something beating the door of the locked room. I felt bad for lying to Femi, but what else could I say? There were too many things I couldn't explain.

*

Down in the kitchen, Jeannie was waiting. 'You angel,' she said, looking up from our laptop. 'I hope you didn't get too wet.'

'No,' I said, although I was wearing different clothes. If she noticed, she gave no sign. I put the eggs away in the ceramic hen on the sideboard. 'How are you getting on?'

Jeannie sighed. 'I can't get used to this keyboard!'

'Is it different from yours?'

'It's bigger. I keep hitting the wrong buttons and it's rather slowing things down.' The keyboard wasn't any bigger. We had the same laptop. I slid into the chair beside her to take a look, but she said, 'Would you be a dear . . . ?' and pushed the computer towards me. There was another half-written email on the screen:

Darling Suzanne s o. sorry i missed our lunch!!! not like me as you know not to be on top of these things HOWEVER would you believe we have had the most terriblet rr trouble at home.

I glanced up at Jeannie, wondering what she wanted. A proofreader? She looked back at me expectantly.

'Oh,' I said, realising. 'Yes. Sure. I can help.' I pulled the laptop closer, laid my hands over the keys.

'Wonderful,' said Jeannie. 'So: '"we have had the most terrible trouble at home. Do you remember back in 1998 when Hugo and I had all those awful rows about the roof . . ."'

I began typing. Although I kept all Jeannie's passwords, I'd always tried to respect her privacy: it would have been rude to go around reading her emails. But that morning, taking dictation, I saw first-hand how little of her day was filled with the work we ostensibly did together.

After an hour or two, she got up to make sandwiches for her and Edward while continuing to dictate. '"Those long Saturday nights on the terrazzo were magical. Do you ever miss England? We miss you, although of course we understand it's better for Markus's health . . .'"

'Sorry, can you go a bit slower?'

'Mm-hm,' she said, licking piccalilli from her thumb. 'Sorry, Danielle. Your typing is wonderfully fast. I don't know how I would have got through so much without you. Is it all right if we take a break for lunch?'

'Sure.'

'Then I might see if I can persuade the man of the house to blow the cobwebs off,' she said cheerfully. I supposed this meant that she and Edward were going for a walk. 'So you can get on with whatever else you need to do.' That was just as well. A lot of the emails Jeannie and I had sent involved some version of the sentence, *Danielle, cc'd, has my diary and can sort this out.*

'Sure,' I said.

She tossed the dirty knives, spoon, chopping boards into the sink. 'Would you be an angel,' she trilled, and skipped upstairs with the sandwiches, not waiting for a reply.

I stood, went over to the big, old-fashioned enamel sink. Jeannie's used cutlery lay at the bottom. That was what she'd meant, of course: she expected me to do the washing-up.

*

When I woke, the attic room was bright with moonlight; I must have forgotten to close the curtains. It was the middle of the night, but I was strangely alert. Then I heard something from the empty bed.

I didn't move. Couldn't. I just lay on my side, watching. Because it was an old house, things scratched and fidgeted sometimes, mice – but it was obvious that whatever was moving was too large to be an animal. The weight of something raising the blankets, lifting them.

I watched as somebody sat up in the other bed.

I tried to speak but my mouth, like every other part of me, was immovable. I wanted to leap up, run for the door, but of course I couldn't do that either. And yet, this couldn't be sleep paralysis, I was sure I was really awake, as I watched her climb from the other bed, pale elbows in the moonlight, plaits. Not a monster. A woman.

She stood at the basin in the corner of the room while I lay watching. If she could hear the sound I was making, frightened, low in my throat, she gave no sign. Slowly, carefully, she washed and dressed. Boots. Apron. Cap. Dark, sensible dress. The maid. I'd seen her before, I knew, in every dream since I came here, and not just dreams. I'd seen her, passed her, in the house. She'd been watching me.

When she was finished, she turned to meet my eyes.

'Come on then,' she said. 'Are you getting up?'

I woke to light on the ceiling. It was still raining, but not as heavily. I checked my phone; just after 7.30. I didn't want to move or think, not yet. I lay and scrolled for a while. Twitter. Instagram. Puddles, sandbags, village children on inflatable boats. Endless photographs of traffic jams, people sitting on suitcases in train stations, sleeping in airports. I opened a travel app to confirm what I already suspected, that the train line between here and Leeds was still down, then shut my phone, and stared at the ceiling.

Images surfaced in my mind, disconnected from each other. Moonlight on the waterlogged grounds around Westerley. Fresh eggs in the palm of my hand. The woman in the dark dress, in my nightmares: the maid. I could remember everything quite clearly. It didn't feel any more like a dream, now, in the morning, than it had at the time. Perhaps it hadn't been one at all. None of it had.

Hadn't I been thinking exactly this before Jeannie arrived? And pushed it down, and doubted myself, and tried to be *rational*. But maybe it wasn't stress, or tiredness, or spending too much time alone, or drinking too much – maybe there wasn't anything wrong with me. Maybe there was everything wrong with Westerley.

Rolling onto my side, I picked my phone back up, looked at my face in its black mirror. Bags under my eyes. I opened the internet, searched *find out if house haunted*, and was immediately irritated with myself. What was I expecting to see? A little automated pop-up, perhaps:

Looks like you're searching from a <u>haunted house</u>! Your local spirit appears to be <u>Beatrice</u> who died of <u>cholera</u> in 1783. Click <u>here</u> to find out more!

What actually came up, as always, was lots of articles plagiarised from one another, the first called *Ten Signs*

Your House Is Haunted. I clicked and scanned through. Cold spots, whispering voices, flickering lights; none of this was really the kind of thing I'd been experiencing, and the advice seemed to focus on salting window ledges and burning sage, things I couldn't imagine doing, especially now Jeannie was here.

I didn't know what I was looking for, and anyway, I was out of time. I had to get up, go downstairs, face the day. I had work to do.

*

Good as her word, Jeannie had made Edward clear his uncle's old computer from the study. I hadn't been in much, except to clean, but it was a nice room, good light, big windows, with a large desk, oak and green leather, taking up most of the space. I came in after breakfast to find Jeannie sitting on one side of the desk with my laptop open, waiting for me to put the password in. Her smiling, expectant face reminded me of a hundred other mornings at Hodgepodge, seen through a funhouse mirror.

'Lovely,' she said, seeing me. 'Let's begin.'

Jeannie wanted me to do the typing again, so I sat at the laptop while she paced around. I read the new emails out to her: a reply from Tamara about next summer, a reply from Suzanne about lunch, something from Mollie about a panel Jeannie was meant to be chairing on the cost of living crisis. A classic Hodgepodge *real issue* that we wanted to get *ordinary people* thinking about; I was sure that ordinary people who could barely afford their weekly shops would be glad to get financial advice from Jeannie.

'Let's give her a call,' Jeannie said, then rang Mollie from her mobile and put her on speaker. 'Hello, Mollie! Here we are!'

They talked for a few minutes, and agreed it would be best to take the panel online now, with plenty of notice, 'things being what they are': between travel disruptions and Jeannie's home repairs, who knew how long she'd need to work remotely? The panel was in eleven days. I remembered my call with Femi: despite what Jeannie had told me, she was clearly planning to be at Westerley for some time.

'Well, this is all great,' said Mollie, wrapping up. 'Thanks for calling, Jeannie. And did I say before? I was so, *so* sorry to hear about your home.' Suck-up. It buoyed me a little to imagine how jealous Mollie must be that I was up here with Jeannie, while she was stuck in London – but it was cold comfort. If anyone was stuck, it was me.

I took dictation for another hour or so after the call ended. Then we moved on to Jeannie's 'to-do' list. I wasn't surprised to discover that only a few things were related to Hodgepodge, and most were about Westerley: pipes that needed to be bled, drains cleared, work on the grounds. 'Mrs Waddingham was never up to it,' she said. We spent a long time building a list of potential landscape gardeners, and were in the middle of writing to a man called Paul Perennial, which surely couldn't be his real name, when there was a knock at the door.

'Come,' said Jeannie.

Edward appeared, hair messy and unkempt. 'I'm bored.'

'We're *working*,' she admonished, with a conspiratorial glance at me, like we were the adults and he the child.

'Can't we go for a walk or something?'

'After lunch.'

He rolled his eyes. 'Shall I make us lunch now? It's gone twelve.'

Jeannie laughed. She looked slightly flushed, flattered by the attention, and I wondered if this was a weird psychosexual thing they had going on, or if he was usually horrible to her, and she was just pleased he wanted to hang out. Maybe both. 'Fine,' she said. 'Be right down.' He shut the door. 'Sorry about that, Danielle.'

'No problem.'

We finished the email, and then she followed Edward, leaving me alone in the study. I listened to the sound of her footsteps retreating, the quiet of the house. I thought about that morning. I thought about last night. Then I opened a private window in my browser and searched *Westerley Hall + ghost stories*. There seemed to be another stately home in Devon called Westerley Hill, which did Halloween sleepovers for local schools; most of the articles were about them. I couldn't see anything about this house – though I wasn't sure what I was looking for. And yet. Glancing over my shoulder, like Jeannie might burst back in at any moment, the searches began to pour out of me:

Westerley Hall + dead
Westerley Hall + maid
Westerley Hall + dead maid
Westerley Hall + dead maid ghost
Westerley Hall + Yorkshire + haunted
Yorkshire haunted houses Westerley Hall
Yorkshire haunted houses ghost maid Westerley

Of course, I'd looked up the house before I came, finding only the Wikipedia page. There wasn't much else online: a Victorian engraving someone was trying to sell, part of a job lot on eBay; an article from 1999 about the grounds being used for a summer fete, kids from the local village burying a time capsule. No ghosts. Obviously.

Perhaps I should find out more about the history of the house, people who'd lived here? I wasn't sure what I was looking for, or how I'd know if I'd found it. It wasn't like the maid had ever stood over my bed shouting I AM THE GHOST OF MARY MILLER. But five minutes later, I was taking out a free trial to an ancestry website and setting several reminders to cancel it. If I forgot, the website would charge me nearly £200, an absurd amount of money, but I guessed amateur gene- alogists were a captive audience. The problem with the free websites was that they assumed you were looking for family: you could search by surname, first name and place of birth to find out if your great-grandad had been a butcher, baker, candlestick-maker – but if you wanted to search by address, it was harder. I had to pay up, or at least sign up, to be able to look for Westerley.

I started in 1911. The house came up easily, PDFs of scanned-in papers with old-fashioned writing, like my nan's, and lists of names. Jeannie's ancestors were recorded with *landowner* as their job title, other names underneath with *cook*, *butler*, *housemaid*, *gardener*, *under-gardener*, all the people who'd lived in this house or on its grounds over a century ago.

It was weird, and interesting, but it didn't tell me much. Whatever I'd expected to know or feel was absent. No tingles. No signs. No ghostly hands pointing at the screen or writing AVENGE ME on the window in blood. 'This is stupid,' I muttered.

Then I remembered the very real fear I had felt, watching the blankets moving in the other bed, the shape of a person. I could still hear her voice: 'Come on then. Are you getting up?' I shuddered. I could be as arch as I wanted, but for now, I was stuck here, with the prospect of another night like that, or ten, or twenty, stretching ahead of me.

I clicked back through the censuses for 1901, 1891, 1881. Silly that the first list had seemed so long to me when, going backwards, they only got longer, scullery maids and laundry maids and nursery maids. The house must have been shrinking the whole time. Even before the wars, its best days were already behind it. The 1871 census had a funny coincidence, a son of the house named Edward, in his early thirties – though it was probably a family name. Posh people did that, didn't they? I lifted my hand to click back to 1861, then stopped, heart in my mouth. She was at the very bottom:

Sarah Price, 16, housemaid.

An inane thought, but immediate: Price was my mother's maiden name. Hadn't her dad's family been servants? I was sure she'd told me that. I had a creeping, horrible feeling, even though I knew I was being ridiculous. My family weren't from Yorkshire, they were from the Midlands, and there must have been thousands of Prices in service, it was an incredibly common name. It meant nothing, proved nothing. But looking at the carefully handwritten *Sarah Price*, I wondered. She wasn't at Westerley ten years later, and however much the Victorians loved child labour, she wasn't going to be on the 1861 census, working as a maid, when she was six. (I checked, just in case. Obviously not.)

I wondered how long Sarah had spent here, who she was, why she left. It was only a coincidence, the surname, but how funny if we *were* related: it would mean my family had been fetching and carrying for Jeannie's for a full century and a half. Not funny ha-ha.

My phone started ringing. Jeannie. I panicked, shut the laptop as I scrabbled to answer, like she'd be able to see my search history over the phone. 'Everything all right?'

'Danielle,' she said. 'I'm in the kitchen. Would you be an angel and come down? I need help with these bowls and you've got such steady hands!'

I stood up from the desk. 'Sure,' I said. 'Coming.'

*

Down in the kitchen, I ate a sandwich while Jeannie and Edward had their soup upstairs. She came down with their bowls while I was washing up, put them carefully at my elbow. 'We're off out,' she said.

'Have a nice walk.'

'Yes, we'll try and do better today. Pitifully short yesterday. You'd think Edward was made of sugar, the way he acted about the rain, but then, that's your generation, isn't it? Always indoors.'

I turned to look at her. She seemed distracted, searching for something. I thought about protesting, saying, *well, the pandemic*, but then I decided it was fair enough. Phones.

Jeannie found what she was looking for, a scarf she'd thrown over a chair, silk and patterned with swirls. She picked it up and wrapped it around her head, crown to jaw, like a film star from the 1940s. 'Well!' she said, heading back towards the stairs. She stopped before she reached them. 'Oh, Danielle, you wouldn't be a darling, would you, and put some tea things out in the living room in about an hour? Edward has hollow legs, I just know he'll come back absolutely *famished* and in such a rotten temper.'

'Tea things?'

'Nothing grand. Just a pot, some cake, a sandwich or two?'

It took me a moment to catch up – and then, of course, I understood. Strangely, it was Sarah Price I thought of. Sixteen. It must have been heavy, carrying the big trays up all those stairs.

'Danielle?'

Jeannie was looking at me, waiting for me to say yes. Last tug of reluctance in my sternum, last instinct to say that I wouldn't do it, but how could I not? I was in her house – and I had never said no before. It didn't seem possible to start now.

'Fine,' I said quietly.

Jeannie smiled. 'Thanks so much, Danielle. You're an angel.'

She left me alone in the kitchen and I stood for a while at the sink. I don't remember what I thought about. The sound of the front door closing woke me up: I had wet hands, and the water in the sink was cold. I ran it again, finished the washing-up.

This was the logical extension, I supposed, of the tray I'd had in London. Maybe it wasn't that surprising. Besides, for better or worse, making Jeannie happy, comfortable, was my job – and I had done it, now, for nearly half a decade. It was the only thing I was really good at. Most of the time, she didn't even need to ask me for things, I just knew. I was very attentive to her needs.

When I had finished, I went up to the first floor, strolled the empty rooms, glanced through the door of the master bedroom. Already it felt strange, an intrusion, which I suppose it was. Jeannie's brushes were spread out on the dressing table, her perfume. They looked right there, I had to admit. My things had looked messy in comparison. Cheap.

I knew I should use the time while they were out to do something for myself. But what? I stood, oddly dazed, staring out of windows. The time passed anyway. Eventually I realised that they would be back soon – that I needed to go downstairs and get the tea things ready.

I'd been using a one-serving pot for Jeannie's breakfast, it wouldn't be big enough for two. So I took the old china tea service down from the kitchen cupboard, with proper cups and saucers and a big, old pot. I washed out the film of dust inside everything. I filled the kettle, and while it was boiling, took out a large tray and filled it with the china I needed: two teacups, saucers, teaspoons, a sugar bowl, a milk jug, a plate for biscuits and one for the ginger cake Jeannie had brought, which I sliced into smaller pieces. I had done this kind of thing for her meetings back in London, after all. It was easy.

I filled the pot with hot water and held it between my palms, rolling it around until the water warmed each part of the china. I wasn't sure why, it just felt like the right thing to do. Perhaps I'd read about it in a book once. Once the teapot was warm, I poured the water away, spooned in the tea leaves and filled it back up. I was bringing everything upstairs when I heard the front door open.

Jeannie saw me coming up with the tray while she was taking her wet things off in the entrance hall. Edward, behind her, looked sodden and grumpy.

'Danielle! Brilliant. Just in there,' she said, gesturing to the drawing room. I struggled to push the door with my elbow, but got it eventually, laying the tray out on the low table between the uncomfortable-looking sofas. From the paintings, a young, pale Regency woman watched me with an expression that said I Have Since Died of Dysentery. I stood there a moment, uncertain, then took the china off the tray and laid it all on the table. I could bring the tray back later. That seemed best.

Jeannie and Edward came in just as I was about to leave, so I ended up holding the door for them while they entered the room, bickering about Edward's older brother, who was doing something in the city that they both seemed to think was immoral, but for slightly different reasons. Jeannie caught my eye while I stood there. 'Lovely,' she said, smiling at the tea things. 'You can go.'

I nodded, slipped away without another word.

*

All the days that followed were the same. Grey. Raining. The line between Westerley and Leeds stayed down. We fell into a routine, the three of us: in the mornings, I'd work with Jeannie in the study. We found a gardener, made plans, agreed fees. She was getting the patio repaved in the spring. In the afternoons, Jeannie and Edward would go walking while I had lunch alone in the kitchen, then I'd prep the tea things while they were out. My days were longer than they had been: Jeannie liked to start early, and gave me a lot to catch up on in the afternoons. But I didn't mind. Keeping busy seemed to help me sleep through the nights.

In the evenings, the two of them would cook first, eat in the dining room, then leave their plates on the table for me, while they retired to the snug with a brandy – or Jeannie did, while Edward went back to his music. He'd brought several synthesisers up with them and worked in the blue bedroom most of the time. It sounded less dancey than Feather Gamblers' old stuff, more ominous and repetitive, a strange, low underscore that bled through the floors of the house and made me uneasy.

But I was all right. I slept through the nights, most of them, at least. Time passed. Then one morning I woke up, and she was back.

I'd been dreaming about Ben, the last night in his flat. In the dream, we lay side by side in his bed, and his hands were on my face, but he was angry. He wouldn't look at me. When I woke alone at Westerley, I was disorientated. It was a few moments before I realised where I was – before I saw her.

It was the same as before, dressing in the dawn light, only this time, I could move. A finger, an arm, a hand. If I could move, I could get up. If I could get up, I could reach her. I don't know why I wanted to do these things. Dream logic. But I did. It was hard, like waking from an operation, limbs heavy as I dragged myself out of bed. Slow. Dazed. The maid turned to look at me. 'Careful,' she said, and I dropped.

I woke on the floor with a bitter headache and a strange taste in my mouth. Daylight, morning, and everything ached. But there was no going back to bed. My alarm was ringing, had been ringing, I realised, for some time – I must have been quite deeply asleep on the floor. Now, if I wasn't careful, I was going to be late for work.

I found Jeannie waiting for me in the study. 'Sorry,' I said. I was holding a cup of tea, but hadn't been able to face breakfast, my stomach still roiling with bad dreams.

'That's okay,' Jeannie said, without much inflection. She was standing at the window, and gestured to my usual place, the chair closest to the door. 'Sit down.'

Something was wrong in the room, something had changed. But I did as I was told and slid into the chair, taking my laptop out. 'Okay,' I said. 'I'm ready. Wait. Is it the desk?'

'Is what the desk?'

I paused, staring. 'Something's different.'

Jeannie laughed. 'No,' she said.

It was, though. Nigel's desk had been a big oak monstrosity, but this was smaller and more delicate. A writing desk for the woman of the house, where she'd sit to do her letters, organise the menu. It was elegant, classical, very refined. 'This desk wasn't here yesterday.'

Jeannie looked at me, then came round to my chair, laid a palm against my forehead. 'Are you feeling all right?' she said. 'You're not warm.'

'No, I'm okay. Just tired. Are you sure—'

'This desk,' Jeannie interrupted. 'Was my grandmother's. I promise, it has always been here.'

I wondered if I was dreaming. But everything felt real. The padded leather chair against my back. The smell of dust, old wood, laundry. Grey sky outside the window. My half-drunk cup of tea was warm in my hand, and my mouth was dry and sticky, tasted of tannins, because I'd left the teabag in too long. This was real, all of it, it had to be. I was here, inside my body, behind my eyeballs, where I always was.

'Danielle, are you sure you're okay?'

'Yes,' I said. 'Sorry, I just had some – bad dreams.'

Jeannie sat down across the desk. 'Sorry to hear that,' she said. 'I sometimes think the whole day after a nightmare feels strange.'

'Yes,' I said. 'It's such an old house. And,' speaking slowly, 'and nobody says, do they, that it's haunted?'

Jeannie looked at me. Then she began to laugh. 'Danielle!' she said. 'I've always thought of you as such a *sensible* girl.'

I tried to laugh too.

'Well, anyway,' she said, rolling the sleeves of her cardigan up. 'If you're feeling better, we ought to get on.'

I wasn't feeling better; I wondered where she'd got that impression. But I was ready to work. We did the

Hodgepodge emails first – there weren't many – and soon we were on to the timings of the gardener's visit next week; a man popping in to look at the Aga. The work of Westerley spread around us, familiar and safe.

Jeannie's reaction had seemed sincere enough. You wouldn't laugh like that if there was some awful family secret you were hiding, a dead girl in a box. But I didn't feel relieved. I was disappointed. If she'd lowered her voice, leaned towards me with her face in shadows, *oh God, tell me, what have you seen?* then, yes, I would have been frightened, but it would have been a relief, too. Knowing for sure that it wasn't all in my head. I wouldn't have felt so alone.

Perhaps if I told someone, anyone, I would feel better. Perhaps I just needed to talk. Besides, Jeannie hadn't lived at Westerley for forty years – there could easily be stories she'd forgotten, or not been told. I would ask somebody else. I knew just the man.

*

'Mitch,' I said. 'How's it going?'

Mitch was hunched over his paper in the corner of the bar, only a third of a pint left in his glass. When he heard my voice, he looked up, eyes narrowing like a mole's, struggling to focus. I wondered how drunk he was.

It was mid-evening; I'd foregone my usual kitchen dinner to walk to The Hart's Salvation as soon as I could get away from work. The rain had finally stopped, leaving a bright, clear night that felt like winter.

'Oh!' he said, seeming to recognise me at last. 'Danielle, wasn't it? Do you want to sit down?'

I didn't: I was agitated, jittery, having had a lot of caffeine and not a lot to eat that day, but it felt rude to say no. I forced myself into the chair opposite. 'Thanks.'

'So what can I do you for?'

Great. Cut to the chase. Good man, Mitch. 'When we met,' I said, 'you seemed like you were going to tell me something – a ghost story about Westerley. Could you tell me now?'

'Ahh.' Mitch grinned like an evil portent. 'Spooking yourself out, all alone in that big house, are you?'

I didn't have the heart to explain that I was less alone, but somehow more 'spooked out' than ever. 'I'm not scared,' I lied. 'I just think it's interesting.'

Mitch looked at me, eyes narrowed, saying nothing.

'You do remember, don't you?'

He nodded. 'Yes, I remember. Ted stopped me telling you.'

My eyes flicked towards the bar, then back to Mitch. Ted wasn't in today. I nodded.

'Well,' he said. 'I'm happy to repeat what little I've heard.' He took a tin out of his pocket and began rolling a cigarette, fingertips yellow on the paper. 'Want one?'

I shook my head.

'Places that old, there's always stories, aren't there? Westerley's all right, not a bad family, not as far as people say, anyway. That's not to say they made their money in good ways. That kind of money, those kinds of times, you couldn't, could you? Anyway. There's not many stories about Westerley. But there is one.' He flicked his tongue across the paper, dabbing, and then rolled. 'Come out with me so I can smoke this, will you?'

We headed through the pub to the beer garden at the back. Mitch was definitely pissed, but not egregiously so – just enough to enjoy having an audience, want to draw it out. As we walked, I wondered what I was about to hear. A maid, trapped in the kitchens, or up in the attic where I slept. Servants slept in attics, didn't they? It made sense. A girl my age, younger, homesick, or worse. Beaten. Killed in a fire. I'd read enough novels to be able to fill in the blanks. Sarah Price, sixteen, who wasn't on the census ten years later.

Mitch held the door for me. I hadn't been out to the beer garden before; it was small and scrubby, with a couple of picnic tables, grass growing between the paving slabs. Maybe it looked better in the sun. I stood next to Mitch as he lit up. 'So the story runs that there was this woman,' he said. 'Turn of the century.'

I braced myself. 'Right.'

'Last one, obviously – century, I mean. Victorian times. She's the daughter of the house, so her whole job is to marry, get a good husband, bit of money in. She nets some duke or other – only she gets left at the altar. He'd got some other girl in the family way. And this lady, she's heartbroken, so what does she do?' He

took a big drag of the cigarette and looked at me signi-
ficantly. 'Throws herself in the river. Stones sewn into
her dress, and – poof.' Mitch blew the smoke out
through his nose, voice tight. 'Course, the river's dried,
these days it's more of a stream, at the bottom of
Thornley Patch . . . They say her spirit stalks the halls,
dripping, calling the name of the fella that threw her
over. A woman in white, or a grey lady or – you know.
That sort of thing.'

I blinked. 'No,' I said. 'That's here. A woman in white,
that's the pub, you already told me that one.'

'Did I?' Mitch laughed. 'That's most places, love.
Ghostly women pining away. I think it's cos you can
hear their dresses: swish, swish.' He did a surprisingly
delicate mime. 'That's why they make better ghosts.
Because you can hear them, can't you? Their dresses,
moving around.'

I felt like I'd been exposed to a gas leak. 'No. I mean,
this place and Westerley, it's the same story. A woman
getting left and then killing herself. It's bollocks.'

Mitch looked offended. 'Is not.'

'They're just – tropes.'

'This pub was nearly on *Most Haunted*.'

'That's – it wouldn't even be a good story if they'd
actually been on it, Mitch. Nearly on – nearly! Nearly on
Most Haunted. Oh my God. That is so shit.' I started to
laugh, harder than I meant to. I sat on one of the benches,
covered my face with my hands.

Mitch sat opposite me. 'Are you all right?'

'Yeah,' I said. 'No. I don't know. Go on then,' I nodded at his cigarette, 'I will have one, please. I just thought . . . aren't there any stories about a maid? From Westerley.'

'A ghost maid?' The fresh air seemed to have sobered him up. He began rolling me a cigarette with one hand while smoking with the other, leaning forwards to flick ash into an empty pint glass. 'You don't get 'em.'

'What do you mean, "don't get them"?'

'Well, what I mean is . . . Do you believe in ghosts, Danielle?'

A lad came out to the beer garden with a tray of pints, looking not quite old enough to get served. His friends, waiting on a table at the back, cheered, and he flushed red to the roots of his hair. I tried to ignore them.

Mitch's question had surprised me, which was stupid, because it was exactly what I'd been wondering myself. 'I don't know,' I said slowly. 'I think places can . . . feel a certain way? If something happens there.' Was that what I thought? I wasn't sure anymore. A month ago, I would have just said no.

'Like stone tape theory.'

'What's that?'

'Just what you said, really. The idea that when big, awful things happen, the bricks and mortar sort of record it. Store it up. And replay it later, like a tape machine.' Mitch's lined, weather-beaten face split into a grin. 'You're probably too young to remember those. I mean, like one of your – you know. An iPod.'

I was too tired to laugh anymore, though I dimly registered that this was funny, iPods not being much more modern than tape players. I rubbed my face with one hand. 'Sure,' I said. 'Like that, I guess. And you?'

'What about me?'

'Do you believe in ghosts?'

Mitch shrugged, rather decorously. 'I don't know. They're good stories, aren't they? That's what I think. They tell us what we value, what we think about the world. They promise things – a kind of immortality. Life after death. And these big houses . . . well, they have to have a ghost story. Connection to a lost world, status – it's marketing. That's why none of the ghosts are maids, isn't it?' I must have looked blank, because Mitch sighed. 'You visit a big stately home, there's a ghost story, you want it to be about one of the people in the portraits, don't you? Someone that mattered.'

I wasn't sure what to say. Mitch had finished rolling, held the cigarette out to me. 'There you are. Sorry I wasn't much use. Shall I get the drinks in?'

*

It was clear and cold, the waxing moon nearly full, as I set off back to Westerley. I was hoping the walk over the fields would sober me up. I was hungry, and quite drunk. I'd stayed out longer than planned, Mitch chain-smoking his way through the time normal humans ate dinner, though at least I'd stopped at one borrowed roll-up.

He was an interesting man who'd done a lot of different jobs: teacher, handyman, three marriages, travelled all over the world before he washed up here. He seemed intrigued by how I'd ended up at Westerley, and I tried to give enough detail to make the story fun without embroiling him in my personal life. He didn't know Jeannie, but he'd come across her brother in the pub, and said he was a prick; I was pleased, even though I'd never met Nigel and had no reason to dislike him.

My phone buzzed in my pocket: voice note from Anita. It seemed so long since I'd heard from anyone. I played it, her voice echoing strangely in the dark field.

'Hi babe. Just going into the cinema but wanted to send this first. Um. I've sent you lots of messages but I'm not really hearing much and I'm worried our chat the other day has freaked you out, so, yeah. Don't be mad at me. Have you called Ben? I think you guys should talk. Okay, love you. Bye.'

I played it again, twice, just to hear her voice. What did she mean, she'd sent me lots of messages? I hadn't heard from her in ages. And why would I be freaked out? What chat? There was a pain in my head, a pressure, and: the kitchen. I'd stood in the kitchen, the last night I spoke to Anita. Her new enemy at work, the guy that wouldn't talk. But after that, it was all blank space. Headaches. I remembered how I'd woken on top of the covers, lost time, been too unsettled, too embarrassed to ask her what we talked about. But now I nudged a little, and Anita's voice was in my ear, her laughter, 'Ben had that crush on you for ages, it was a whole will-they-won't-they thing, wasn't it?'

I kept walking. One foot in front of another in the darkness. The night had that quality of beauty everything has when you're a little drunker than you meant to be. I was alone out here, and free, and almost had it; like trying to remember a dream, the way images slipped through your fingers, but: yes. The stairs. The hall. I'd been pacing, shocked, I'd heard the knocking from the locked room, like a nightmare. But real. Real, of course; I knew that, because it had happened again. Not that I wanted to think about any of that now, the house, the maid – for the moment, at least, I no longer cared. I only cared about remembering what Anita had told me. Her conversation with Ben, years ago, how she'd warned him off. Yes. Because I'd thought for weeks that Ben had been appalled. I thought he'd seen the longing in my face that night, known I wanted him to kiss me, that he'd been disgusted, angry with me for betraying our friendship. I thought he'd worked everything out and begun avoiding me. But the things Anita had said . . .

Maybe I had got the whole thing wrong. Maybe Ben really had wanted to kiss me. Maybe I was the one who'd pulled away, run off, stopped calling.

I took my phone out, flicked through my contacts, pressed the button. It rang for a long time.

'Hi,' said Ben's voice. 'You're through to Ben Wright. I'm not around right now, so leave a message, and I'll get back to you.'

What could I say? My mind was as clear and empty as the winter sky. My mouth began moving on its own.

'Ben, I miss you. I don't really know what's going on with us. We had that stupid fight and maybe you're still angry with me, or maybe you're not, maybe I've just been weird, because of – because the night before I went, I – but look, this is – this is shit, Ben, I've been shit and this is shit.' Going well so far. I sighed, stopped walking, covered my face with my hand.

'Jeannie's here,' I said. 'She's come up, and she – she's living in the house with me, which is weird, actually, and – and I can't drive, so I'm just stuck there, all the time, and I don't – feel – well? Like I'm not sleeping well.'

I was beginning to wonder if this was a bad idea. 'Look,' I ploughed on, 'I don't know why, I don't know why I thought it, but I did, I thought you were going to kiss me, and I want – I wanted – God! This is so stupid! Will you just, I think we need to have a real conversation, in person, and I can't come to London because I can't fucking drive, so you'll just have to – yeah, I think you should, can you come and get me, please? Because I hate it, okay, I hate it here, so just. Yeah. Okay then. Bye.'

I hung up my phone and thought about throwing it into a hedge, or down a well, somewhere I could never get it back. I was full of adrenaline, like I'd been running from something. Worse than I'd felt when I thought someone was robbing the house, much worse. I shoved my phone in my pocket and started walking again, quickly, as if I was trying to escape from something.

What had I said? Had I apologised? Explained myself? I wasn't sure. I also wasn't sure why I'd left a *voicemail*, like someone in the 2000s, instead of texting, or voice noting, or doing anything I could *delete*. By the time I reached the outskirts of the house, I'd given up, taken my phone back out, begun writing a text:

Don't listen to my stupid voicemail lol sorry bit tired and emotional but can we chat soon?

I stood in the entrance hall, toeing off my shoes. Deleted the message. Tried again.

Just got a bit drunk and lonely PLEASE don't listen to that voicemail lollll call you tomorrow?

I deleted this one too, thinking it might be worse than the first, then wasn't sure if I'd deleted the message for everyone, or just myself. I was stood wondering exactly that when somebody said, 'Wow.'

I looked up. Edward was leaning against the drawing room door, watching me. 'You look spaced out,' he said. 'Like you need a drink.'

I stared back. In days of moving around inside the same house, he'd barely spoken to me. Anyway, he was wrong: I'd definitely had enough.

'I'm okay,' I said. 'But thanks.'

Edward snorted, quite wetly, like the air coming out of a particularly damp balloon. 'Don't believe you,' he said. 'Come on.' He went back into the drawing room. The door swung shut behind him.

I hung up my coat, thought about going down to the kitchen to make food. I could hear someone moving around on the floor above: Jeannie must be in her bedroom. If I went downstairs and had dinner, everything would be better, except that I would be staring at my phone from now until I passed out, waiting to hear from Ben. The lure of another drink was strong.

In the drawing room, Edward was sprawled on one of the uncomfortable sofas and was, I thought, quite drunk. He was refilling his glass unsteadily from a decanter of amber liquid. A fire burned in the grate.

'Good girl,' he said, as I crossed the room. 'Come sit by me.' I tried to hide my wince. But Edward didn't notice, too busy reaching across the low table to fill a second glass. I wondered where it had come from. Had he been waiting for me? Or perhaps he'd thought his mother might join him. Whatever.

I took the drink and sat on the sofa, as far away as I could. 'Thanks.'

'Go on then,' he said. 'Tell me about yourself.'

I was surprised by the sudden interest, but not charmed. If Edward had approached me in a bar, sat beside me like this with his legs absurdly spread, taking up so much space, I would have made my excuses and left. But I was in his house. I worked for his mother. 'Tell you what?'

He shrugged, smiled. Definitely drunk. 'I dunno. We're living in this place together and I barely know the first thing about you. I don't even know your last name.'

'It's MacKinnon.'

'MacKinnon?' It sounded absurd in his mouth, all the wrong vowels. 'Scottish, is it?'

'My dad's from Glasgow.'

'Cool. I like the Scots.' He raised his whisky glass to me, as if to illustrate his point. 'Chin-chin.'

'Chin-chin,' I repeated, because I'd seen it in films, and knew you had to say it back. The whisky tasted peaty, expensive, so I told him it was nice. It turned out he knew a lot about whisky. He began talking about the difference between single and blended malts, the ages of different casks, the angel's share, all that stuff. I'd gone to Edinburgh once to see Ben in a Fringe show with friends from uni. When it finished, we all went up the country for a few days, did a distillery tour, so I knew everything Edward was saying, but I didn't stop him. It was easier to let him talk.

I drank my whisky quietly, checked my phone. Ben hadn't seen his messages since 9 p.m. Could be working a shift at The Prince; if so, he wouldn't see it till midnight.

'I've got a friend who's a collector,' Edward went on. 'He hooks me up. Macallan Reds, the whole thing, I swear to you he's got them all, a forty, a fifty, a sixty … Too rich for my blood, though. I'm a musician, so, you know, bit outside my price range.'

'Yeah,' I said. 'I mean, I know you're a musician.'

Edward shrugged, false-modest. 'I guess you've heard me fooling around up there.'

'Actually, I've seen your band.'

He lit up immediately. 'Wow,' he said, then schooled his glowing face into a mock frown. 'So what the hell, MacKinnon, what's the deal? You some kind of stalker?'

I smiled, like it was a joke we were sharing. Surnames. So public school. I held out my glass while I said, 'Your mum made us – I mean, Jeannie, she – she organised a kind of work trip to that festival you played. The one in Victoria Park.'

'Oh, wow, sure,' Edward said, refilling my drink. 'Yeah, that was a good one. Fun. Did you have fun?'

I remembered drinking a warm pint in the sunshine, very slowly, because I didn't want to embarrass myself in front of my boss. The way Jeannie waved and jumped when they took to the stage. It was sweet. She was proud of him. 'Yeah,' I said politely. 'Yeah, it was great.'

'Yeah,' Edward repeated. 'You know, I always knew I wanted to be a musician.'

'Really.'

'It's hard. Like obviously it's a lot of work. But I love it. I love what I do. You know?'

I knew he made little to no money, because Jeannie was always complaining about it. I hadn't enjoyed Edward's band, but the music industry seemed badly paid and unstable, so I had some sympathy for him – though it also seemed unfair that he was able to keep ploughing badly on, earning nothing, living with Jeannie, when other, better musicians had probably had to give up and work in a bank. It made me think of Ben, who was so talented and had so little time to do the things he was good at. All the pub work and the call centres, all the shame. *I don't know why I live in this stupid way*, he'd said. Edward probably never felt like that. He just did what he did. He didn't have to keep justifying it to himself, weighing it against the ghost of a more stable life.

Man, I wanted to talk to Ben. I wished he'd see his stupid phone and call me already. I didn't care if he was angry, I didn't even care if he laughed at me, I just missed him.

'It's streaming,' Edward was saying. 'Streaming's kind of our bread and butter so I can't really slag it, like, it's given us a lot, we're an internet-age band, you know? But the numbers don't add up, MacKinnon, let me tell you. They do not add up.'

Edward, I realised, was still talking, and I'd nearly finished my second whisky. God I was tired. And drunk. And hungry. I sat back on the sofa, pushing myself into the corner as I tried to focus on Jeannie's son and the boring things he was saying. Something about the magic of creation. How alive it made him feel. 'That's amazing,' I said, or thought I did.

Edward had been edging closer to me on the sofa the whole time, and as I pulled my jumper off – he'd stoked the fire too high, the room was boiling – I saw his eyes flick to my cleavage, and felt a kind of full-body exhaustion. Though I also, briefly, considered how much it would piss Jeannie off if I fucked her son. It wouldn't be worth it. But it would be funny.

'So what do you do?' he asked.

I snorted. 'I work for your mum,' I said, more unkindly than I'd meant to. But I also thought: cop on, I'm not sending emails all day for my health, am I?

Edward rolled his eyes, nudged my shoulder with his own. 'I know that, you silly prick,' he said, surprising a laugh out of me. 'I mean, what do you really do?'

'What do you mean?'

'I mean, a job like that, you must be working towards something else. You can't want to make coffee for my mum forever. Because you seem quite clever, so . . . ?'

I wasn't sure what to say. My mouth opened, then closed.

'You look pissed off. What did I say?'

'I'm not,' I said quickly, though I wasn't sure if I was or not. I imagined myself saying *I actually don't know what I want to do*, and of course I could see what would happen after that. How Edward would write me off as somebody without an inner life, retract the limited beam of his attention, his interest in me, and maybe that would be fine, because I knew what his interest meant and I didn't want it, but still – it made me angry. The thought of being dismissed as a person just because of how I made my money. Just because I had to make money at all. Fuck him. Then I wondered how I could be angry, when I judged myself for it so harshly. Didn't I lie to strangers at parties and hate that I was 'only' Jeannie's assistant? Like that meant anything real, like it mattered.

I didn't need to tell Edward what I did to know what he thought of me. The world was full of Edwards. It was made by them, for them, and the things they thought about me were already inside of me: they were the things I thought about myself. I believed the work I did all day made me matter less, and the world said, *Yeah, obviously.* And didn't I think that I deserved it? And didn't I sometimes think, when Jeannie ordered me around, that I was in my right place?

'Hello?' said Edward.

I'd been quiet too long. 'Oh, yeah,' I said. 'I'm actually, uh. I'm an actor.'

'Wow,' he said. 'Acting's cool. Wouldn't have expected that.'

I hadn't expected it either, but I was still slightly offended. 'Why not?'

He shrugged. 'I don't know, most of the actresses I know are just like, *super* thin. But it's cool if you haven't let that whole thing trap you.'

I started laughing. 'Okay,' I said. 'Sure.' I finished my drink, put the glass down, bracing myself to stand up and leave. But Edward was straight in, pouring another, letting his arm brush against mine as he did it. He was bored, I guess, and I was there. And I belonged to his mum, to the house. Maybe he just thought I came free with the package.

'No, look, I'm fine actually, thanks,' I said, gesturing to the whisky, but he'd already filled my glass.

'Come on, be fun,' he said. 'It's Thursday night. Thursday's the new Friday.'

Already? Christ. How long had I been in the attic?

'Go on then,' he said. 'How you liking the house?'

I should go. I knew I should. But I was so tired, and already holding my drink, and then I found myself saying Westerley was *so* beautiful in such a stupid, annoying, museum-visitor voice that I thought, *Jesus Christ, Danielle.* Anyway, I didn't have to finish the drink to leave, did I? I hadn't asked for it.

Edward told me some things about the house, when it was built, that I already knew from Wikipedia, and meanwhile I moved to check my phone, and realised it wasn't there. It must have slipped between the sofa cushions. I tried to search for it discreetly.

He'd stopped talking. I cast around for something to say. 'Did – did you grow up here?'

Edward laughed. 'God, no. Mum did. But I'm, you know, a London boy. From ends.' He did a gesture with his hand that I immediately tried to memorise, so I could do an impression later.

'Right,' I said.

'I like it though. We've always come up here for like, summers and stuff, sometimes Christmases. I didn't board, so there was just home and here.'

'Yeah,' I said. Still no sign of the phone.

'I'm glad you like it too. The house. I mean, it's good you're here. If it was just me and Mum, I'd go crazy.' He put a hand on my leg, a little above my knee. I saw a panic muscle twitch through my jeans.

'Ah,' I said. 'Look. No. Sorry, but . . .'

Edward didn't take his hand away. He was watching me intently, eyes slightly unfocused. 'Don't tell me you're not interested,' he said. 'I've seen how you look at me.'

I tried not to laugh. It was important to strike the right balance between friendliness and being firm. I felt irritated with myself for accepting the drink at all. 'I'm sorry,' I said again. 'I, uh – I'm seeing someone.'

Edward squinted at me. 'I thought you just split up with your boyfriend. Isn't that why you're here? Mum said you're like, homeless. She said you cried about it.'

Could I convince myself this was funny and not humiliating? At least I was drunk, so it sort of bounced off. 'Yeah, look,' I said, too loudly. 'That's true. We split up. But we – we actually might get back together.' Why did I always lie in such a loud voice? Who, at the back, was I projecting for? 'We've been together years. We've been texting. It's really complicated, so I can't just . . .'

'No, no, sure,' he said. He looked at me, then at his hand, which was still on my leg, which had remained on my leg this whole time, holding my thigh too tightly, higher up than I was comfortable with.

Edward took his hand away. I exhaled.

'You're not really my type anyway,' he said.

I laughed. 'Well, no, sure.' I thought about trying to high-five him, or shake hands. Could I push this somewhere pally, fun, before he started to feel rejected? God, I was drunk. I wished he'd just go to bed already, so I could search for my phone properly. What a stupid situation. No such thing as a free drink.

'I mean, obviously,' he added.

I'd lost the thread a bit. 'Obviously?'

'Obviously we're not compatible.'

'Sure,' I repeated. There was an edge to his voice that was unsettling.

'Do you want to know why?'

'Why what?'

'Why we're not,' his eyes were unfocused, struggling to land on me, '*compatible*.' He spelled out every syllable. I said nothing. I just watched him, waiting.

Then he pointed at himself, and said, 'Upstairs.' Then he pointed at me, and said, 'Downstairs.' Then at him, and said, 'Downton.' At me, and said, 'Abbey.' Him, and said, 'Wooster.' Me, and said, 'Jeeves.' Then he laughed. It was a big, showy, full-throated laugh. Braying. I sat still, watching him.

'Oh come on,' he said, seeing my face. 'It's a joke, Jesus. Like, you work for my mum, right? So you're the staff. I was *joking*.'

I tried to smile, but I wasn't sure what my face was doing. He kept laughing as he stood up, squeezed my leg again, said goodnight, left. I think I said, Yeah. I think I said, You sleep well too. Maybe I even laughed. I don't know. But I stayed there a long time after he went, breathing, listening to the house settle around me. I knew I had to get up, eat, find my phone, go to bed, but I couldn't make myself do it, not yet. I couldn't make myself do anything. I was so tired.

*

The drawing room was pink in the dawn light coming through the open curtains – and of course, she was there. The maid knelt in the fireplace, sweeping the ashes away with a long-handled brush. She was too absorbed in her task to notice I was awake. I didn't try to get up this time. I just watched her.

When I woke again, it was later, the room full of sickly grey light. I was still on the sofa in the drawing room: I must have passed out instead of going to bed. I felt dreadful, queasy, and very cold. I reached for my phone to check the time, but it wasn't in my pockets or on the table. I remembered groping around for it last night. Somehow, just sitting here, I had lost it.

I made myself get up, pull the sofa cushions out, feeling a lurch in my stomach as the various different stages of the evening returned to me. My phone wasn't there, but maybe I'd never had it on the couch? I must be getting confused.

It would have to wait. I needed to warm up, have a bath, eat something. Downstairs in the kitchen, the wall clock said it was 6.45 a.m., a time I rarely saw by choice. The end of the evening was fuzzy. I hoped I hadn't fallen asleep before Edward went upstairs, although I tried to convince myself that I didn't care either way. He'd been hammered, would probably remember less than me. He might even be embarrassed, apologetic, in the cold light of day.

I put some bread in to toast and was opening the cutlery drawer when I saw the stains on my palm. I turned my empty hands over and back again: both were ash-black, like I'd been messing about in the fireplaces. I remembered the maid in my dream, the intensity of her focus.

Had I been sleepwalking? Had I imagined her, when really I was the one kneeling in the fireplace? Surely I hadn't moved: I'd sat on the couch last night and woken in the exact same place this morning.

I ran the taps as hot as they'd go, scrubbed my palms with soap. I ate my toast, felt worse, went upstairs to run a bath. While it was filling, I came back to the entrance hall, checked again for my phone. It wasn't on the side, under the couch, in my bag. At the front door, I retraced my steps. I'd definitely brought it home: I remembered standing here, taking my shoes off, sending and deleting messages to Ben—

Jolt of horror. The voicemail, the fucking voicemail, God. But there was no time now to worry about what I'd said, or what he thought. I pushed it all down. In the bathroom, I took off the clothes I'd slept in and stood, shivering, looking out of the windows. It was going to be one of those days where the sun didn't really come up. No phone anywhere, and even though I'd scrubbed and scrubbed, my empty palms were black with soot.

*

Jeannie talked and I typed while underneath it all, my hangover whirred. I tried to comfort myself by thinking how much worse I'd feel if I'd slept with Edward. It was weird enough, to be honest, being here in the study and remembering his hand on my leg, where I very much did not want it to be. Embarrassing, even though I hadn't done anything wrong.

'And then just wish them lots of love,' Jeannie said, without turning around. She was posed artfully at the window, contemplating the view, in a way that seemed self-conscious, like a portrait: *the lady of the house surveys the grounds.*

'Done,' I said, and pressed send.

'Anything else we should answer?'

'Um,' I said. I made a show of scanning through Jeannie's inbox, while actually flicking back to my own. I was relieved to see a reply from Anita already. I'd emailed her that morning, to say I hadn't been getting her messages, that I was sorry for the radio silence, missed her – and also that I'd lost my phone in the house somehow, so could she please tell people I wasn't dead.

Oh no babe that is mad!! I'll text your mum / Ben / uni group chat but lmk if there's anyone else you want me to message? Just off to spin class before work but I have a spare phone at home so if you send me your address I can post it to you, big love Anita xxx

I was glad she was going to tell Ben even though I hadn't been able to face asking about him specifically, asking her to tell him, because just typing his name had made me feel sick. I wished I had a less vivid imagination, couldn't picture him so clearly, walking home from a shift at The Prince last night, listening to my voicemail with an expression of horror and disgust. That was the hangover talking, of course – but it was very persuasive.

'Danielle?'

'Yes, sorry, just reading.' I flicked back to Jeannie's emails. There was a new one from a name I vaguely recognised. 'Who's Howard Markham? Isn't he an MP?'

'Oh, lovely Howard,' she cooed. 'Has he written me a note?'

'"Dear Mopsy,"' I read aloud, trying not to let the second-hand embarrassment show in my voice. The email said he would be passing through London soon for a big vote, and he'd love to catch up over lunch. I remembered him now, a Tory MP from my childhood who'd faded into obscurity after losing a leadership bid. He was in the Lords now.

'How do you know Howard Markham?' I asked.

Jeannie laughed. 'He was at school with Nigel! We had a little,' she fluttered her fingers, vaguely, 'but years ago and not at all serious. He's a lovely man. Actually, we should put him on the list, shouldn't we? For a panel or something.' I must have looked blank because Jeannie went on, 'You know. A talk, or a debate. At Hodgepodge.' Of course. Hodgepodge, where we had both worked for many years, a place I would definitely never forget existed. 'Are you feeling all right, Danielle?'

It had been hard to keep track, recently. So much of the work we did together was the house, the grounds, the handymen. Foliage. Pipes. I pulled my hair back, tied it into a tight, decisive ponytail.

'Yes,' I said. 'Sorry, Jeannie. I haven't been sleeping well, that's all.' I opened the document where we kept a list of Jeannie's contacts: actors, writers, speakers, politicians, old friends. I added Howard Markham's name. 'Do you want to reply now?'

I glanced at Jeannie, who looking at me strangely. 'Was it a late night?' she said, false-casual, and my stomach turned over. She knew. Or suspected. Not that I'd done anything – I hadn't done anything – but surely she was talking about Edward?

'Not that late,' I said, trying for breezy, relaxed; I sounded like someone had died.

'Well, I heard you get in,' she said dryly. 'And it was fairly late. Were you doing anything nice?'

'Just the – The Hart's Salvation.'

Jeannie scoffed. 'That old place? I can't believe it's still open. Nigel used to go at Christmas, when we were teenagers.'

My pulse began to settle. I was being paranoid – she suspected me of being hungover, not of staying up with her son. Not – whatever. His hand on my leg. 'It's quite nice now,' I managed to say. 'It's a gastropub. The food's good.' It felt sensible to imply I'd eaten dinner. I wished I had.

'Hmm,' said Jeannie, eyes narrowed. 'Well, no more staying out on school nights, all right? I need you bright-eyed and bushy-tailed.'

I'd never been in a situation before where my boss knew what time I went to bed, and I didn't like it. Some part of me wanted to say that it was my life, my time, my right to roll in at one in the morning if I wanted to. But the need to get out of this conversation was stronger. If she'd heard me get in, she must have heard Edward offer me a drink, our voices, and I would do anything to avoid discussing last night. Nobody wants to tell their boss her son is a sex case.

'No,' I said. 'Fine. Of course. Shall we – do you want to get back to Howard?'

'Yes,' she said. I scrubbed a hand over my face, sat up straighter, put my fingers to the keys as she began to dictate.

*

While I was washing up from lunch, I looked out of the high windows at the grounds. Already the sky had begun to darken; the days were so short now, they felt barely-there. Soon, it would be night again. A shudder of something ran through me and at that moment, Edward came downstairs. He was unshaven, dishevelled, said nothing as he crossed the room to the fridge. I don't know what I'd been expecting. An apology, maybe; friendliness. Maybe he was only friendly when he was drunk.

I was stuck at the sink, scrubbing butter from one of the plates in my pink rubber gloves. He took a can of something from the fridge and started back towards the stairs.

'Edward,' I said. I pulled my hands from the water with such speed that it was loud in the quiet kitchen, and he looked faintly surprised, like he'd just noticed I was there. 'Sorry,' I said. 'I meant to ask. Last night, did you, when we – did you maybe take my phone? Like, by mistake.'

It was all I could think of. I was sure I'd had it on the couch, remembered looking at it, refreshing my messages. Edward stared as if he knew my face was familiar, but couldn't place me.

'No?' he said slowly. 'Why would I do that?'

I felt stupid. 'I don't know. If you thought it was yours, you might have ... I thought you might have picked it up by mistake.' We looked at each other. 'I don't know,' I said again.

'You're a weird one, MacKinnon.' He shrugged, smiled. 'Sorry. Haven't seen it.'

Then he went out, leaving me alone in the kitchen. I wondered which version of him I would get tonight: this one, disinterested, barely talking, or the one I'd had last night, pouring whisky down my throat and propositioning me.

I wasn't going to be here to find out.

It was a strange feeling, like waking up from a dream: why had I stopped trying to leave? I hadn't even looked the trains up for days. Like I'd given up.

Well, I was awake now, and I was going back to London. I couldn't ask Jeannie for a lift without explaining a lot of not-great things, but what about Mrs Waddingham? Lovely Mrs Waddingham, who'd brought me here, and run me round, and taught me how to make a fire. She was kind. If I threw myself on her mercy, she would be happy to help, I was sure. She'd drive me wherever I wanted to go. Maybe it was an imposition, but I wanted to leave too much to feel guilty. She wouldn't mind. I'd send flowers.

I went to the cupboard under the stairs where they kept the landline, found her number on the corkboard. It rang a long time before I heard her voice.

'Hello, you've reached David and Helen Waddingham. We're not here at the moment but please leave a message.'

For a moment, I was too surprised that she had a first name to say anything. 'Er – hi, sorry, it's me. It's Danielle. Um. My phone got lost and I'm wondering if you can give me a lift. I need to get to the train station, or – somewhere – I need to get back to London. Could you call me back, please? Thanks so much.' Then I hung up too heavily, sound echoing in the empty kitchen.

For a while I stood there, waiting, in case she called straight back. I stared at the handset. When it didn't ring, I told myself that was fine. She might be anywhere – out for lunch, at the shops, down the garden – and would hear my message in an hour or two, call back then. Or maybe she would just turn up to fetch me? I'd see her car in the drive and that would be it. Freedom. For a moment I stood in the cupboard and closed my eyes, let myself picture it.

Then I went out and shut the door behind me. I couldn't just stand around all day. I had work to do.

*

I took out the china tea service, warmed the pot and then the cups. I sliced the cake, put the slices on the plates, the plates on the tray. My hands moved of their own accord, the actions second nature now. I spooned tea into the pot. I fetched the milk jug, sugar. Poured the boiling water. Carried everything upstairs.

In the drawing room, Edward and Jeannie sat talking. She looked windblown from their walk, her hair flyaway, and was trying to clip it back. Edward lounged beside his mother, insouciant, half his attention on his phone.

'Mama always gave such lovely parties when I was young,' Jeannie was saying. 'Thank you, Danielle, pop down there.' She turned back to Edward. 'And if we're going to be up here anyway, we might as well put something together.'

'No, sure. What you thinking for the music?'

'We'll probably want something a little more traditional than your tastes, darling.' I crouched by the low table, taking things off the tray. The pot, the sugar, the milk, the cups. Jeannie was watching me. 'I don't know. I think it always was at the beginning of Advent. So it would be nice, a tradition.'

'How many people?' he said.

'Well, a lot of the families we knew locally have moved away, but perhaps if we wrote to them, they'd come back. And there's a school not too far from here. We could ask the children. What do you think?'

I realised she was talking to me. I'd finished unloading my tray, stood to leave. 'About what, sorry?'

'A party!' Jeannie cried. 'For Christmas – the first Saturday of Advent. There always used to be such lovely parties here, I think the old place misses them . . .' Edward rolled his eyes at this, but said nothing, and Jeannie didn't notice. 'Well?'

They were looking at me, waiting for an answer. But I would be gone long before any party. 'I like Christmas,' I said. 'Yeah. A party sounds good.'

'A big event like that is loads of work, Mum,' said Edward. 'Are you sure you're up to it?'

Jeannie clapped her hands together with excitement. 'Of course! It's lucky we have help, isn't it?' She gazed up at me and smiled.

*

Mrs Waddingham didn't call back that day. She didn't call the next day either. Late that evening, after dinner, I went to the kitchen cupboard, left another voicemail.

'Hi, sorry, don't know if I said, but I lost my mobile. So just in case you're trying to call me on there, it won't work. I'd love to talk about getting a lift, hope that's still okay. Call anytime. It's Danielle, by the way.'

I put the phone down, stood for a while. The cupboard smelled stale and slightly savoury. There were other cards on the corkboard: takeaways; handwritten phone numbers for *Gina*, *Abi*, *The Droves*; washed-out old business cards for taxi companies. Jeannie treated my laptop like her own, so now that I'd lost my phone, I was entirely without internet. But here were all these taxi numbers. Maybe I didn't have to wait for Mrs Waddingham to come and get me? Even if it cost a hundred pounds, I didn't care.

I called Amber Cars and waited, listening. It rang for a while and then cut out, dial tone. I called again and the same thing happened. The next card was for a company called Get Me There! but when I dialled the number, it was the same. None of them rang. They must be old firms, gone bust years ago.

Who else could I call? Who would help me? For a while I stood, holding the receiver to my ear and listening to the dial tone. Then, on impulse, I dialled the only number I knew by heart. She answered in three rings.

'Hello?'

'Mum?'

'Danielle! Hello, sweetheart. How you doing?'

Her voice washed over me, unbearably familiar. 'Yeah,' I said, because if I said anything else, I might cry. 'How are you?'

'Nice surprise, I wasn't expecting to hear from you. Anita said you lost your phone, is this your new number?'

'No, it's the landline here.'

'Oh, that's nice,' she said. Nice that Jeannie had a land-line or nice that I'd thought to call her? 'Was there something you wanted, love? Not in a bad way – just, I was about to head out.'

I thought I'd called for no reason. But now, I realised there was something. 'Do you remember you told me about your dad's family who were servants?'

'Course. Nanny Doreen and all that side.'

'Yeah. And was that in the Midlands?'

'No, sweetheart,' she said. This was why I had called, of course it was. *Sarah Price, 16.* Dream logic, story logic, if I found out what had been happening to me here, maybe it would stop. Maybe it would let me go. I braced for Mum to tell me about Yorkshire, Westerley, Thornley Patch where the river had dried; braced to find out that Sarah Price was my great-great-whatever. 'They were down in Essex, actually,' she said. 'Norfolk and Essex, anyway. They moved up to the Midlands, ooh – just before the First World War, I think?'

'That can't be right.'

'Why not? I did one of those websites. I tried to tell you all this years ago, you said it was boring.'

'No—'

'Oh yes you did. But it was Christmas, we'd probably had too much to drink.'

'No, I mean, they . . . I mean, are you absolutely sure they didn't work round here, in Yorkshire?'

Mum laughed. 'No. Why?'

I thought of the maid, ash on the palms of my hands, days slipping away from me. I thought of Mitch, telling me ghost stories about the lady of the house, how she'd drowned in a river that was all dried up, and I hadn't believed a word of it. Jeannie had laughed when I asked if Westerley was haunted, but now I knew I really, really wanted it to be. Because if there was nothing wrong with the house, there was something very wrong with me.

'No reason,' I said.

'Sorry, sweetheart, I've got to go. I'm late for Aunty Shan. But you'll call again soon?'

'All right. Yeah.' I told her I loved her, and put the phone down. I went out, closed the cupboard door behind me.

Alone in the kitchen, I thought of Sarah Price, who wasn't my great-great-grandmother. She wasn't anything to me at all, just a girl who'd passed through the house, the same as all the other girls on the list, hundreds of them, and hundreds more who'd never even made it to a census, whose presence at Westerley was fleeting, unrecorded. Like mine.

*

Late afternoon. Jeannie was handwriting a list at the kitchen table, while I cleaned. Behind me, the tap dripped into the sink. Out of the high windows, a grey day, the start of a cold snap. The rain-soaked earth had begun to freeze over.

'The real question is, caterers or no caterers?'

I turned to look at her. 'Sorry?'

'For the Advent party. If it's a 7 p.m. start, we'll need to feed everyone, won't we?'

I leaned against the kitchen cabinets. I'd forgotten about the party. 'How many people?'

'Well, I'm still looking at lists. I thought you could help me with the invites tomorrow. But if we invite about three, four hundred, probably half of that will come – so two hundred, say? One fifty?'

I was amazed. 'I thought it was just a small, local thing.'

Jeannie smiled at me, slender and glamorous in cashmere, her hair in a bun held together by some kind of pale green scarf. She took off her reading glasses to get a better look at me. 'The parties Mama threw when I was a girl were much bigger and grander than that. Wouldn't it be nice to give the children something really lovely to remember?'

I wondered which children she was referring to. Her own? I sat down next to her at the table, glanced at the handwritten list.

Music
Decorations
Food – caterers?
Guest list
Invitations

This was a much bigger thing than I'd anticipated. I'd barely thought about the party since Jeannie mentioned it, kept thinking I would be gone any day. Now, for whatever reason, I wasn't sure.

I remembered catering events at Hodgepodge. Crisps and wine and hummus for thirty people. Nothing ever went as far as you thought it would. 'Two hundred people will need a lot of food,' I said carefully.

'So you think we *should* hire caterers?'

I wondered what the alternative was, me and Jeannie drawing tray after tray of sausage rolls from the oven. Then I thought, come on. It would just be me. 'Yeah, caterers are a good idea, I think. Hot buffet? Hog roast? If you decide what you want, we can get quotes tomorrow.'

Jeannie reached out and gripped my wrist, once, briefly. 'Thank goodness for you, Danielle. I don't know what I'd do without you!' My wrist was warm from her palm. 'Edward was right, it's going to be a lot of work.'

I looked back at her list. 'Do you have Christmas decorations here, or will you need to order some? A lot of shipping's been messed up by the weather.'

'Actually, I was thinking about getting some greenery in from the garden, putting it up in the entrance hall. It was a Westerley tradition for a long time. But it drops quickly, so we'll have to do all that the morning of the party.' There was a buzzing in my ears, like panic. 'We've got shears in the old gardeners' hut on the grounds. You and I can gather everything, and then I'm sure I can persuade Edward to give us a hand putting it up ...'

'Jeannie,' I said. 'What if I'm not here for the party?' She looked at me levelly, without speaking, but there was something dangerous in her expression that surprised me. 'The rain's stopped,' I went on, falteringly. 'So the trains are probably running again, and I was thinking . . . I might go back to London soon. Because – because it's your house, you and Edward, and I don't want to get in the way here, or—'

Jeannie frowned. 'Nonsense,' she said. 'You're not in the way. You've been very helpful. And really, the bulk of your work is with me, isn't it? So it wouldn't be very convenient if you left.'

'Yes,' I said. 'But . . .' I was thinking of video calls, emails, everything else. I could leave my laptop here for her. I didn't care.

'And Danielle,' she interrupted, lowering her voice, like here was something very delicate. 'I thought you didn't have anywhere else to go?'

The tap was still dripping.

'That was what you said, wasn't it?' Jeannie went on. 'I'm not mistaken?' She said it like: *You weren't lying, were you?* I hadn't been lying, of course.

'No,' I said. 'It's true. Not until December.'

'Fine,' said Jeannie. 'Well, the party's on the third. You're free to go back after that, of course! I can drive you to the station myself.'

I had half an instinct to protest, insist on leaving sooner, but didn't know how. Jeannie was right. Where was I trying to get to? I thought of Ben with a rush of queasiness. No word from him since my voicemail. He was the last person in London I could have asked to let me stay, and it was obvious that he was no longer speaking to me. Maybe we weren't even friends anymore. There was nowhere. I had nowhere to go.

*

I set out one evening, just after nine, when Jeannie and Edward were drinking together in the snug. I knew nobody would miss me – but, to be safe, I went loudly upstairs to my bedroom, then crept back down, toed my shoes on quietly.

I'd promised Jeannie that I wouldn't go back to The Hart on a weeknight. But really, I thought, she had been asking me not to be hungover at work – fair enough. I would drink lime and sodas all night. I just needed people, normality, conversation, needed to see life outside Westerley. Without my phone, I felt so cut off.

I closed the front door as softly as I could manage. Outside, the fields were black, moon waned to a thin crescent. I had no torch, but my eyes soon adjusted to the dark, as I picked my way over the footpath where the grass was trodden down. I thought of the noise and bright lights of The Hart, an oasis on the horizon. Soon, soon, soon.

But when I pushed the door open, the pub was quieter than usual. I scanned the room. It wasn't that there were no people – there were old men on the bar stools, a couple in the corner, what looked like a vicar doing a crossword, but there was no music, nobody playing pool.

The pool table, actually, had gone entirely, perhaps moved to a different part of the warren-like pub, but it made the room feel different, wider. And there was nobody behind the bar.

'Hello?' I called. Ted came through a door at the back. 'Oh, hi,' I said, relieved. I'd begun to feel like maybe I'd gone to the wrong place.

'Danielle. What are you doing here?'

I laughed at the joke: haha, didn't expect to see you At The Pub. He'd probably pretend to faint when I ordered a soft drink. It was all so different, though. 'Have you redecorated?' I scanned the wall behind him.

Ted didn't answer. He was looking at me oddly, grey hair sticking up at funny angles.

'What?' I said.

He came around the bar, right up to me, and said, voice low, 'I'm not to serve you.' His lined face looked even more lined than usual. If he was joking, this was going a bit far. 'Orders from up top. The lady.'

'What lady? Your wife?'

Ted shook his head. 'The lady,' he repeated. 'I'm sorry for it. Truly.'

I still couldn't work out what he meant. He was the landlord, wasn't he? It was his pub. Then I realised what was different: everything. It wasn't just the pool table. The TVs had gone from their brackets, sambuca bottles vanished from behind the bar. There were only dark walls, little tables, lines of ales on tap. It looked like a pub from an old film. 'Why have you taken the TVs down?' I asked.

Ted frowned. 'What?'

I wondered if they were filming something here, some ITV period drama. No time to worry about that now. 'Look, I only want a lime and soda.'

He shook his head again, touched me on the arm. I was comforted. Then I realised he was moving me, kindly but firmly, towards the door. 'She says you've a lot to do. Don't need me distracting you.'

'Wait. Jeannie? Is that who you're talking about?' I should have felt angry, but I didn't. There was a static, white-noise sound in my ears, like the world contracting around me.

'You're a nice girl,' he said. 'And I'm sorry. But they own everything round here. They rent us the land. I can't just . . .'

'No,' I interrupted, stepping back, out of his grip. I didn't want him to push me out. I would go myself. 'Don't worry about it. Really, Ted.' With my hand on the handle, I waved. Then I walked back out into the dark.

Moonlight. A rabbit. The shape of Westerley rising out of the fog. All these things were older and stronger and bigger than me. I wondered if I should just give up, and what giving up would look like. As I picked my way over the fields, I laughed. The sound was strange in my ears, which were ringing, as after something very loud, like a concert, or an explosion. Then I was back. Back again. Back again.

*

I worked. I didn't know what else to do. I took the cleaning things from the kitchen cupboards. Swept the floors. Polished the bannisters. I warmed the pot and then the cups. Took notes. Wrote down the things Jeannie told me to write down. I spooned tea into the pot, fetched milk, sugar. Scrubbed the kitchen surfaces. Washed the dinner things. Carried tea to the drawing room and laid it out. Time passed, as it had always done. That was what time did.

*

One afternoon, I heard a car pull up in front of the house. My heart leapt. I was in the kitchen washing up, but I pulled my gloves off, tossed them onto the side, left half the plates unfinished and bounded upstairs. It was Mrs Waddingham. She'd come for me. But Jeannie was already at the door, speaking in a low voice.

'That's all right,' I heard Jeannie saying. 'Thank you anyway.'

Before she could turn and see me, I slipped into the drawing room and ran to the patio doors. I didn't have any shoes on, but that was okay. I stepped out into the grounds, wet grass soaking my socks, then went as quietly as possible around the edge of the house, keeping low, so I couldn't be seen from the windows.

I don't know why I did these things. In the moment of doing them, I felt I had no choice.

When I got to the front of the house, I heard Mrs Waddingham call, 'Sorry about that. Bye then,' before the front door closed. I was just in time.

I watched Mrs Waddingham walk back to her car, stand for a moment looking up at the house, before I called out to her. 'Mrs Waddingham. Helen!' Stage whisper.

She looked at me, and our eyes met. I don't know what I was expecting. A hug, a greeting, an open passenger door. We just looked at one another – then she shook her head. That was all. A small gesture, but it was enough.

I stood watching as she got into the car, and drove away.

*

We sat at the desk writing invites. Jeannie kept it so well organised: one drawer for letters that needed answering; one for letters that had been answered already, which she wanted to keep; one for things to do with the house; one for letters waiting to be posted. Almost all her correspondence was about the party now.

The pen in my hand was heavy, expensive, and the invite cards were beautiful. Gold leaf.

'It's going to be lovely,' I said.

'Yes,' Jeannie replied.

I smiled to myself, picturing all that food and clamour, all the decorations. Only a week to go, now. Nearly December. I'd always loved Christmas and couldn't wait to see the hall full of greenery again. Then I wondered why I'd thought that: I hadn't seen Westerley at Christmas before, I hadn't been here long enough.

Perhaps I'd seen it in my dreams.

*

In the mornings and at night, I saw her watching me. The maid. Dressing in the dawn light, sweeping fireplaces, taking the cups in. The movement of her hands was practised and familiar. I tried to copy her, walked in her footsteps. Then one night I woke and she wasn't working at all; she was lying in the other bed, beside my own.

The attic room was white with moonlight. I had left the curtains open again. I must have forgotten. I was always so tired.

I watched the sheets lift as she turned over in bed, to face me.

'Hello,' I whispered. The relief when she opened her eyes, smiled, held a hand out.

'Can't sleep?' she said.

'It's,' I said vaguely. 'The moon. It's so bright.'

'Ah. Don't let it spook you.'

'I wasn't.'

'You look frightened.'

She was still holding her hand out towards me. I took it. 'No,' I said. 'I'm not. I'm not frightened.'

*

Days passed. The frost came, and everything outside our windows was white. It was a relief after so much rain. Christmas coming. Always a busy season at Westerley. There was so much to do, from the fireplaces in the morning to the final dinner service; I was glad the other girl had come to help.

*

It was late when Edward called me into his room, I'd been about to go to bed.

'MacKinnon,' he said. 'Come and look at this.'

I wavered in the doorway, not wanting to go inside. I tried not to be alone with him. But he rolled his eyes. 'Don't be a prude. I've got you a costume, for the party.'

'Is it a costume party?'

'Come on,' he repeated. I followed him into the room. The dress was hanging on his wardrobe door: dark, severe and sober. White collar, white apron. A cap. A maid's clothes.

'It's funny,' he said. 'Because of what we said before. Our joke.' He was laughing. I touched the collar of the dress with my fingers. It smelled musty and familiar. Heavy material. 'Don't you get it, MacKinnon?'

I said nothing.

'Look, it's fine.' He gestured behind me. I turned to see the other girl standing in the doorway, wearing the same clothes. Dark dress. White collar. Cap.

'She doesn't mind,' he said. 'So why should you?'

*

I woke in the attic room at dawn. There were streaks of orange on the ceiling, and the other girl was already up, standing at the dresser, washing her face and hands from the water jug. There was a layer of ice on the window panes from our sleeping breath. It was going to be another cold day.

As she stood plaiting her hair, I could tell she wanted to talk, that she was half watching me, trying to work out if I was already awake. I rolled over so she wouldn't be able to see my face. I wanted to enjoy the peace a few moments longer, the feeling of being warm inside my sheets.

Soon, I knew, I would have to rise, wash my wrists and hands and neck, pin up my hair. I would have to dress and go downstairs. There were fires to be swept and lit, water to be warmed.

'Come on then,' she said. 'Are you getting up?'

It was the day of the Advent party. There was so much to do.

IV.
The Echo

THE LADY FOUND US shortly before midday. She came into the kitchens with her hair flyaway, falling out of its pins. I stood as soon as she entered, went to wash my hands in the sink. She wouldn't come down to fetch us unless it was urgent, so I had best be ready. I'd worked in the house long enough that we no longer needed to discuss such things; I was attentive to her needs.

Preparations for the party had been ongoing for weeks, but Cook liked to make a lot of things as fresh as possible, so we'd spent the morning helping with the pastry. She pushed out great rolls of it with her thick, strong forearms, while the other maid and I did the measurements, the cutting and egg-washing, simple jobs that we could be trusted with. It was unusual, to work in the kitchens, but I'd enjoyed it.

'It smells wonderful down here,' said the lady, and Cook blushed. They talked for a while about the food: meat pies, boiled ham, baked potatoes, roast beef; there would be bowls of beans from the greenhouse, and sprouts, and buttered leeks; there would be savoury pies, sweet pies, mince pies, puddings, oranges and chestnuts, and lots of gingerbread for the children. 'You're a marvel. What would we do without you?'

'Oh, you're all right,' said Cook, shy again. 'Thanks for letting the girls help.'

'Can you manage alone from here? I have another job for them.'

'Course,' said Cook.

The lady gestured to us to follow her. 'Come, girls. Time to start on the decorations.'

We went upstairs to the entrance hall. The elderly gardener had already brought a lot of greenery in from the grounds: there were huge sprigs of holly with bright red berries, batches of eucalyptus, trails of variegated ivy, as well as dried things he'd been keeping back from summer, larkspurs, roses from behind the kitchen garden, pots of red poinsettia. The party was for Advent beginning, and Christmas coming, and although Mr Edward had complained that we would have to decorate for Christmas twice – once now, and once again in several weeks, when the cut greenery had died – I knew that in truth, we were all equally excited.

'All right, girls,' said the lady. 'First I'd like you to help me make the wreaths. Then we'll put them up.'

The lady had an eye for these things, so she did the arranging, and we copied. Some of the plants became sprigs, some went into vases, others wreaths and garlands. I enjoyed the festive smell of fir and eucalyptus. Even though the holly bit my hands until they bled, it was a pleasant way to spend the afternoon; much pleasanter, I thought secretly, than sweeping and polishing.

After an hour or so, we'd made enough. The lady had us carry the gardener's workbenches inside and stand on them, then directed us as we lifted the wreaths and sprays and tied them to the walls. The smell of crushed eucalyptus filled the entrance hall as the other maid and I worked.

It took both of us to pin the ends and hold them in place, tying off to the brass sconces by the door, and the catches on the windows, wherever we could find a place to hold the string.

We'd finished most of the hanging when the front door swung open, almost throwing me from the bench. I cried out in shock.

'Careful!' It was Edward. He caught me by the elbow, and I steadied myself just in time.

'You're the one who ought to be careful,' said his mother. 'You knew we were doing this today. And where have you been all this time?'

'Out in the grounds,' said Edward. 'Securing the boundary line. There was a tear. You remember.' His voice was commanding, but he looked evasive. It was obvious he'd been wanting to avoid the preparations.

'Well,' the lady said vaguely. She looked cross, though she never stayed angry with him for long. Then I heard her turn towards me. 'Higher,' she called. 'A little higher, there. That's it. Tie off.'

While I followed her instructions, Edward closed the door and stepped around me into the hall. I was relieved: it was bitterly cold outside and the entrance hall was not much warmer, but worse with the door hanging open. My hands were numb, almost blue; it was a struggle to tie the string.

Edward tutted, stamping frost from his boots. 'This house looks absurd,' he said. The floor was littered with greenery we hadn't got to yet. He crossed to where the lady sat, directing us from the stairs, and seated himself beside her. 'Those maids could break their necks.'

She laughed. 'They'll be fine. Go and change, darling, you look a fright.'

'No tea?'

'And who'd serve it? We are all quite busy, as you can see. Go down to the kitchens and help yourself, if you like.'

Edward sighed. I pulled down the sleeves of my dress to try and warm my hands. It would be worth the pain, of course. Mr Edward was wrong: the house looked beautiful. I was jealous of anyone who'd be riding up to us tonight. With the sprigs of greenery everywhere and candles lighted in the windows, it would look as warm and inviting as a scene from a Christmas card.

I got down from the bench and picked through the greenery that was still to hang. 'What next, ma'am?'

'That one, there,' she said, indicating a smaller wreath. I took it up. 'Yes,' she said. 'Good girl. Put it next to the last one – to the left, a little higher.'

I was climbing back onto the bench when I heard Edward saying, in a lower voice, 'By the way, Mother. Something funny.'

'Up, girl, up,' the lady called out to the other maid. I heard her scrabble to raise the wreath higher, almost higher than her arms could reach. The lady told her to tie off, then turned to Edward and said, in a voice that was low like his, 'What is it?'

'When I was coming back, I saw a man at the treeline, watching the house.'

I suppose they thought we couldn't tell what they were saying. But I had good hearing, and could do more than one thing at a time: my arms were hanging the eucalyptus wreath while my ears followed their words.

'A man?'

'Yes,' said Edward. 'I thought so. He stepped back as I passed, and there's no way I could have reached him in time, but I saw him, plain as day. Skulking around, looking up at the house.'

'Could be a guest.'

'So early? And by such a route?'

The lady said something I didn't catch, but I thought it was about the gardener, how Edward should ask him to take the shotgun around the grounds before dark. Edward nodded. Then she caught me looking at them. 'Ah!' she cried, clapping her hands sharply. I overbalanced in shock, and had to grab one of the sconces for support. 'Haven't you enough to do, girl? Don't eavesdrop.'

'Sorry, ma'am,' I said. I climbed down to fetch more greenery, feeling all their eyes on me: the lady, angry; Edward, wryly amused; and the other maid, watching me for a moment before she turned to continue with her work. As I stooped to pick up another wreath, and follow her example, the back of my neck burned hot with shame.

*

Once all the greenery was in place, Cook asked if I could go across the fields for eggs. The cat had got up on the side, she said, smashed three or four, and now she didn't have enough to finish the pudding. The lady said she could spare me for half an hour and handed me some coins, so I pulled my scarf on, took a wicker basket and set out from the house.

Usually, for a party, the lady would pay girls from the village to come up and help, but Cook was getting old and impatient, and this year she'd said those girls did more harm than good, and she would rather do without. It meant a lot of extra work for me, but I didn't mind. I liked to keep busy. It made the time pass.

Already there wasn't much left of the day. I walked quickly. The stile was frozen under my palms, full of water from last month's rain, which had turned to ice and swollen up the wood. I got across, and took the fields almost at a run. By the time I reached the farm, I was out of breath. Luckily, the farmer was close by.

'Shouldn't run like that,' he said. 'You could slip.'

'Sorry,' I said, panting, though I didn't know why I'd apologised. It would hardly be his problem if I fell: it would be my own. But he'd lost interest in me already. He was holding one of the hens, doing something to its feet, and seemed absorbed in the task. 'Could I please trouble you for some eggs?'

He nodded without looking up. 'Good eggs, these.'

'I know,' I said. 'I've come from Westerley.'

'Right you are.' Eventually he put the hen down and went to their pen. I waited while he chose the best eggs, and put them into my basket. The other hens stood around, like they were waiting their turn.

'Thank you,' I said, handing him the coins.

He nodded. 'You give my regards to the lady.'

I went back slower than I'd come, afraid to slip, break the eggs and be punished for wasting them, but when I noticed the light was failing, I tried to walk more quickly. Mr Edward's talk of the stranger had frightened me, and I've never much liked the dark since I was a girl. I watched my feet, avoiding patches of ice, and was glad when I came in sight of Westerley again. It looked so lovely and welcoming, with the windows lit in gold and green. And we had made it like that, I had, with my own hands. Then came a voice from the half-light, 'Who's there?'

I jumped, alarmed, held the basket closer to myself. The air smelled of woodsmoke. I could make out, now, what I was seeing: in the dark I'd thought it was a stranger, but it was only the gardener with his shotgun and crest of grey hair. He came a little closer.

'Oh,' he said. 'One of the little maids. Sorry if I frightened thee.'

He must be walking the perimeter, like the lady had suggested, to ensure there was no stranger lurking in the woodlands. But as I'd learned all this from eavesdropping, I thought it better not to ask. 'Fetching eggs,' I said, holding up the basket.

He nodded gravely. 'And which are thee? Sorry to say I get you little maids mixed up, still.'

'You mean what's my name?'

He laughed. 'Aye, I did. Sorry.'

I shook my head, opened my mouth to say that I was not offended, but he interrupted, 'Wait a moment. I'm an old man, it will come to me. Sarah, is it?'

'No,' I said, but somehow, I was not sure how to answer. 'I – I'm . . .'

Quiet. Crows calling to each other in the dusk. The gardener frowned at me. 'Tha cannot have forgotten, surely?' he said.

'I'm Sarah,' said the other maid. She was standing on the steps, watching us.

He laughed, and the moment was broken. 'Aye, course,' he said. 'Course you are. Sorry, Sarah.'

'Come on,' she called to me. 'Cook's going spare for those eggs.'

I ducked around the gardener with an apology. Perhaps he thought me shy. I hope he thought that – rather than strange. I felt his eyes on my back as I fled up the steps, into the safety of the house, and closed the door behind us. The sound of it rang in the entrance hall. Here was the greenery, just where we'd put it, looking somehow different, grander in the dying light.

'I went as quickly as I could,' I said.

'It's all right. I didn't come to rush you.'

We kept our voices low in the main house, force of habit. I frowned. 'Then why were you waiting for me?'

'It's nearly dark,' she said simply. 'I thought you'd be frightened.' We smiled at one another.

*

Every surface in the kitchen was covered with used dishes and bowls and dirty spoons. Sarah was at the sink, helping with some of the cleaning. Cook was red-faced, and I wondered when she would be too old for these parties. At least she wasn't cross with me for dawdling.

'Can I do anything to help?' I asked her.

'The lady was looking for you,' she said, but I watched her waver. Then she handed me a bowl of potatoes. 'If you could just peel two, three of these before you go, I'll will you something lovely when I die.'

Sarah raised her eyebrows at me. We had a joke that Cook was already at least a hundred and would outlive everyone in the house. But I said, 'Of course,' and took the bowl.

I stood at the counter to peel. I wasn't nimble, had to go slowly so as not to cut myself with the knife, but I managed to tackle a few. I was on the third when Cook slipped me the corner of a pie she was cutting into slices. Steam rose from the filling. 'Here,' she said.

I took it in wet hands and nibbled the edge, trying not to burn my mouth. It was perfect: soft beef, rosemary, buttery pastry. I hadn't realised I was so hungry. I was still eating when I heard the sound – a high, unnatural bell, calling from the corner of the room. 'What's that?' I asked, my mouth full.

'Swallow before you speak,' said Cook, rolling her eyes. It wasn't the first time I'd had to be told. I blew out, mouth full of steam, and forced the last mouthful down my throat.

'All gone,' I said, and stuck my tongue out.

Sarah laughed. Cook hit me with a dishcloth. 'Filthy girl.'

The sound was still going. I wondered if it was a signal for Cook, like a bell from the upper floors. I peered around to see where it was coming from.

'Really,' I said. 'What is that?'

'What's what?' Cook muttered, distracted. Sarah had gone back to washing up, Cook to slicing the pie into sections, all her focus on the crust, the knife.

'But it's coming from here,' I said, as I followed the sound to the cupboard beneath the stairs.

I stood at the door and listened. Ring, ring. Strangely familiar. Could they really not hear anything? I reached out and pulled the door back.

'What are you doing?' said Sarah.

Of course, there were only Cook's cleaning things inside. A broom, bucket, packets of unopened soap and piles of mouse traps. What had I been expecting? I closed the door again, unsettled. The sound had stopped.

I turned to find them both watching me.

'You all right, girl?' said Cook. There was a smudge of flour on her cheekbone, and an expression of alarm on her face. 'What on God's green earth did you think was gonna be in there?'

'I . . .' I said, frowning. 'I don't know. A – a telephone.'

'A what?' said Cook. They were both looking at me like I was strange. Perhaps I was.

'Hello down there?' It was the lady's voice. Looking for me.

'Sorry,' I called. 'Coming.' I ran up the kitchen stairs without looking back.

*

I brought up water for the lady's bath, hot, with lavender salts. While she was bathing, I built up the fire in the master, so it would be warm enough for her to dress. It was half past five and dark at the windows. She came in while I was pulling the curtains closed. 'Nice bath, ma'am?'

'Lovely,' she said, and sat at the dressing table in her robe. It was cold outside, but I was sweating beneath my collar as I brushed her waves of hair with silver-backed brushes.

I didn't overly like being in the lady's bedroom. There was something about it that I found, if this isn't strange to say, too familiar. I sometimes dreamed about waking there and would feel unsettled all day. In another life, perhaps – although it wasn't befitting of my station to think as much. Still, there were other rooms in the house that unsettled me too, especially when I first arrived. I wasn't used to anything so large and grand, to all that space.

The lady's dress had been brought up from London, pressed, and hung now in the dressing room. I had dreamed about this, too, nicer dreams, about the moment I would get to bring it through, velvet beneath my palms; knowing the Advent party had finally come. The lady looked at me. 'Go on then,' she said.

I went to fetch the dress, holding it carefully on its hanger, like it was something alive. Dark green velvet with a gold trim, rich and seasonal. It would match the plants we'd brought in from the garden. The lady had jewels of emeralds to wear it with, on her neck and in her ears, and there was holly on the dresser, waiting to be cut, which I would pin at her temples.

The lady painted her face while I pinned up her hair, and put her jewels on. 'And what of you?' she said, while I worked.

'Me, ma'am?'

'What will you wear to the party?'

I looked at myself. I had taken my apron off, dirty from the day's exertions, before I touched the lady's clothes, and was wearing my dark dress. I had no other.

'Wait a moment,' she said. She took a piece of cut holly from the pile, threaded it into a hairpin. Then she stood, removed my cap and pushed the sprig into my hair. I felt lovelier already. 'There. For all your hard work.'

I was grateful for her kindness. When I first came to Westerley, I had given the lady cause to speak harshly to me. I had been ungainly, made mistakes, been homesick, cried. I'd kept Sarah awake nights, weeping and wanting to go home. But the lady rarely ever had to punish me anymore. I was glad that she was pleased.

'Now, go outside and wait a moment, will you?' she said. 'I want you to get the effect of everything together, and tell me what you think.'

'Yes, ma'am.' I left her to change. In the hall, I pulled the door to, and stepped back. While I waited, I went to the staircase and walked a little way down, to enjoy a view of our hard work: the entrance hall windows were full of greenery, and beyond them, snow had started to fall. I was smiling at the sight when I noticed Sarah at the bottom of the stairs.

'What did you say, down in the kitchens?'

I opened my mouth, closed it again. 'Nothing.'

Sarah took a step towards me, then another, until she drew level with me. Everything about her was small, small nose, small hands, and she was shy around Edward and the lady, but she wasn't shy in private. She was forthright and quick-witted, and now she was looking at me very directly. 'It was not nothing. What did you say about the cupboard?'

I shook my head.

'The thing you were looking for. What was it?'

I had a headache. Though perhaps it was only from the heat of the master bedroom. 'A telephone,' I said vaguely.

'And what is that?'

'I don't know.'

'But you must, or you wouldn't know to look for it.'

I rubbed at my temples. 'Don't be a bully, Sarah, my head hurts.'

'I'm not. It's just, you don't even seem to remember . . .' She shook her head. She was looking at me strangely. 'You don't seem to remember where you come from.'

I felt a jolt, and tried to laugh it off. 'You mean where I was born?'

Sarah lowered her voice. 'I mean that you weren't here. That it used to just be me. That you—'

'Girls?' We turned. The lady was behind us, at the top of the stairs, slender and upright in her velvet dress. The sprigs of holly set it all off perfectly. She looked like a painting. 'What do you think?'

Sarah said nothing. I could feel her trembling beside me and I wondered why.

'We love it,' I said. 'You look wonderful, ma'am. Perfect.'

*

The first guests were to begin arriving around six. I was to wait by the door, taking coats and making people welcome. Down the hall, the furniture in the morning room had been cleared, all the carpets pulled back, food brought up and laid out on the tables. There was even a band; as I took up my post, I could hear them warming up, tuning their instruments. A fiddler! That meant there would be dancing. I could hardly wait to see it.

Edward came through the entrance hall. 'Got you standing sentry, has she?' he said wryly. 'Keep the ruffians out?'

I laughed politely. 'Yes, sir.'

'Hmm,' he said, looking at me. He took a step closer. 'I suppose you heard what I was saying earlier, you little eavesdropper.'

I hesitated, not wanting either to lie or give myself away, but my silence must have spoken for itself. Edward laughed. 'Yes, well, just you give any strangers trying to get in what-for, won't you?'

'Yes, sir.'

Edward was still watching me with a strange expression. Then he said, 'Aha.' He reached up and flicked the sprig of holly in my hair. 'Thought you looked different. Suits you.'

My cheeks warmed. 'It was a present from your mother.'

'Right. Well.' He let his hand linger for a moment, touched a finger to my cheek. I stared at the floor, waiting for it to be over. He stepped back. 'Where's that Sarah got to? Have you seen her?'

I hadn't, not for a while: the lady had given us different roles for the evening, and mine was here, at the door. I did not know what hers was. I hadn't seen her since – the staircase, when she'd said—

'Hello? Are you awake, girl? I asked if you'd seen Sarah.'

I looked up at Mr Edward. 'No, sir. I'm sorry.'

'Oh well,' he said, sounding irritated. Then his mood changed. To my surprise, he clicked his heels together, held up a hand in salute. 'Good luck, sentry,' he said, and left me alone to wait.

The guests began to arrive. There were ladies in dark velvet and furs, fox, ermine, men in suits and hats, little girls in red and gold, babies in arms. They wore bright colours and dark colours, dresses that looked like port being poured from a bottle, dresses that looked like candlelight. One after another they came, old people alone, and young people together, and families, all wearing looks of amazement. The house was startling in its beauty, and I was glad of my role in its transformation, glad of my place. As I took their coats and cloaks and mufflers, laying them out on the tables and racks we'd moved into the billiards room, I was grateful to be part of Westerley, part of its ancient magic, magic that would go on and on long after I was gone. And a piece of me would still be here. It was a safe and wonderful thing to know – like never having to die at all.

Eventually, the stream began to tail off. The noise from the party was very loud now, talking and music. I was able to catch my breath and think. The grandfather clock in the hall said that it was after eight: they must already be eating the food, and soon there would be dancing. Surely, at this time, there could be no more guests.

In an hour or two, families with children would begin to leave. I would have to help them find their hats and coats. I went to the billiards room to straighten things out. It had been so busy earlier that I'd piled everything up haphazardly, and now I arranged it in a better order, hanging as many coats as I could fit on the racks.

Everything smelled of velvet and damp wool. I worked for a long time. I was so focused on what I was doing that I barely noticed when Edward stepped into the room.

'Sarah,' he said. 'You've been avoiding me.'

'I'm not Sarah,' I said, surprised, as he shut the door behind him. The room had been lighted only by the hallway, and the darkness now was sudden and profound, like hands around my throat. I closed my eyes. The sound of his breath, his footsteps, getting closer. 'Please,' I said. I wasn't her. I wasn't even supposed to be here.

Then the knocking started: a loud, firm beating on the front door.

I opened my eyes to find that I could see quite clearly. I was alone in the billiards room, surrounded by wet coats and furs.

'Sir?' I called. 'Mr Edward?'

There was no sign of him. And the door was still propped open, as it had been, the small room full of light from the hallway. What strange, waking dream had made me think he was with me?

First the ringing in the kitchen, then Sarah's comments on the stairs, and now this. I was losing my wits.

The knocking came again, echoing strangely in here, so that it sounded quite unfamiliar – but it must be the front door, because where else could the sound be coming from? Another guest. I left the billiards room, crossed the entrance hall, pulled the front door open. 'Sorry about the wait,' I said. 'It was—'

I stopped, looking about me. It was bitterly cold out here, the snow falling quite heavily now. Some footmen waited shivering by the carriages, a horse stamped its feet against the gravel road. But there was nobody to let in. No late guest. So where had the knocking come from?

Then, through the growing blizzard, I saw it: the shape of a man in a black coat, twenty feet from the house, watching the doorway. The stranger at the treeline, the uninvited guest, the man Edward had seen that morning. He was real. Looking at me. And as I stood there, staring, shivering in my dark dress, he raised an arm in something like a greeting.

There were footsteps behind me. I shut the door with some force, turned to see Edward approaching from the morning room. This was no dream: he looked different, red-faced from the heat of the party, hair sticking to his forehead, the top buttons of his dress shirt undone. He didn't seem to be looking for me, or to notice any disturbance to my manner, but as he approached, he said, distractedly, 'Still at it, then?' as a father might to a child who always hung on him for entertainment.

It wasn't quite a question, but I felt I should answer all the same. 'Yes sir, although I think most people have arrived now.' My voice was level. Like I hadn't seen the stranger at all. 'Does your mother want me?'

'What's that?'

'I said I think I should be able to leave the door now, sir. I wondered if your mother wanted me to help Cook bring up any more food?'

By now, Edward had stopped, and his eyes settled on me with a surprised expression, as though seeing me for the first time. 'No,' he said slowly. 'No, actually, you can help with something.'

'Help you, sir?' I never took instructions from Edward. His mother ran the household; she was the one who told me which rooms to clean and in what order, which beds wanted warming, which fireplaces sweeping. But he seemed in a hurry.

'Come on, girl, don't stand around. Follow me.' He went to the main staircase and began to climb.

For a moment I hesitated. My strange presentiment in the billiards room had made me anxious of him. I looked about me. Heat was pouring from the morning room and some of the greenery in the windows had begun to wilt. What I was looking for, I do not know. For the lady to come with instructions of her own, perhaps. But I was not the lady's maid; I was the family's.

I followed Edward upstairs, our footsteps creaking on the wooden boards below the carpet runner. He said no more to me, did not speak or turn, as we moved down the corridor towards the blue bedroom, where he slept. I had been inside it many times, of course, to change the sheets, beat dust from the curtains, but never like this, alone with him.

The wind outside was picking up, turning the snowfall into a storm, and the house moved around us, a slow and steady creak. Edward was holding the door of his room open, waiting for me to go in. I felt quite strongly that I did not want to, that it was not proper, but the words were not available to me.

'Well,' he said, irritated. 'Go on then. Hurry up.'

'What is the matter that you need my help with, sir?'

Edward didn't notice the crack in my voice, or perhaps he just didn't care to. 'What's the point of standing around describing something I can more quickly show you?'

I had no evidence that he meant me harm, only the sheer and sudden force of my fear, and his eyes. The way they travelled over me. Not with desire, but with the bland confidence of possession.

'Sir,' I said, still hesitating, and he snapped, 'For God's sake, do as you're told.' He seized my arm and pulled, but I was no longer afraid. Or that is not quite true: I was more afraid of going with him than of anything else.

I kicked at Edward's leg, and he pulled me off balance. I stumbled towards the doorway, braced myself against his chest and kicked again. I felt the toe of my boot connect with his shin, heard him cry out and, in surprise, let go. I ran.

'Stupid girl,' he called at my back, but I kept going. I ran from the staircase, along the top hall, towards the attic. He was right, I was stupid: if I'd fled the other way, towards the stairs, I could have been out of the house, across the grounds, into the night. Instead I had run unthinkingly, like a child, towards my own bedroom – a dead end.

At the foot of the attic stairs, I stopped. I would be trapped up there. Edward's footsteps behind me, sluggish at first, were now gaining speed. I must get away. Then I saw something I had not noticed before: a door on my right, leading away from the attic, down into the house. Without further thought, I went through and slammed it behind me.

I found myself standing in a hallway I had never seen before.

No, worse than that: I was standing in a hallway that should not exist. There had never been another door at the foot of the attic stairs. So how had I arrived here?

I turned to look behind me. The doorway was no longer there: just more corridor, long and dark, stretching away in both directions. The sound of my own breath in my ears. I was panting from the chase, but there seemed little point in thinking about what I had left behind, or what I could possibly be moving towards. I began to walk.

This was Westerley, but not as I knew it. The hallway went on and on into the dark, and all the doors of all the rooms were open to me, branching off, forever. I did not stop at any, but as I walked, I saw inside each one.

There were morning rooms and sitting rooms and drawing rooms and bathing rooms, rooms for eating or sleeping or hiding or praying, rooms to die in; the house had every room you could ever need in all your life, and she was there in every one, the maid. Some of the rooms had pale walls and stone floors that she scrubbed on her knees. Some were very grand; she stood in silence, waiting at the table. I saw the drawing room at Westerley as I had known it, portraits and large windows, and she knelt in the fireplace, sweeping ash from the grate.

Sometimes she was dressed in black, sometimes faded linen. There was a room where she stood with a wooden bucket, white-washing the walls, and another where she made beds. A kitchen, but not like ours, older, darker, she was bringing pails of water from the garden; I could see the grounds stretching away through the window. It was like a magic trick: sometimes I was on one side of the house, sometimes another; I moved between the lower and the upper floors, although I walked no staircases. I passed through sweet-smelling bedrooms where she dressed the lady of the house in corsets, shifts, stays, petticoats, pale blue ruffles with empire waists, dresses and dresses and dresses. Or sweeping. Polishing. Washing sheets. She cried in the corridors from homesickness when she thought no one could see her. I could see her. I saw all of them. The rooms stretched out around me, endless corridor like a hall of mirrors, matryoshka, and in every room there were servants and servants and servants and servants. I saw her in the library, turning the pages of a book she was meant to be dusting; the shape of the object in her hands called down the years to her, although she had not been taught to read. I saw her polishing silver. I saw her taking a cloth to the floor on her knees.

Something whistled past my ear, and took out part of the wall. I gasped, and it was a shock to realise that I could, that I had a body at all. But I did. I was not just eyes: I was a person, in a dark dress, and I stood in a kitchen that was not at all familiar, seeing blue sky where, a moment ago, there had only been plaster. She was there too, staring through the hole in one of the walls. It was dusk and the grounds were full of soldiers. Metal helmets. Roundheads. 'Girl,' someone called. 'Come away from there.' But she stayed at the window because she wanted to watch, even as the room filled with smoke from the cannon fire. Westerley was burning to the ground, and Westerley was rising from the ashes, and Westerley would last forever.

I ran from the flames. The house was older now, and unfamiliar to me, but the maid was still helping her lady to dress. Mantuas and overskirts. Farthingales. Kirtles. Stockings. Partlets. Velvet and linen, gable hoods and brocade. As the years fell away, the circles of the ladies' skirts contracted and widened, and so did the circumference of the routes she took about her mistress.

I saw every room Westerley had ever held, hundreds and hundreds of years, and she was in all of them. The shack, the timber-clad house with soldiers in the stairwell, hunts in the grounds, Christmas greenery in the entrance hall, year after year. She was the flat-faced girl with large eyes, bruises on her forearms, plucking feathers from a duck. She held a baby boy to her chest, the master's son, and let it devour her. She was part of the house, and it was happy, and it ate and ate and ate, and in the half-light of a vanished past, a man in rags said, *Please, my lord, the people of your land are starving*, and the house said, *Let them starve*. A woman beat on the door with an infant in her arms. The sound of her knocking was everywhere, all around us, thud, thud, thud, but still, the doors stayed closed to her. And the house was as hungry as a hundred years are hungry, and it would never, ever, ever be full.

I was in the corridor again, smoke spilling from one of the open doorways. The distant sounds of flames, cannon fire, shouting. It was all breaking apart; I had to get out.

I ran. I ran in my dark dress past living rooms and drawing rooms and dressing rooms and bedrooms, past the blue room with its door closing tight and the dining room, where the maids were laying out breakfast, strawberries, melon, a bowl of glistening peaches. I ran past the study where Mrs Waddingham was cleaning windows, past the sawdust kitchen where a stuck pig hung from the rafters, past the windowsill where Jeannie, aged fourteen, sat reading, nothing where it was meant to be, nothing at all in a line. Time was a jumble, catastrophe, noise and smoke and hunger, and it was all here, still happening, everything at once.

I couldn't breathe. My head swam, and I leaned against the wall, coughing. 'Sarah,' said a man's voice, and I looked up.

The smoke was gone. I was in the billiards room. Dark night, snow at the windows, the sound of a fiddler down the hall. And he was standing in the doorway, the man with the deep voice and the beautiful clothes, staring past me to where the maid stood, piling up wet cloaks and coats on the table. He did not look like Edward, but there was a hunger in his face that was the same.

'Sir?' said the girl. Small hands.

'You've been avoiding me.' He shut the door behind him and the room, lit by the hallway beyond, became dark. The sounds of the Christmas party quietened.

'Sir,' she repeated, frightened as he moved towards her, put a hand across her mouth. Something in her eyes spoke to me so strongly that, for a moment, I thought she could see me. But she couldn't: neither of them could. I was just an echo. When he held her down, his knuckles were white.

I tried to say, 'Stop,' but there was smoke in my lungs and the dust of a hundred years choking me. They couldn't hear me anyway. I turned away from them, beating my fists on the locked door of the billiards room, throwing myself against it, screaming and screaming for someone to help her. 'Hello,' I called. I stood there, beating the door, as the years fell away. Thud. Thud. Thud. 'Hello? Help. Please help.'

'Hello?' said a voice on the other side of the door. But I knew it was no use: the voice was just my own, and she was no help. She didn't even know how to help herself.

I turned back. The pile of coats and cloaks was gone, the girl was gone, the master of the house was gone. I was alone in the billiards room, bare floor, scrubbed wooden boards and endless, endless night. The moon outside. The sound of a plane. I was tired. No more shouting. 'Please,' I said.

My voice was hoarse as I let go of the door. A roar of laughter from somewhere. Christmas music. How could there still be Christmas music when everything else was finished? When it had all been and gone so long ago?

I was sick, dizzy; if I didn't lie down, I would faint.

I lay down. Clammy face. Pain in my head. Silence.

*

I opened my eyes. I was lying in the ground floor hall at Westerley, beside the locked door of the billiards room, the sounds of a party drifting towards me. Tinny, pre-recorded carols faded in and out, like a radio tuning. Jeannie's party. Of course. It was happening, it was tonight.

I sat up. Everything span, but I held onto the wall, and then it slowed. I pulled myself to my feet with the handle, but the door of the billiards room was locked. Still locked. I tried to laugh, mouth tasting of metal. I was going to be sick. For some reason, I felt certain that, whatever else had happened, I couldn't be sick here, now, on Jeannie's carpet.

I pulled myself along the corridor and across the entrance hall, shaking, stumbling as I wrenched the front door open. Night air hit my face, cold and damp. I knelt in the bushes to throw up.

'Mac?'

Someone was there, but I couldn't speak while my body was turning itself inside out. My head hurt so much. I emptied my stomach into the rhododendrons and then knelt back, shaking, and realised my hair was soaking wet. Why had I thought it was snowing? It was pouring with rain out here, of course; it always was.

'Mac, is that you? Are you okay?' It sounded like Ben, though it couldn't be. His hand was cool on the back of my neck. 'Jesus, you're boiling. Are you ill?'

I looked round. Ben was crouching beside me, hair hanging damply into his eyes, wearing a black raincoat that was soaked flat against him. He was very still, watching as I reached out to grip his shoulder. It was warm and solid. 'Are you real?'

'Why wouldn't I be?'

My mouth tasted like beef and rosemary and stomach acid. There weren't words for it, of course: things that had happened to me and never happened to me. I reached up, touched the sprig of holly in my wet hair.

'Are you okay? You're freaking me out,' he said. I shook my head.

We couldn't stay here in the rain. I needed to think clearly, get warm, be more than a foot away from my own vomit. I wobbled to my feet, and Ben gripped my elbow. The ghosts of words formed themselves at the back of my throat, but I was scared to ask why, how, he was here – scared that if I poked at the impossibility of it, Ben might blink out of existence right in front of me, like a dream. So I just said, 'Come on. This way.'

We went back through the front door of Westerley Hall. I closed it behind us. The entrance hall was quiet, but I could hear a tumult of voices from the drawing room: laughter, shouting, Christmas music from a CD, playing on Edward's sound system. For a moment, I wanted to run, but I would leave soon enough. I felt braver, anyway, with Ben beside me. We climbed the main staircase wordlessly, passed the master bedroom, study, blue room, all the way up to the top of the house. The room was as I'd left it: twin beds, mine unmade; my suitcase in the corner with clothes spilling out.

'Is this where you've been sleeping?' Ben said, and I nodded, but I was too tired to say anything else. I sagged down onto my bed – the bed that had been mine, for a while, at least – and closed my eyes.

You couldn't hear the party, up in the attic. Just wind, rain on the roof of the house. Then, with a jolt, I heard her bed creak. My eyes snapped open.

'Don't sit there,' I said.

Ben stood up. 'Okay,' he said quickly. 'That's fine. Can I sit by you?'

I nodded. He eased down next to me the way a vet might approach an animal it was going to sedate. I wished I *was* going to be sedated. Anything would be better than trying to understand what had happened. But of course I would have to, because Ben was saying, 'What's going on, Mac?' I'd never heard him sound so scared before.

How could I explain when I didn't know myself? Sarah, the boarded-up room, the son of the house. Hallways that went on forever. Soldiers. Fire. The blank-eyed scullery maid with a fistful of feathers. I wanted to ask if he thought a place could remember the things that had happened inside of it, like an echo. Mitch's stone tape. I wanted to say that it had been something to do with time. How it still wasn't over: none of it was over, the wasting of people, theft, doors closed. What I actually said was, 'Hundreds and hundreds and hundreds of years.'

Ben nodded. 'Right,' he said. 'And on a scale of, like, normal things – should I be phoning the police, or . . . ?'

There was a sound in the room that was at once familiar and strange. I realised it was the sound of my own laughter. Ben was looking at me. 'You've not cracked, have you?' he said, trying for lightness, but there was fear in his voice.

I stopped laughing. 'No, Ben. Sorry. I don't want to call the police. I want to pack my things and leave.' He nodded. 'But I want to smoke a cigarette first. A whole one.'

Now it was Ben's turn to laugh. 'Sure,' he said, patting his pockets. 'Okay. I can tell this is a medical emergency.'

We got up from the bed, opened the high window in the attic's sloped ceiling, which meant we could stand side-by-side, with the glass keeping the rain off our heads, and enjoy the view. The roof descended from here, falling away into darkness. Inside that darkness, I knew, was the front of the house, the edge of the grounds, the drive. I could picture it all so well.

Ben lit two cigarettes and passed me one, a little damp from his pocket, but functional. 'Nice place you've got here,' he said.

'Yeah,' I said. 'It was, for a bit.'

Hadn't it been? And hadn't I loved it? How could I not? I was temporary, and it was forever.

I took a drag of my cigarette, a strange feeling curling in my empty stomach. I pictured myself a few minutes from now, distracted, packing my things, leaving my half-smoked cigarette to burn down on the ledge. Forgetting. I thought about the way a spark could drift and catch; the curtains first, and then the bedsheets. Before long, the whole attic would be on fire. It would make its way lower and lower, through the bedrooms, the drawing room, the billiards room; all the guests standing on the lawn in their finery as Westerley burned down to nothing. The house had burned before, after all. Maybe once wasn't enough.

How lovely the light would look, gold and red and orange in the night sky. A plume of smoke. I could almost see it, ruins smoking in the dull winter dawn, and then – nothing. When spring came, you'd be able to watch the rabbits in the garden from the gravel drive. You'd be able to see all the way to the woods. Pile of ash. Dead house.

I wouldn't do it, of course. Despite these last weeks, I wasn't actually insane, or at least, I didn't think I was. Besides, I didn't really believe that destroying the house would help. The things that had happened to me here, things beyond my ability to articulate, hadn't started at Westerley, they had started in London. Weeks of fear on Anita's couch, dark shadow watching me sleep, a shape that had become a maid that had become a witness, watching me in the dark, my fear and isolation. And I had been a witness too.

I wasn't sure I would call it a haunting, though I didn't know what else to call it. Perhaps it didn't matter. It wasn't about whether the house was haunted or not; I was haunted by it, by its presence, by the things it said about the world I lived in. Perhaps I always had been.

Besides. Nothing would burn after weeks of rain, would it?

'Ben, what are you doing here?' I said. 'How did you even get here?'

He looked surprised I'd spoken. I'd been quiet a long time.

'Well,' he said. 'I drove. Did you forget I could do that?'

I had, actually. Driving didn't seem like something he should be allowed to do. 'Er,' I said, and he laughed.

'Anita gave me the address. She said you lost your phone, and then you just kind of . . . dropped off the face of the earth. We were worried.'

'My phone,' I said vaguely. 'Yeah. The house ate it, I think.'

'And you left me a voicemail. You told me to come and get you.'

'But I didn't think you actually would.'

'But you asked me to.' Ben shrugged, like it was obvious. He'd driven two hundred miles to fetch me, just because I asked.

The voicemail. God. And all the things I'd said. My stomach turned over as, for perhaps the first time, I realised it was really Ben, he was here, this was happening. It was like being dropped back into my body from a height: I was suddenly aware of the burn in my throat, sweat under the band of my wristwatch, wet hair on my neck. And Ben. His alive-ness. The heat of his body through our damp clothes. I stared at him. 'I can't believe you came all this way. I thought . . .' I shook my head.

There was too much I needed to say, and no words. 'Ben. I thought you hated me.'

'That's a stupid thing to think,' he said, half laughing. 'But I can't talk, because I kind of thought the same thing. I mean, that you hated *me*.'

'Never.'

We were still looking at each other. Ben stubbed his cigarette out on the windowsill, then reached out slowly with his free hand, and touched my face, fingertips curling against my jaw. He was so warm. 'Is this okay?' he said.

It was strange. Frightening. But on the scale of strange and frightening things that had happened lately, it also wasn't, really. 'Yes,' I said quietly. 'It's okay.' I gripped his waist through his raincoat. He was soaked to the skin. I should tell him. But before I could, he leaned forwards – slowly, very slowly, like he was giving me time to run away – and kissed me.

'And that?' he said, looking at me intently. 'Is that okay?'

I made a face. 'I was sick, Ben.'

He laughed. 'But you can't tell. Because of the smoking.' I kissed him again. His hand in my hair, breath in my mouth. He tasted of smoking, too, and strawberry chewing gum, familiar and unfamiliar all at once, like something I shouldn't be allowed to do. He was cold from the rain as I pulled him closer. How simple it was. My relief was a physical thing, a pulse beating in my abdomen, a weakness in my legs. My life. It was real. It was waiting for me. Ben had come to take me home.

Something creaked behind us, a sound like weight on one of the beds – her bed – and Ben froze. 'Did you hear something?' he said, pulling away.

'No,' I said, smiling because, for the first time in a long time, I could imagine the future – not see it, or picture it, but imagine it. Imagine there was one. 'No. I didn't hear anything.'

*

We walked downstairs. I went ahead with my backpack; Ben carried my suitcase. And then we were in the entrance hall, listening to the distant sounds of the party from along the corridor. The front door was ringed by greenery from the gardens. Holly with bright red berries, batches of eucalyptus, trails of variegated ivy. I tried to remember putting it there: me, Jeannie, Edward, but it couldn't have been just us, could it? Blank space in my mind.

'Shall we go, then?' said Ben. He was standing by the front door, watching me.

It was tempting, the thought of just disappearing. Jeannie looking around, after the party, for someone to help clear up. Her and Edward in the empty house, walking from room to room, calling my name. I could do better, though. I took Ben's hand and started towards the drawing room. 'What are you doing?' he asked. But I didn't answer, and he didn't stop me.

I pushed the door open, and saw –

Ladies in dark velvet. Furs, fox, ermine. Men in suits and hats. Little girls in red and gold. They wore bright colours and dark colours, dresses that looked like port being poured from a bottle, dresses that looked like candle-light. More greenery in here, that Sarah must have hung, because I hadn't touched it, hadn't even seen the morning room like this, with all the furniture pushed back against the walls, and people everywhere you looked, a riot of them. The fiddler with his leg up on the table, couples talking in corners with their heads tipped together, children running between the adults' legs, already some of them beginning to dance, and around the walls, Cook's food: pies, ham, potatoes, beef, beans, gingerbread, oranges, chestnuts. A smoking bishop being lit on fire. Smoke at the back of my throat . . .

And then it was gone.

Ben squeezed my hand, and I realised I'd stopped in the doorway, staring at nothing more exciting than Jeannie's Christmas party: tinsel, mulled wine and glasses of fizz. A tastefully catered buffet of quiche, coleslaw, jacket pota-toes. A Nigella ham. Edward's good sound system playing 'Carols from King's'.

'You okay?' said Ben.

'Yeah. Come on.'

We crossed the room, and the party quietened around us, middle-aged women in John Lewis clothes holding glasses of wine, children begging for sweets, waiters from the catering company in their white shirts, black bowties, waistcoats. I don't know what it was about me that made all those people stop talking. Perhaps I looked a fright, dripping rainwater in my black dress, trailing mud and fury – or perhaps I carried something stranger, some smell still clinging to my clothes, from the vanished past, that would not vanish at all.

By the time I reached Jeannie, the only sound left was the music, 'Once in Royal David's City', tinny and suddenly too loud.

'Danielle?' said Jeannie, startled. She was sitting at the edge of the room, in a gold dress, talking to an old woman with beautifully dyed hair. They stared at me. Everyone was staring.

Beneath the Christmas carol, I heard the sound of water dripping from Ben's raincoat onto the wooden floor, and fought an urge to laugh. I looked at Jeannie, trying to find the words. I wanted to say that it wasn't her fault: we'd both been playing the parts that were written for us. I understood that now, understood that she believed, in some deep part of herself, in the order, and her place in it, and mine. I had believed it too; in all my actions, I had believed it, day after day for years and years, wearing me down to nothing. It wasn't her fault any more than it was mine.

Jeannie looked angry. Maybe because I wasn't talking, because the silence made her uncomfortable. Or maybe because I had walked through the middle of her party, wild-eyed, dragging a damp actor and a suitcase, and ruined everything. 'Danielle, please,' she said, glancing from me to the guests, trying to smile. 'Shouldn't you be doing something useful?'

'Jeannie,' I replied. 'I'm not your fucking servant.'

Somebody gasped. Dimly, I remembered that we'd invited the local vicar to this party.

Jeannie climbed shakily to her feet, the old woman gripping her hand, like I was a threat. 'I know that,' she said, with quiet dignity. 'You're my PA.'

I smiled. 'Not anymore. I quit.'

Jeannie stared. 'Danielle, for goodness' sake,' she said, but we didn't wait for her reply. We turned away, crowd parting, shocked faces watching us pass. Three sets of footsteps in the quiet. The song had finished, and my wet boots squeaked on the parquet floor. I wondered, guiltily, who was going to have to clean that up. Not enough to stop me leaving. I threw the patio doors open: out we went, all of us, into the night.

*

'It's five minutes to the car,' said Ben, as we started down the drive. 'If you're okay to walk?'

'I'm fine,' I said. I didn't feel sick anymore – actually, I felt hungry. I wished I'd taken something from the tables at the party. I would make Ben stop at a service station.

It was no longer raining, the night crisp and full of stars. I pulled my coat tighter around me. I was no longer afraid.

'That was cool, Mac,' said Ben. 'Do you feel free?'

I felt unemployed. But that was a problem for the future, so I just said, 'Yeah.'

We walked in silence for a while. Ben smoked with one hand, pulled my suitcase with the other, and didn't ask any questions, though I knew he must have a lot of them. I was grateful.

'Wait,' I said. 'Where did you even get a car? You don't have a car.'

'I went round Anita's for a crisis talk and her housemate said I could borrow it. Whatshisname? You know, the rich kid.'

'Nice Pete?'

'That's the one.' I laughed, and he went on, 'Hey do you ever wonder: who's Un-Nice Pete? You know, like, where's the other Pete? What do they call that guy?'

'I do wonder that.' Ben had thrown his cigarette away, so I reached out and took his free hand before he could light another. 'Ben. Thank you for coming to get me.'

He smiled at me from the corner of his eye. 'Yeah. Of course.' Something uncharacteristically shy about him that filled me with tenderness. 'Here we are, look.'

We stopped at a dark blue Peugeot that I didn't recognise. Ben pulled the keys from his pocket, clicked to open the boot, and lifted my suitcase inside. We went round to the doors, us to the left and Ben to the driver's seat on the right. I climbed into the front while she got in the back.

There was a blanket, so I wrapped myself in it, curled against the window. I was still wearing my sober black dress, soaked and half frozen. It was strange to be leaving Westerley after all this time. I thought about my first afternoon: the drive with Mrs Waddingham, golden sunset catching in the windows. I thought about the year ending, and the new one coming. The grounds would be lovely in spring. But of course, we wouldn't be here to see it.

Ben was watching me. 'Are you sure you're okay?'

I nodded. Then I looked away from him, met the maid's eyes in the rear-view mirror. She was sitting patiently in the back seat, dark dress, dark eyes, white cap. Hands folded on her knees. 'We're going home,' I told her, and she nodded.

Ben thought I was talking to him. 'Yeah,' he said, and gripped my hand. 'Yeah, that's right. We are.'

Acknowledgements

Thank you to the team at Manilla for believing in this book, and for all you've done to make it the best version of itself, particularly Sophie Orme, Helen Reith, Clare Kelly – and of course my brilliant editor, Zoe Yang. Fast, incisive, supportive, always with a sense of humour, you are a dream collaborator. Huge thanks to Jake Cook for the beautiful cover design, as well as Flora Willis, Sahina Bibi, Kelly Samler, Kevin Hawkins and Alex May.

Thanks to all at David Higham Associates, particularly my brilliant agent, Veronique Baxter, to whom I am deeply indebted. She believed in this book even when it was a mess, helped so brilliantly to shape it, and found it a home – nobody could ask for more. Thanks also to Georgie Smith, her assistant Jem Dryer, and Veronique's assistants, Sara Langham and (previously) Becca Challis.

I was a part-time student on the MA in Creative Writing (Prose) at the University of East Anglia from 2018 to 2020. It changed my life. Thanks to DHA for the scholarship that made it possible, and to everyone I learned with and was taught by – far too many people to name, but particularly my first workshop tutor, Andrew Cowan, for the most inspiring weeks of my life. Naomi Wood,

Tom Benn and Giles Foden taught me many valuable things. Hugest thanks to Bede Yolland and Shandana Minhas, for friendship and fellowship. I'm also grateful to all my undergraduate teachers, especially Jill Rudd and Alexandra Harris, and everyone at the University of Liverpool.

This book owes a debt to the music of Mitski, Fever Ray and Young Fathers, and was written largely to Stasis by Pye Corner Audio and MORE D4TA by Moderat. I'm grateful for the writing (in various mediums) of Pat Barker, Lolita Chakrabarti, Michaela Coel, Mark Fisher, David Graeber, In Bed With My Brother, Shirley Jackson, MR James, Nigel Kneale, Alison Light, Daphne du Maurier, Sh!t Theatre, Sharlene Teo, Miya Tokumitsu, Laura Wade and Sarah Waters.

Service has its roots in a piece of theatre I tried to make in 2017. Thanks to Sara Joyce, Sami El-Enany, Ralph Thompson, Battersea Arts Centre and Arts Council England. Very glad I never finished that show. Sometimes ideas need to cook for a decade longer, and change in every conceivable way.

I wouldn't have written this book without a decade of making theatre. There are too many people to name, but David Byrne and Will Young, none of this would be happening without your encouragement and support. I'm grateful to my theatre agent, Imogen Sarre, her assistant William Byam Shaw, and all at Casarotto Ramsay & Associates. Biggest thanks to James Yeatman, my Kandinsky compatriot, for a decade of friendship, deep anxiety, rich joy and sometimes, when it all works, magic. Let's never get real jobs.

Service was made in London and about London, a city I loved, lived in for thirteen years, and left while editing this book. Thanks to everyone who filled that time with joy: all my housemates, particularly Liam Welton and Heather Doole; the Sunday Funday gang; everyone I did office jobs with, especially Sam Sedgman, Mazin Saleem, Tricia Rich and most of all Harpreet Purewal, for the affogatos, the hawks and everything since. My best friends, Erin Hopkins, Alice Marples, Cat Stroud and Maddie Wilson, you are the funniest and stupidest people I could hope to know – thank you for filling my life with laughter and floorbeds. I'd also like to thank Maddie for the incisive notes on an early draft, and Maddie's parents, Karen and Andrew Wilson, for all their kindness over the last two decades.

I'm grateful to my family: Julie, Nigel and the Bs, who looked after me while I was finishing this book; Karen, Howard, Heather and Iona, for letting me be part of your bright and brilliant gang; Winifred, who started all this; and my late grandmother Margaret, much missed. Most of all, I'm grateful to my parents, Carol and James. Mum and Dad, you taught me to read, and to love books, and gave me the weirdest tastes any kid could wish for. Thanks for owning the entirety of *Sapphire and Steel* on VHS and showing it to me when I was way too young, you lunatics. I love you both so much.

Finally, love and thanks beyond my ability to articulate go to my husband and occasional writing partner, Stewart

Pringle, to whom this book is dedicated. All those words, and none of them are enough, but here's a few anyway: you're the funniest person I know. Your little songs are very catchy. Your belief in me makes everything possible. I'm grateful beyond words for our days, our tortoise, and (at time of publishing) almost eighteen years of friendship, and over a decade of love. Thank God for bad pubs, worse theatre, and C Venues.